Miss Read, or in real life Dora Saint, was a teacher by profession who started writing after the Second World War, beginning with light essays written for *Punch* and other journals. She then wrote on educational and country matters and worked as a scriptwriter for the BBC. Miss Read was married to a schoolmaster for sixty-four years until his death in 2004, and they had one daughter.

Miss Read was awarded an MBE in the 1998 New Year Honours list for her services to literature. She was the author of many immensely popular books, including two autobiographical works, but it was her novels of English rural life for which she was best known. The first of these, *Village School*, was published in 1955, and Miss Read continued to write about the fictional villages of Fairacre and Thrush Green for many years. She lived near Newbury in Berkshire until her death in 2012.

D1151774

Books by Miss Read

NOVELS

Village School * Village Diary * Storm in the Village
Thrush Green * Fresh from the Country
Winter in Thrush Green * Miss Clare Remembers
Over the Gate * The Market Square * Village Christmas
The Howards of Caxley * Fairacre Festival
News from Thrush Green * Emily Davis * Tyler's Row
The Christmas Mouse * Farther Afield
Battles at Thrush Green * No Holly for Miss Quinn
Village Affairs * Return to Thrush Green * The White Robin
Village Centenary * Gossip from Thrush Green
Affairs at Thrush Green * Summer at Fairacre
At Home in Thrush Green * The School at Thrush Green
Mrs Pringle * Friends at Thrush Green * Changes at Fairacre
Celebrations at Thrush Green * Farewell to Fairacre
Tales from a Village School * The Year at Thrush Green
A Peaceful Retirement * Christmas at Thrush Green

ANTHOLOGIES

Country Bunch * Miss Read's Christmas Book

OMNIBUSES

Chronicles of Fairacre * Life at Thrush Green
More Stories from Thrush Green
Further Chronicles of Fairacre * Christmas at Fairacre
A Country Christmas * Fairacre Roundabout
Tales from Thrush Green * Fairacre Affairs
Encounters at Thrush Green * The Caxley Chronicles
Farewell, Thrush Green * The Last Chronicle of Fairacre
Christmas with Miss Read

NON-FICTION

Miss Read's Country Cooking * Tiggy
The World of Thrush Green
Early Days (*comprising* A Fortunate Grandchild &
Time Remembered)

At Home in Thrush Green

* * *

Miss Read

Illustrated by J. S. Goodall

An Orion paperback

First published in Great Britain in 1985
by Michael Joseph Ltd
This paperback edition published in 2009
by Orion Books,
an imprint of The Orion Publishing Group Ltd
Orion House, 5 Upper St Martin's Lane,
London WC2H 9EA

An Hachette UK company

5 7 9 10 8 6 4

A CIP catalogue record for this book is available
from the British Library.

ISBN 978 0 7528 8387 8

Typeset at the Spartan Press Ltd,
Lymington, Hants

Printed and bound in Great Britain by
Clays Ltd, St Ives plc

The Orion Publishing Group's policy is to use papers
that are natural, renewable and recyclable products and
made from wood grown in sustainable forests. The logging
and manufacturing processes are expected to conform to the
environmental regulations of the country of origin.

www.orionbooks.co.uk

For
Nina and Bill
with love

Among new men, strange faces, other minds.

TENNYSON (1809–1892)

The house of every one is to him as his castle and fortress.

SIR EDWARD COKE (1552–1634)

CONTENTS

* * *

PART ONE

Work In Progress

1	June Afternoon	3
2	Problems at Thrush Green	15
3	Market Day at Lulling	27
4	Family Demands	40
5	The Longest Day	52
6	The Fuchsia Bush to the Rescue	65
7	Summer Visitors	76

PART TWO

Moving In

8	New Neighbours	91
9	Some Malefactors	102
10	Settling Down	114
11	Preparing for Bonfire Night	126
12	The Fifth of November	137
13	Old People's Fears	149
14	Visitors	161

PART THREE

Getting Settled

15 Christmas   175
16 Winter Discomforts   187
17 Nelly Piggott Meets the Past   200
18 A Hint of Spring   214
19 Various Surprises   225
20 Richard's Affairs   235

PART ONE

Work In Progress

* * *

1. JUNE AFTERNOON

'I must pay a visit to Thrush Green this afternoon,' said Dimity Henstock to her husband Charles.

They were breakfasting in the kitchen of Lulling Vicarage. Charles buttered a slice of toast carefully.

'I can drive you there before two, my dear, but I have this meeting in Oxford at three.'

'Don't worry, I shall walk. Ella is clean out of light blue tapestry wool for her lovers' knots, and I have some here.'

'Her lovers' knots?' echoed Charles, toast poised.

'Round the edge of the chair seat,' explained Dimity.

She rose and began to clear the table. Charles, still looking bewildered, chewed the last mouthful of toast.

'I must get on, dear,' said Dimity. 'Mrs Allen comes today, and I like to get things cleared up.'

'I always thought that we employed Mrs Allen for the express purpose of clearing up for us.'

'Yes, one would think that in theory, but in practice, of course, it really makes more work to do.'

'Then I will go and water the greenhouse,' said the vicar of Lulling, rector of Thrush Green, and general priest in charge of Lulling Woods and Nidden – otherwise Charles Henstock.

He stepped out of the back door into the dewy freshness of a fine June morning, and made his way happily through the vicarage garden.

*

3

As he tended his seedlings in the pleasantly humid atmosphere of the greenhouse, Charles pondered on the felicity of his life in Lulling.

His present vicarage and its garden were both mellow and beautiful, owing much to the care given by his immediate predecessor, Anthony Bull, who now had a living in Kensington, where his good looks and slightly dramatic sermons were as much admired there as they had been at Lulling. Charles and he remained staunch friends.

Charles had been twice married, and after the untimely death of his first wife, life had been bleak. Soon after, he had been appointed to the living of Thrush Green, where he dwelt in the ugliest and coldest house there. Most of the dwellings round the large area of grass which gave the place its name, were built of Cotswold stone and tiled to match. Why a Victorian builder had ever been allowed to erect the gloomy pile which had been Charles's home for so many years, remained a mystery.

The good rector, the humblest and most hard-working of men, seemed oblivious of the draughts, the murkiness, and the sheer discomfort of his home. When he married his second wife, Dimity, who had shared a cottage with her friend Ella Bembridge nearby, he was perplexed to hear her complaints about her new abode, and did his best to help her to render the rectory more comfortable.

In fact, it was a losing battle. The house faced north-east, was shoddily built, and had a long corridor, leading from the front door to the back, which acted as an efficient wind tunnel and chilled the atmosphere whenever either door was opened.

Two or three years before the present June morning, the whole place had been consumed by fire, and very few local people regretted its passing.

Charles himself was devastated. He and Dimity had been away from home on the night of the fire, but he knew that he could never forget the sight of the smoking ruins which greeted him on his return.

He shuddered now at the remembrance, standing upright, a minute seedling of Cos lettuce held between thumb and fore-finger, and his gaze fixed, unseeing, upon the present splendour of his Lulling garden beyond the greenhouse glass. His mind's eye saw again the blackened heap, the drifting smoke, and the pathetic huddle of his salvaged possessions at some distance on the green.

And then he remembered his neighbours, the comforting arm about his shoulder, the stricken looks of those who mourned with him, their blackened hands offering mugs of steaming tea, their eyes reddened with the acrid smoke. It was their sym-pathy and practical help which had supported him and Dimity through the weeks that followed. He would never forget.

A sneeze shook him back into the present. With infinite care he lowered the threadlike roots of the seedling into its tiny home, and gently made it secure.

Dimity set out for Thrush Green as soon as lunch was over, leaving her husband sorting out the papers he would need for the afternoon's meeting at Oxford.

It was a time of day that Dimity always enjoyed, the slack period when most people were digesting their midday meal, the streets were quiet, and an air of torpor hung over the little town.

Most of the Lulling shops still closed for an hour or more. Old customs die hard in this part of the Cotswolds, and some shopkeepers still lived above their businesses, or near enough to go home to lunch. Dimity approved of this sensible practice, and did not rail, as many of her friends did, about the difficulty of shopping in the middle of the day.

The two modern supermarkets, made hideous with garish window stickers, seemed to be the only places open, as Dimity made her way along the High Street. Even they appeared remarkably quiet, she noticed. So far, Lulling folk seemed to keep to their usual ways, and would not be emerging from their rest until the older shops turned the CLOSED notice to OPEN, unlocked their doors, and pulled out the awnings to shade their wares should the sun have arrived.

Dimity did not hurry. The sun was warm, and she was pleasantly conscious of its comfort on her back as she admired, yet again, the honey-coloured stone of the buildings, the fresh green of the lime trees, and the plumes of lilac, white and purple, which nodded from the front gardens, and scented the warm air.

A tabby cat was stretched across the sunny doorstep of the draper's shop. Dimity bent to stroke it, and it acknowledged her attentions with a little chirruping sound and a luxurious flexing of its striped legs. Hard by, in the dusty gutter, a bevy of sparrows bathed noisily, but the cat was too lethargic to stir itself into action in the present warmth.

Dimity made her way through the somnolent town, crossed the murmuring River Pleshey, pausing to watch its eddies and dimples for a few minutes, and then faced the steep hill which led to Thrush Green and her friend Ella Bembridge.

Ella was one of those squarely-built, gruff ladies of mannish appearance whose looks belie their gentleness.

Her large hands, rough and brown from gardening, were equally at home with weaving, smocking, embroidery and tapestry work. Those hands had also tackled pottery, carpentry, painting and metalwork in their time, but now that Ella lived alone she preferred to enjoy the handiwork which she could do in her own home, without the complications of potter's wheels, lathes, soldering irons and the like.

She and Dimity had spent several happy years together. Though different in looks and temperament, the one had complemented the other. When Dimity had been carried off by Charles, first to the rectory across the way at Thrush Green, and later to the vicarage at Lulling, Ella had missed her old friend, but rejoiced in her good fortune.

She was not one to pine, and her innumerable projects kept

Ella busy and cheerful. It was lucky that Dimity lived so near, and that the two could see each other frequently.

As Dimity was puffing her way uphill, Ella was kneeling in the front garden of their home planting out a row of pansies, a cigarette dangling from her lips. She looked up as the latch of the gate clicked.

'What a nice surprise!' she exclaimed, scrambling to her feet, and wiping her hands energetically down her skirt.

'I told you I'd bring the wool,' replied Dimity. 'On the phone.'

'Well, I didn't cotton on that you'd come this afternoon. To be honest, Dim, I believe I'm getting deaf. Don't hear half people say on the blower.'

'Probably only wax,' said Dimity, sitting down exhaustedly on a rustic seat under the eaves of the thatch. 'Get John Lovell to squish it out.'

'He'd perforate my ear drums, more like,' commented Ella. Her opinion of medical practitioners was low. Good health had kept her largely from their clutches, and she was suspicious of their professional activities.

'Want a cuppa?' she continued. 'You look whacked.'

'No, no. It's only walking up the hill. Don't let me stop you working. Can I help?'

'No, I've only a few more to bung in. You sit there and tell me all the news. How's Charles?'

'He's off to Oxford for a meeting.'

'Poor thing! Rather him than me. What on earth do clergymen do at these meetings? Do a bit of re-editing of *Hymns Ancient and Modern*? Make a list of their fellow priests who need censuring? Or defrocking?'

'Oh, nothing like that, I'm sure,' replied Dimity, somewhat shocked. 'I think it's more to do with money. Upkeep of the church property, allocation of funds, that sort of thing. Though I must admit that Charles never talks about church matters to me, and I'm very glad he doesn't. One can so easily let out something innocently that is supposed to be private.'

'Your Charles is a wise old bird. If you don't want a thing known, say nowt to anyone. I can't abide people who tell you some titbit and then add: "But don't say a word. You are the only person I've told!" You can bet your bottom dollar she's said the same to a dozen others before telling you.'

She rammed home the last pansy plant, and came to sit beside Dimity in the sun. Out from her skirt pocket came the battered tin which Dimity knew so well, and Ella began to roll one of her pungent and untidy cigarettes.

The two old friends sat in silence. They were both drowsy and pleasantly tired from their recent exercise. A chaffinch pottered busily in the garden bed, occasionally giving a satisfied chirrup, and a light breeze rustled the budding may bush by the gate.

In the distance, they could hear the school children at play across the green, and the rumble of traffic from the main road at the foot of the hill. It was all very soporific and the ladies could easily have dropped off. But suddenly the rattling of machinery close at hand made them alert.

'That dratted cement mixer,' said Ella. 'They're still mucking about with those new houses. Putting in steps, or a terrace, or some such, the foreman told me.'

Dimity stood up to see what was happening across the road, on the very site of her demolished old home.

Eight one-storey houses in the form of a south-facing L were being built for old people, designed by the local architect Edward Young, who lived close by in what was readily acknowledged as the handsomest house on Thrush Green.

'What a time they're taking!' commented Dimity. 'They were started ages ago.'

'Poor old Edward's having the deuce of a time with some of his suppliers, I gather. He's having handles fixed to the baths, and rails by the loos, and they had to be sent back because they weren't to his specification. Then he'd planned underfloor heating, and it was practically complete when another chap told him that some old people had complained of foot trouble after some time in a place in Northamptonshire. So off he went to investigate, and decided to rip it out and start again.'

'When does he hope to have them ready?'

'You tell me! One thing, there are plenty of people around with their names on the list. Is Charles mixed up with this?'

'He's on the committee, I know.'

'Well, he's got my sympathy when it comes to selecting eight deserving cases from the roll. The fur will fly for some time, is my guess. Why, even Percy Hodge has put his name down.'

'Percy Hodge?' echoed Dimity. 'But he's already got a house! And a wife to look after him!'

'Not now he hasn't. She's left him for good, has our Doris.'

'But he can only be sixty at the outside,' expostulated Dimity. 'That's not old by today's standards.'

'True enough, but he's not the only sixty-year-old to try it on. I hear Mrs Cooke at Nidden's applied too, and those mercenary old twins at Nod whose name I can never remember.'

'But Mrs Cooke has heaps of children to look after her, and those Bellamy twins have pots of money, and a bungalow of their own!'

'We all know that. All I'm saying is, Charles will have his work cut out when he's one of the panel trying to make a choice.'

Dimity looked troubled as she gazed across the hedge to the new buildings.

'Well, at this rate he won't be making any decisions yet a while,' she said at last. 'Maybe things will be easier when the time comes.'

To Ella's mind, this was a forlorn hope. But, for once, she forbore to say so.

'You don't have to hurry back, do you, Dim? Stop and have a cup of tea.'

'I'd love to. Charles won't be home before six, I imagine.'

'Good, then we'll go down to Dotty's to collect the milk. It will save Connie a trip. Incidentally, Dotty sent me some biscuits she'd made. Shall we try them at tea time?'

Dimity laughed. 'You can, I shan't! I had a fine bout of Dotty's Collywobbles when I went there last.'

Ella smiled behind her cigarette smoke. 'Don't worry. I was only teasing. They went out to the birds within half an hour, and I can't say they were too keen either.'

Later the two ladies crossed the green and entered the narrow lane that led across fields to Dotty Harmer's cottage, and then on to Lulling Woods.

The cement mixer by the new buildings was now at rest, and the site deserted. The low terrace of houses was going to be very attractive once the builders' mess was removed, lawns and shrubs planted, and the final lick of paint applied.

'Almost makes you think of putting your name on the list,' commented Ella as they walked on. 'Not that I'd stand a chance, and in any case I should hate to leave our little place.'

At Dotty's there was evidence of building too. Their eccentric old friend had lived there for many years with numerous animals and a large garden erratically tended. She had been the only daughter of the headmaster of the local grammar school. He had had a fearsome reputation for stern discipline, and grown men in Lulling still quailed at the mention of his name.

On his death, marked by a packed church at his memorial service ('Relief rather than respect!' as some wag remarked later), Dotty had moved to her present abode and enjoyed her freedom. As well as caring for her animals with passionate devotion, she experimented with the bounty of the fields and hedgerows, making chutneys and preserves of dubious plants and berries which she pressed upon her apprehensive friends. John Lovell, the Thrush Green doctor, was well aware of the local stomach trouble known as Dotty's Collywobbles, and it was the first question he asked of his suffering patients before turning to more orthodox complaints.

Dotty's own health was the concern of her friends for several years, but when her niece Connie came to take charge they breathed a sigh of relief. Now Connie had married Kit Armitage, a handsome widower, who once had attended Lulling's grammar school and known Dotty's ferocious father only too well for comfort. The enlargement of Dotty's thatched cottage was the result of their marriage.

It was Connie who opened the door to Ella and Dimity, and greeted them with affection.

'Do come in. Aunt Dotty's in the sitting-room. Kit's shopping in Lulling. Have you had tea?'

They assured her on this point and went through the hall to see Dotty. They found her semi-prone on a sofa, a tapestry frame lodged on her stomach, and mounds of wool scattered around her.

'Don't get up!' exclaimed Ella, as Dotty began to thrash about. 'What are you making?' She gazed with an expert eye at Dotty's efforts.

'A cushion cover, so the pattern says,' replied Dotty. 'It's called Florentine stitch, and supposed to be quite simple.'

'It is,' said Ella. 'Let's have a look.'

She removed the frame from Dotty's stomach, tightened some nuts, and then studied the work closely, back and front.

'You've missed a whole row of holes in some places,' she said at last. 'See these white lines? That's the canvas showing through.'

'Oh really?' said Dotty, yawning. 'Does it matter?'

'It does if you want the work to look well done,' said Ella with spirit. 'Tell you what, I'll take it home and put it right for you.'

Dotty lowered her skinny legs to the ground, and pulled up her wrinkled stockings.

'Oh, don't bother, Ella dear. I quite like the white lines. Rather a pretty effect. In any case, I'm gather busy sorting out a drawerful of old photos at the moment, and I think I'll put this work aside till the winter.'

She took possession of the frame and thrust it under the sofa. There was a yelp, and Flossie the spaniel emerged, looking hurt.

'Oh, my poor love!' cried Dotty. 'I had no idea you were there! Let me find you a biscuit as a peace offering.'

She scrabbled behind a cushion on the sofa head and produced a crumpled paper bag. From it she withdrew a piece of Rich Tea biscuit, and offered it to the dog. It was warmly received.

'Now,' said Dotty, rising to her feet and wiping her hands down her skirt, 'come and see the new building.'

'Aunt Dotty,' protested Connie, now entering the room, 'there's nothing to see yet. Let Ella and Dimity have a rest after their walk.'

'No, let's see it,' said Ella, stumping along behind Dotty. 'How long have the men been here?'

The four women surveyed the piles of building material scattered about the garden. Dimity thought the sight depressing. Planks were propped against the fruit trees. Piles of bricks lurched drunkenly on what was once a lawn. Buckets, wheel-barrows, hods and spades all jostled together, and the inevitable cement mixer lurked behind the lilac bushes which were already covered in white dust.

'Full of hope, isn't it?' cried Dotty, eyes shining through her spectacles. 'Of course, there will be rather a mess when the thatcher comes. All that straw, you know, and his little hazel spars. I'm so looking forward to that. I shall have a chair out here and watch him at work. I think it must be rather a lonely job up on a roof. A little conversation should help him along.'

No one dared to comment on this appalling plan, but Connie hastily blew her nose, and looked towards the distant Lulling Woods.

'And when do you hope to see it complete?' asked Dimity.

'Edward says it should be ready by the winter,' replied Dotty. 'It's not a very big project, after all. The garage will be there.' She pointed to the powdered lilac bushes. 'And behind that will be a sitting-room, or is it the larder, Connie dear?'

'The sitting-room. And a bedroom above with a bathroom.'

'For Kit and Connie,' explained Dotty. 'A *large* bedroom, you understand. I think married people should have plenty of *air* at night. Two of them, in one room, you see. Now I only need that *small* room of mine. Plenty of cubic space for one sleeper. If ever I married, of course, I should have the wall knocked down between the two small rooms at the other end of the house.'

The hope of matrimony for dear old Dotty, now in her eighties, seemed so remote to all three ladies that they made no comment upon these wild conjectures, but contented themselves with picking their way among the muddle, and making polite noises.

'We really came to collect the milk,' said Ella at last, tired of stepping round piles of bricks, and circumventing wheel-barrows.

'It's all ready,' said Connie, turning towards the kitchen door.

Ella and Dotty followed the younger woman, but Dimity lingered in the garden.

The air was warm, and heavy with the scent of hay lying in the field beyond Dotty's hedge. Soon the baler would be thumping the crop into neat oblongs, grass and flowers and aromatic leaves compacted together, to carry the smell and comfort of summer into the winter byres where the cattle store stood, or to the snowy fields and the hungry sheep.

Of all the seasons, summer was the one that Dimity loved best. Thin and frail, she dreaded the cold Cotswold winter which dragged on, more often than not, into a chilling April. But a sunny June, with its many blessings of roses, hayfields, strawberries and long warm evenings, raised Dimity's spirits to near ecstasy.

She sighed with deep contentment, and made her way after the others. It was good to live in the country. It was good to have so many friends. It was good to feel warm and in splendid health.

Dimity paused by the kitchen door to pick the bright bud of an Albertine rose to thread in her buttonhole. 'Perfect!' she said, entering the house.

2. PROBLEMS AT THRUSH GREEN

The hawthorn blossom along the hedges gave way to the showy cream plates of elder flowers, and sprays of wild roses, pink and frail as sea shells. The gardens of Thrush Green were bright with irises and peonies, and the air was murmurous with the sound of lawn mowers.

But not all was idyllic.

Albert Piggott, caretaker, sexton, and erstwhile grave-digger at St Andrew's, found the June heat a sore trial, his nature being inclined to melancholy and excessive self-pity. But it was the mowing which gave him his present reason for complaint.

Some years earlier, Charles Henstock had decided that the tombstones of the Thrush Green forefathers should be moved, with due reverence, to the edge of the graveyard, and the turf flattened, so that a mower could keep the area tidy with the minimum of effort.

For too long it had been an eyesore. Albert, whose job it had been to scythe the grass over and around the mounds, was clearly beyond the work, and it seemed impossible to get a replacement.

There was some opposition to the good rector's proposal, but eventually it was accepted, and now, years later, it was generally agreed that the churchyard of St Andrew's was an exceptionally pleasant place, and the change had been quite successful.

Albert did not agree, as he told his long-suffering neighbour, Mr Jones of The Two Pheasants, one bright morning as soon as the pub was open.

'Them dratted tombstones was put too close to the outside wall when they done the job.'

He took a noisy slurp of his beer.

'Young Cooke,' he went on, replacing the dripping glass on Mr Jones's carefully polished bar counter, 'can't get the mower between them and the wall.'

'Oh-ah!' replied Mr Jones without much interest. Albert and his young assistant had been at loggerheads for years now. The publican had heard both sides of the many arguments between the two, and for far too long.

'Means as I has to get down on me hands and knees with the bill-hook, round the back, like. Not that easy at my age. Not after me Operation.'

A shadow fell across the sunlit floor. Percy Hodge, a farmer from the Nidden road hard by, was seeking refreshment.

'You ain't still on about your innards, are you?' he queried. 'I reckon all Thrush Green knows about them tubes of yours. And fair sick of 'em too. Half a pint, please.'

Albert's face grew even more morose. 'All right for you. Never had a day's illness in your life!'

'Ah! But I got my troubles.'

He pulled some coins across the counter and settled on the next stool to Albert.

'Oh? Your Doris come back?'

Percy drew in his breath noisily.

'Now, Albert,' began Mr Jones. 'We don't want no trouble between old friends.'

'Who's talking about old friends?' enquired Albert nastily. Percy's breathing became heavier.

'You keep Doris's name out of this,' he said. 'I don't keep on about your Nelly, though we all know what she is!'

'*Gentlemen!*' cried Mr Jones in alarm.

Percy and Albert fell silent, and turned their attention to their glasses. A distant clanking sound, followed by a steady chugging, proclaimed that the cement mixer was at work.

'By the time them places is finished,' said Albert, 'our lot'll all be in the graveyard. Be about ready for young Cooke, I reckon.'

'Wonder who they'll choose?' asked Percy, secretly glad to pick up this olive branch. 'You put your name down?'

'What, with my Nelly to look after me? And my girl Molly across the green at the Youngs? No point in me havin' a try. They'll be looking for old folk on their own.'

'Well, I've put my name forward,' said Percy. 'I'm old, and on my own.'

His listeners seemed taken aback. Albert was trying to work out how much younger Percy was than he himself. Mr Jones was shocked at the cheek of a man who was only middle-aged, and had a house and a living, in applying for one of the new homes. But he forbore to comment. He did not want any trouble in his respectable hostelry, and both customers were touchy.

'You'll be lucky!' commented Albert at last, putting his empty glass down. 'Must get back to my bill-hook. I'd like to meet the chap as set them tombstones round the wall. I'd give him a piece of me mind.'

'He got hurt in a car crash, other side of Oxford,' volunteered Percy. 'My cousin told me. Broke his arm, he said.'

'No more'n he deserved,' said Albert heartlessly, and hobbled back to his duties.

Later that morning, as the church clock struck twelve, the noise of the cement mixer growled into silence.

Two of the workmen appeared, hot and dusty, and ordered pints of bitter across the counter.

'And how's it going?' asked Mr Jones.

'Not bad,' said the one in a blue shirt.

'Just doin' the steps,' said the other, who sported a black singlet.

'*Steps?*' echoed Mr Jones. 'I should've thought there'd be no steps at all in a place for old people. Bit of a hazard, surely?'

'That's what the orders are,' said Blue Shirt.

'Only three of them,' said the second man. 'Shaller ones, too.'

'And a rail to hang on to,' chimed in Blue Shirt. 'You'll be safe enough, Dad, when you move over there!' He winked at his companion.

Mr Jones smiled a shade frostily. If he had spoken to his elders in such a way, when he was young, his father would have boxed his ears for him.

'Well, I'm sure Mr Young knows best,' he said diplomatically. 'He's reckoned to be a top-notch architect.'

But privately, the good publican found the thought of steps, no matter how shallow, and even when accompanied by a rail, a somewhat disconcerting feature of an old people's home.

'Could lead to trouble,' he confided to his wife that afternoon when the pub door was closed.

He was to recall his misgivings later.

Almost facing The Two Pheasants across Thrush Green stood the house where Winnie Bailey and her maid Jenny lived.

Adjoining it was John Lovell's surgery. Old Dr Bailey had died a year or two earlier, and sorely did his younger partner miss the wisdom and local knowledge of his senior. The practice was a busy one. John had two junior partners, both keen young men well up in modern medicine. The older folk in Thrush Green still viewed them with some suspicion, and tended to hark back to 'good old Dr Bailey' and his methods. But gradually the newcomers were beginning to be recognised, much to John Lovell's relief.

He himself was glad to have Winnie Bailey at hand. Her memory was prodigious, and she could frequently give him a brief history of a family which he found enormously helpful.

He was now very much a part of Thrush Green. As a junior partner to Donald Bailey, he had met and married Ruth Bassett, sister to Joan Young, the architect's wife. They lived some half a mile or so from the green itself, and as well as their own two young children they cared for old Mrs Bassett who had made her home with them since the death of her husband.

John was a serious and conscientious man, deeply appreciative of his good fortune in having such a settled marriage and a rewarding job. He enjoyed his trips to outlying villages, for he had a great love of country life and was knowledgeable about flowers and birds. These interests were of particular value to him for they helped him to relax.

His wife Ruth knew that if his nature had a flaw at all – which she would have denied hotly, if challenged – it was in the very seriousness which his patients found so reassuring. She did her best to lighten his load, but books, music and theatre, in which she had always delighted, could not engage his attention for any length of time.

'You are always telling your patients,' she said, 'that they must have a few hobbies to relieve any tension, but you don't take your own advice.'

'Doctors never do,' he told her.

It was with Winnie Bailey, as much as anyone, that John Lovell really found some relief from the pressures of his practice.

As soon as surgery was over, on this sunny June morning, he saw Winnie in her garden picking the dead heads from the roses.

'I was coming to get some directions from you, Winnie,' he called, putting his case in the back of the car.

'Come in and have a cup of coffee. I know Jenny's just getting some ready.'

'I dare not stop, many thanks.' He walked across the lawn. 'I've had a call from a Leys Farm. Do you know it? Somewhere off the road to Oxford, I gather.'

'Who lives there?'

'That's what all my patients asked,' said John smiling. 'Why is it in the country that we know the names of the people and never the names of their houses?'

Winnie laughed. 'I don't think I ever heard of Leys Farm, and I'm sure Donald never mentioned it. Could the owners have renamed it?'

'Quite likely. One of my patients said it was once known as Trotters. Does that mean anything?'

'Yes, indeed. A large family used to live at Trotters. They were Bells. Some vague relation of Betty Bell who cleans the school, you know?'

'And where is it?'

'Now you're asking! If you go about two miles out of Lulling on the Oxford road you will come to a narrow lane on the left. There used to be a fir tree there.'

'No gate? No sign?'

'Nothing. It's just a rough track. Heaven help you if you meet a tractor, John. But it's about another two miles to the house. I went there once with Donald.'

'Well, many thanks, Winnie dear. I'll go and blaze a trail to Leys-Farm-once-Trotters and, what's more, I'll tell you the name of the people who live there now, when I get back.'

'*If* you get back,' replied Winnie. 'It's that sort of place if I remember it aright.'

He waved, and departed on his mission.

Winnie had her coffee with Jenny in the kitchen. The room was warm and peaceful, and filled with the mixed scents of Jenny's cooking preparations. At one end of the scrubbed table was the chopping board with mint awaiting the attention of Jenny's knife. Beside it stood a punnet of strawberries.

'Percy Hodge brought 'em,' said Jenny. 'His first picking, so he said.'

'He's not courting you again, Jenny? I thought you had nipped that little affair in the bud.'

'He knows my feelings right enough,' replied Jenny. 'But I didn't see any point in turning down some good strawberries, even if his Doris has left him. Anyway, he knows there's no chance here for him.'

'So we can eat his strawberries with an easy conscience, can we, Jenny?'

'Why not?'

'I had a letter this morning from Richard,' said Winnie, changing the subject.

'Coming to stay, is he?'

'He doesn't say so. He'll be in the area next week and invites himself to lunch or tea. I have a phone number. Tea, I think, it's simpler for us.'

'Good. I'll make him some of my cheese scones. Men always like 'em.'

'I'm sure Richard will too, but don't expect extravagant thanks from him,' warned Winnie. 'He's inclined to take everything for granted, I'm sorry to say.'

She rinsed her cup and went upstairs to dust the bedrooms, her mind busy with thoughts of this, her least favourite, nephew.

Donald had always said: 'The boy's head's all right, but he has no heart.' Certainly, he had done brilliantly in his career as a physicist, and was acknowledged as supreme in his particular field. He spent much of his time lecturing abroad on subjects with such abstruse titles as: 'Molecular structures in relation to nuclear principles'. In fact, thought Winnie, that would probably be one of his elementary lectures, for she remembered seeing one listed which had a title four lines long. Richard's world was a vast unknown to his aunt.

She had not seen him since Donald's death, which had occurred while the young man was in America. To give him his due, he had written a very kind letter, expressing sympathy, which had touched Winnie.

For Richard, she had to admit, was quite the most self-centred individual she had ever come across. Perhaps that was why, she surmised, dusting the windowsill, he had never married, although he was now in his forties.

She ceased her work for a moment and gazed across the sun-lit garden. It was true that years before he had expressed a fondness for Winnie's neighbour Phyllida, then a young widow, but she had turned him down, as gently as could be managed, and within a few weeks she was married to Frank Hurst.

'I shouldn't think that dented Richard's armour very much,' commented Winnie to a surprised chaffinch on a nearby twig.

No, Richard would not have changed much, if she knew anything about him. Probably the same old hypochondriac too, everlastingly fussing with his diet and his bodily functions. Well, she would see him before long, and it would be interesting to see if he appreciated Jenny's cheese scones as richly as they deserved.

Time alone would tell.

John Lovell, driving along the busy road to Oxford, was too engrossed in dodging lorries, queuing up behind tractors laden with bales of hay, and trying to look out for the turning to his new patient's farm, to turn his mind to any Thrush Green problems.

As it was, he overshot the turning, for he had been looking out for the fir tree mentioned by Winnie, but evidently it had been felled since her visit, for nothing marked the entrance to the farm track. He managed to execute a neat U-turn in a lull in the traffic, and then was compelled to wait while yet another tractor, and its tail of fuming motorists, held up his right-hand entry into the lane.

It certainly was narrow, as Winnie had warned him, and the surface was gritty. Banks of nettles and seeding cow parsley brushed the sides of the car, and here and there the vivid blue of cranesbill made splashes of colour among the tall grass. With the eye of a born naturalist John noted the variety of butterflies and birds that frequented such richness.

The hedges were high on each side and badly in need of trimming, but John looked approvingly at the cascading wild roses, the brambles and the goosegrass which clambered from the ditch to drape its sticky shoots across the stronger twigs above. Plenty of good forage there for all manner of insect life, he thought.

Now that he was free of traffic he turned his mind to another topic. Soon the new homes for old people would be allotted, and he had been asked to join the committee and to give his advice on the applicants. It was going to be a problem. As far as he could gather from the local grapevine, there would be no shortage of people applying for the houses. Some could be rejected pretty swiftly.

Some, like Percy Hodge, were too well placed with a house and help already. Some were already so old and helpless that they really needed hospital care which the new homes could not provide. It was striking the balance which was going to be the main difficulty.

He knew at least twenty people who would benefit from being rehoused. His work took him into some pathetically inadequate homes, many of them of picture-book prettiness outside. But under many a quaint thatched roof were damp walls, with fungus growth, and the stains of years. Windows were tiny, stairs crooked and uneven, and a menace to ageing limbs. There were still cottages with oil lamps and candles, and

John Lovell had seen and treated the outcome of three fires in such premises, all lived in by frail old people who should have had accommodation in just the sort of homes so soon to be allotted.

He jammed on his brakes as a covey of young partridges ran from the overgrown verge. They took off with a whirring of wings and flew over the hedge.

Shelving his future responsibilities, John continued on his way to the distant farmhouse.

While John Lovell was driving cautiously along the neglected track, the subject which had been occupying his thoughts was also under discussion at Dotty Harmer's. She, with Kit and Connie, sat at the side of the cottage farthest from the noise of the workmen, mugs in hand.

'Joan Young tells me that Edward is quite distraught with all the delays to those dear little houses of his.'

Dotty always spoke of the old people's homes as though Edward owned the lot.

'We're in the same boat,' commented Kit. 'They've just told me that the plumber has been taken to hospital.'

'Oh no!' cried Connie.

'Well, surely,' said Dotty reasonably, 'the plumber has a deputy? When my father was taken ill, the Second Master stepped into the breach, and simply adjusted the timetable.'

'I've no doubt that things were rather better organised at Lulling Grammar School,' said Kit. 'As far as I can see, the work will be put back until Fred's on his feet again.'

'What's the matter with him?' asked Connie.

'Tummy pains. If it's appendicitis he'll be out in a few days. May not be too long.'

'A dear friend of mine,' mused Dotty, 'who nursed at Edinburgh Infirmary, told me that one of her appendectomy patients cycled from there to Glasgow, or Perth, or perhaps Leith – I can't quite recall now – but some distance away, only *four* days after the operation. Wasn't that marvellous?'

'I can't see our Fred returning after four days,' commented Kit, 'even by ambulance, let alone a bike. Still, we aren't quite as desperate as poor old Edward, who is supposed to have all ship-shape and Bristol-fashion by October, I'm told.'

'Winnie tells me that they are going to be quite charming,' said Dotty. She bent down to stroke her spaniel's silky ears. 'But there's a rumour that animals won't be allowed. I shouldn't like that.'

Connie and Kit exchanged glances.

'You aren't still wondering about applying, are you, Aunt Dot?'

'Well, no,' replied Dotty, sounding alarmingly doubtful.

Kit took charge, as he did so often and so admirably.

'Dotty dear, we've had this all out time and time again. You are staying here *for ever*. Understand? You can have all the animals you like. We are here to look after you, and even if you wanted one of Edward's homes, which you know you don't, you wouldn't get one for all those reasons.'

'You don't really want to leave here, do you?' Connie pleaded, taking one of Dotty's skinny paws in her own. 'This is your home, and has been for years. You know you would hate to make a change, and we want you with us.'

'Yes, yes,' agreed Dotty, much agitated, 'I know all that, and I know that's why we are building on, but sometimes I wonder if I shall be a nuisance to you. All young things should start married life on their own.'

'I feel flattered,' said Kit, patting Dotty's bony shoulder, 'to be called "a young thing" when I'm in my sixties. Now, snap out of it, Dotty. We three aging bodies will settle happily under this one roof. That is, if ever it gets round to being thatched, which I'm beginning to doubt.'

'There you are!' cried Connie. 'So stop harking back to those new homes. Your home is here.'

'Tell you what,' said Kit, echoing Ella Bembridge, whose favourite phrase this was, 'if our builders get on at this rate we could probably all move into one of Edward's abodes for our last declining years.'

'I shan't come,' said Dotty decidedly. 'They haven't got any upstairs. Very upsetting to have no upstairs. We're better off here.'

'That's what we've been telling you,' said Kit, smiling at his wife.

3 · MARKET DAY AT LULLING

On Wednesday mornings throughout the year, unless illness, catastrophic weather or matters of extreme urgency cropped up, Ella Bembridge descended the steep hill from Thrush Green to Lulling.

She carried a large basket, for it was market day in the little Cotswold town, and Ella always made a bee-line for the Women's Institute stall where she could be sure of beautiful fresh eggs, crisp vegetables, home-grown fruit and mouthwatering homemade cakes and scones.

Business done, she met her old friend Dimity at The Fuchsia Bush, and over a cup of coffee they exchanged news in the company of many other ladies and, very occasionally, one or two gentlemen.

On this particular morning, Ella was carrying a raincoat as well as her laden basket. The morning was warm and humid, the sky overcast, and the weather prophets had forecast heavy rain.

'Not that they know any more than my strip of seaweed outside the back door,' pronounced Ella, in ringing tones. Dimity hoped that none of those present had close relations at the Weather Centre, although over the years she had become less sensitive to the reaction of others when confronted by Ella's trenchant remarks.

'We could do with it,' replied Dimity. 'The vicarage lawns are terribly parched, and Charles won't use the sprinkler. He says it sets a bad example, when we've been asked to save water.'

'I can't think why these whizz kids of science can't manage to store some of the water we get too much of half the year. One week we're sloshing about in our wellies, and then after a fortnight's sunshine we are looked upon as criminals if we take a can of water to the carrots.'

'Try one of these sponge fingers,' said Dimity placatingly. 'They melt in the mouth. I expect Nelly made them.'

She pushed the plate across to her friend.

'I reckon we did The Fuchsia Bush a good turn when we suggested that Nelly Piggott might help out in the kitchen,' observed Ella, spurning the excellent sponge fingers, but producing her cigarette-making equipment.

'By the way,' she continued, dropping tobacco flakes on to the cigarette paper, the tabletop and the floor, 'I think the Youngs may get Mrs Peters and the rest of the staff here to make some of the goodies for this lunch do.'

'What lunch do?'

'I thought you knew. They are having a fund-raising effort, half the proceeds to St Andrew's roof fund and the rest to Hearts and Chests, or Ears, Noses and Throats. Can't remember exactly, but it's medically inclined, and to do with *tubes*, not *limbs*.'

'A coffee morning, you mean?'

'More ambitious than that. Joan said a buffet lunch one Saturday should bring in much more cash. We shall have a few stalls, jam and cakes, you know, and I've promised some weaving and canework.'

'It sounds marvellous,' said Dimity, trying to appear enthusiastic. 'When's it to be?'

'End of July, I think. I'll tell you when I know definitely. And Joan asked me to tell the Lovelock girls, so I'll bob in as soon as we've paid the bill.'

'The Lovelock girls' lived almost next door to The Fuchsia Bush, in one of the pleasant Georgian houses which are dotted along Lulling's High Street.

The three sisters were far from girlhood, their average age being closer to eighty than eighteen. They were a formidable trio, and had lived all their lives in the same house.

Ada, Bertha and Violet had been left comfortably provided for by a wealthy and indulgent father. But they were renowned throughout Lulling and its environs for parsimony of an extreme kind. Visitors, bidden to lunch at the house, prudently had a snack beforehand, knowing that in winter they might be lucky enough to get one small chop from the neck end of lamb, with a spoonful of potato and half a dozen peas.

If it were a summer lunch party the fare would be even more spartan. Miss Ada had been known to count the rounds of beetroot as she allotted them to the plates, and as the eyesight of all three sisters was now less than perfect, the lettuce was inclined to be crunchy with particles of garden soil.

However, the linen was always snowy, the glass crystal clear, even if it only held tap water at the meal, and the ancient heavy silver beautifully polished.

When Dimity and Ella entered the house the ladies greeted them effusively.

'How lovely to see you!' cried Miss Ada.

'Come through to the kitchen!' called Miss Bertha. 'We are just preparing lunch. Will you stay?'

The two visitors, long familiar with meals here, made hasty apologies.

Miss Violet was putting the finishing touches to the first course. Six slices of corned beef lay along an oblong dish, flanked with parsley at each corner. A few lettuce leaves, and one tomato, cut into four, seemed to constitute the accompanying dish.

Ella wondered idly who would be so bold as to have the quarter of tomato left over. She hoped that there would not be an ugly fight.

Bertha was concocting a small trifle from two slices of stale sponge cake, half a dozen strawberries cut into pieces and a spoonful of runny jam of indeterminate variety.

Dimity and Ella looked upon these preparations as politely as they could.

'I've only to moisten this with the top of the milk,' said Bertha happily, 'and then we can go into the drawing-room.'

That done, they did indeed traverse the hall again, and settle in the beautiful room which looked out into Lulling High Street.

The drawing-room was crowded with old and lovely articles. The sisters still lived in Edwardian style, with a number of small tables dotted here and there on the Chinese carpet, each laden with photographs in silver frames, tiny pieces of exquisite china, and other knick-knacks. The thought of the wreckage one small child or an exuberant dog could cause did not bear contemplating.

An enormous bronze jug stood in the hearth containing the silver pennies of dried honesty, and the blue and green sheen of long peacock feathers. Dark brown velvet curtains were looped back from the windows, and the pictures were by some of the pre-Raphaelites. It was indeed a real period piece, thought Ella, seated uncomfortably, for one of her bulk, on a spindly mahogany chair decorated with fine marquetry work.

'A cup of coffee?' asked Bertha.

'No, many thanks,' said Ella. 'We've just had some next door.'

'Ah! Mrs Peters makes excellent coffee,' commented Violet. 'And seems to be doing very well now that she has Mrs Jefferson and that rather vulgar Nelly Piggott to help her.'

'I don't think,' said Bertha frostily, 'that there was any need for "*rather vulgar*", Violet. She seems a good enough woman of her type.'

Violet looked abashed at this rebuke from her older sister.

'She always cleaned our silver very well,' put in Ada. 'It was the *cooking* which we found disappointing. Not that she did very much here, but we found her very extravagant. Particularly with butter and eggs.'

'Nevertheless,' said Violet, striking a blow for justice, 'her food was delicious, you know. And they say that The Fuchsia Bush is packed every lunch time.'

'So we hear,' said Ella. 'It's partly because of that that Joan Young thought she might ask Mrs Peters to make up a few cold dishes. Pies and quiches and salads, you know.'

She proceeded to outline the plan for raising money by a buffet lunch at Thrush Green. The sisters, Dimity noted, grew steadily more apprehensive. Obviously, the thought of having to spend money was daunting.

Nevertheless, Ella ploughed on with her task.

'I'll let you know the date, and the price of the tickets and so on, as soon as things are settled,' she promised. 'There will be a bring and buy stall too, of course, and probably a raffle.'

The expressions on the three wrinkled visages became more relaxed.

'Oh, I'm sure we can find something suitable for the stall or the raffle, even if we can't fit in the lunch party with our other duties,' said Ada.

'Those ear-muffs I knitted, and the brooches made of beech husks should be quite acceptable,' agreed Bertha, 'and Violet made some excellent elderberry wine last autumn. Not all the corks blew out, if I remember rightly, and I'm sure there are a few bottles left.'

'Well, we'll keep in touch about it,' replied Ella, with rare diplomacy, and she and Dimity rose to depart. The ladies of the house followed them to the front door.

The pavement was now spotted with rain, and Ella began to struggle into her raincoat. Dimity, less well protected, looked dismayed, but turned up the collar of her summer suit.

'You simply must borrow Father's umbrella,' fluttered Miss Violet, darting to a cylindrical vessel, decorated with improbable bulrushes, which stood in the corner of the hall. 'It was a present from the lodge of his Freemasons. He valued it highly, and we always lend it to our friends on just such an occasion as this.'

It was certainly a handsome object, made of heavy black silk, with a splendid malacca handle embellished with a gold ring.

'I hardly like to take charge of it,' admitted Dimity. But the umbrella was already being opened above the three steps leading down to the pavement, the rain was increasing every minute, and she accepted the umbrella's protection gratefully.

The three sisters waved goodbye, and then retired behind the front door, no doubt to discuss the dreadful possibility of having to purchase tickets for Joan's buffet lunch.

'Well, thank God we weren't staying to lunch,' said Ella when they were safely out of earshot. 'I'm going back to eggs and bacon. Like to join me?'

'I mustn't, Ella, many thanks. Charles and I are having some chicken in a casserole, and I've a horrid feeling I forgot to switch on the oven before coming out.'

'You'd better drop into lunch with the Lovelocks,' said Ella, 'if that's the case.'

And the two friends departed cheerfully.

*

The rain grew heavier, and by midday the gutters were gurgling, the thatched eaves were dripping, and the puddles in Thrush Green's school playground grew larger every minute.

Miss Watson, the headmistress, and her devoted assistant Agnes Fogerty surveyed the scene anxiously.

'You would think,' said Miss Watson tartly, 'that parents would have the sense to provide their children with mackintoshes, especially when the weather man specifically forecast rain in the south.'

'He's often wrong,' protested Agnes.

Miss Watson gave one of her famous snorts, much mimicked by the naughtier of the pupils.

'Well, it can't be helped. Those who go home to dinner must hurry along as best they can. Obviously, this has set in for the day.'

Little Miss Fogerty supervised the departure of the few children who went home for their meal, organising the sharing of umbrellas, buttoning the raincoats of those prudent enough to sport them and exhorting her charges to: 'Hurry home, and keep out of the puddles,' a forlorn hope, as well she knew. Meanwhile, Miss Watson and the remaining assistant attended to the distribution of school dinner.

It was impossible for the children to take their break in the playground after the meal, and conditions were just as bad when afternoon playtime came. Out came the dog-eared comics, the jigsaw puzzles, the dominoes and draughts which featured so monotonously in the winter. The past spell of fine weather had made both staff and pupils forget the frustration of wet days indoors.

Miss Watson and Miss Fogerty were quite out of sorts at the end of the afternoon session, and thankful to return to the peace of the school house which they shared.

'Well, I'm glad to be home,' said Dorothy Watson, kicking off her shoes and putting up her feet on the settee.

'Me too,' agreed Agnes. 'I'll put on the kettle.'

'No, no!' protested Dorothy, not stirring. 'I will get tea in a moment.'

'You will stay there, and rest your poor hip,' responded Agnes firmly. She looked like a mouse trying to be ferocious.

'You spoil me,' murmured her headmistress, and closed her eyes.

The rattle of the tea things brought her back to consciousness. She lowered her legs to the floor, and sat up with a sigh.

'Oh, Agnes, what should I do without you?'

'Manage very well, I'm sure, just as you did when you were here on your own,' Agnes reassured her.

'It has just occurred to me,' said Dorothy, accepting her cup of tea, 'that it is Ray and Kathleen's wedding anniversary the day after tomorrow. I always sent them a card, but since their last dreadful visit here I haven't done so. Their behaviour was so appalling, I really haven't felt inclined to get in touch, but now – well, I don't know—' Her voice trailed away into silence.

Little Miss Fogerty broke it with unaccustomed energy.

'I should send a card, Dorothy dear. After all, he is your only brother, and we are getting too old, all of us, to harbour hard feelings. I'm sure he and Kathleen would be very touched to have a generous gesture made to them.'

Miss Watson still looked doubtful. The 'last dreadful visit' she spoke of had taken place in this very room, when Ray and Kathleen had been invited to tea, had been particularly trying, in Miss Watson's view, and had, moreover, brought in their large and obstreperous dog which capsized the tea table, wrecked the sitting-room and frightened everyone.

Tempers had risen, harsh words had been spoken, Ray and Kathleen had flounced off, vowing never to return, and Dorothy had told them flatly that the arrangement suited her perfectly.

Agnes, whose heart was more tender, had grieved over the rift and was delighted to see that Dorothy too was beginning to be willing to offer the olive branch.

Things had been strained between Ray and Dorothy for some time, and the open quarrel was only the culmination of two or three years' coolness. The headmistress had broken her hip in a fall in the playground, and after the operation had expected to recuperate with Ray, but no invitation had been forthcoming, much to her shocked amazement. Little Miss Fogerty, then living in lodgings, had offered to take up temporary abode at the school house, for a few weeks, until Dorothy was more mobile.

The offer was gratefully accepted, and when Dorothy realised how well the two got on together, she suggested that Agnes settled in permanently. The arrangement worked perfectly, but it meant that there was now no spare bedroom at the school house. In the past, Ray had often dropped in, and expected to stay overnight. Now he was offered the sofa, or directed to Lulling's premier hostelry, The Fleece. Looking back, Agnes feared that she had unwittingly been the means of upsetting Ray.

'Write a card now,' urged Agnes, 'and I will run across to catch the five-thirty collection. Even with the post as it is, it should get there on Friday.'

'I suppose so.'

'And I'm sure they would appreciate such a *gracious* act,' pursued Agnes. 'They must know they were in the wrong bringing that poor animal – Harrison, was it? – into this house uninvited. I'm sure they've often felt guilty about it.'

Dorothy had her doubts about that, but the idea of appearing gracious and forgiving appealed to her. And, in any case, as dear Agnes pointed out, they were all getting too old to continue a silly quarrel.

She rose to get her writing case, and scrabbled busily among its contents. 'I know I have some National Trust cards here somewhere.' She withdrew a folder and spread out the contents on the sofa. 'Now which do you think, Agnes? Bodiam Castle or Mottisfont Abbey? Perhaps Bodiam. All that water round it is so attractive.'

She opened the card, and began to write. Agnes looked on with immense satisfaction, and sipped her tea. After five minutes the card was ready for the post, and Dorothy passed her cup for refilling.

'Well, I hope I've done the right thing. I simply said: "Happy remembrances. Hope all goes well with you both. Agnes joins me in sending love." '

'Perfect,' said her friend. 'I'll go over with it at once. Willie Marchant has been known to collect a few minutes early.' Willie Marchant was Thrush Green's thin postman. Willie Bond was the fat one.

'Still pouring, Agnes dear. Put on your raincoat. And a thousand thanks. I'll clear away the tea things.'

Agnes hurried off, and a minute later Dorothy saw her scurrying across the wet grass to the post box on the corner of Thrush Green.

Had she been wise to write? Would she hear from Ray and Kathleen? Come to that, did she really want to?

Of course she did, she told herself briskly, packing the tray carefully. They were her own flesh and blood after all.

But the response to her gracious gesture was to be rather more overwhelming than Dorothy envisaged.

As the wet day turned into an equally wet and dreary evening, Winnie Bailey across the green was talking to her nephew Richard on the telephone.

Could he drop in for tea on Friday, he asked? He was only in the area for another week, and was hard pressed for time.

'It will suit us perfectly, Richard,' replied Winnie. 'About four?'

'Yes, yes. I'm sure I can get there by then. Don't worry if I'm a little late. And by the way, I have some exciting news for you.'

'What is it?'

'I'm married.'

'Good heavens, Richard! You've taken my breath away! Do bring her with you on Friday!'

'Can't be done. She's in London, but I'll tell you all about it when I see you. I've been run off my feet with these lectures, some in Birmingham, a couple at the University of Buckingham, and two more here in Oxford.'

'You do work hard,' said Winnie.

'Till Friday!' cried Richard, and rang off.

Winnie returned to her sitting-room still bemused. What staggering news! And how long had they been married? And why hadn't he told anybody?

What an odd fellow he was! Donald had always said so, and added that he was the most self-centred young man he had ever come across. She was afraid that this was quite true.

She fell to speculating about the new bride. Would she be a quiet submissive little thing, dazzled by Richard's undoubted eminence in his field, and willing to sacrifice her life to his? Or perhaps she had a job, equally important? The fact that she was remaining in London while Richard was on this lecture tour might mean that she too was busy with her own career. Richard would probably choose someone with plenty of brains as a partner.

What amazingly clever children they might have, thought Winnie, her thoughts racing several years ahead. She recalled spending a short holiday, as a young woman, with a dear friend who lived in Sedley Taylor Road in Cambridge. A good many of the houses were lived in then by newly-married university men, and the roads were busy with young children on tricycles and what were known then as fairy cycles. All seemed to be wiry, energetic infants, with spectacles and sandals, and their vocabularies appeared to Winnie to be much in advance of their tender years. Privately, she referred to any precocious children she met later as 'tiddly-widdly children'. Richard had always been one of them, to her, from the time he first sat up in his pram.

When Jenny put her head round the door to say

goodnight, Winnie told her that Richard would be coming to tea on Friday.

'And Jenny, some terrific news! He's married.'

Jenny looked suitably astonished. 'Well, I never! I wonder what she's like, poor thing?'

She vanished before Winnie could reply, but as she rolled up her knitting and switched off the lights, Winnie could not help feeling that Jenny probably shared Donald's opinion of the bridegroom.

The upstairs lights went on one by one as Thrush Green prepared for bed.

Winnie undressed, still excited by the news of Richard's marriage. Jenny was wondering if she had enough cheese in the larder for the cheese scones she planned to make.

Edward Young tossed and turned, fuming at the weather which was holding up the steps, the ramp and the little paved terrace of the old people's abode.

Nelly Piggott, dropping off to sleep in the back bedroom, and ignoring Albert's snores from the next room, congratulated herself on now having three hundred pounds tucked away in her Post Office savings book. With a chap like Albert as poor provider it was a comfort to have a secret nest egg, she told herself.

At the school house, little Miss Fogerty put her bookmark in the novel she was reading, and closed it thoughtfully. Did she really want to go on with this story, and were the characters typical of young people today? In this book not one appeared to have a normal home, parents appeared to be non-existent, marital arrangements much to be deplored, and drug-taking the accepted thing. No one, it seemed, wanted to work either. It was all extremely depressing.

She turned out the light, sighed heavily, and snuggled into her pillow for comfort.

In the next room, Dorothy Watson began to drift into sleep, serene in her belief that she had been forgiving, generous and –

what had Agnes said? Ah yes, of course! *Gracious*, was the word.

She was asleep in five minutes.

4. FAMILY DEMANDS

Thursday was as wet as the day before. The summer flowers were flattened in the gardens, the chestnut avenue outside the Youngs' gate dripped steadily, and the puddles grew apace.

But, on Friday, Thrush Green woke to blue skies and a freshly washed world. Spirits rose, and Betty Bell, always cheerful, was more exuberant than ever as she wheeled her bicycle from the school to Harold and Isobel Shoosmiths' house next door.

She 'put the school to rights' each morning, and on two days a week she worked as well at the Shoosmiths' home. When Harold Shoosmith had arrived in Thrush Green as a single man some years earlier, Betty had looked after the cleaning and also did some cooking, but since he had married, Isobel undertook most of the household work, and Betty's duties were much reduced.

She espied Willie Bond, the fat postman, ploughing his way towards her, and waited to see if he had any post for the Shoosmiths.

'How's tricks then, Willie? Got any letters for us? I'll save you a few steps maybe.'

Willie dismounted heavily, and fumbled in his canvas bag.

'Two from abroad it seems, and one of them Bingo nonsenses as says you're going to win half a million what you never do.'

Betty accepted them. 'And how's auntie?'

Willie Bond and Betty Bell were first cousins.

'Worriting, as usual. Reckons the price of things is enough to give her the dumps. She's wondering whether to apply for one of these 'ere houses, but I don't reckon she'd like it.'

'Well, let's face it, Willie, she never liked anything much. Always a moaner, your mum.'

Willie sighed. 'True enough, Bet, my girl. Well, I'd best be speeding off.'

He clambered again on to his bicycle and weaved his way to deliver letters at the school house.

'At least there are no bills this morning,' said Harold to Isobel, across the breakfast table. Upstairs the hum of the vacuum cleaner joined Betty Bell's voice uplifted in song.

'All's right with the world then,' commented Isobel, looking out at the sunshine, as Harold read his letters.

They had both found a perfect place for retirement, she thought yet again. It was good to be part of the small community of Thrush Green, and she was particularly fortunate to have made such a happy second marriage. She relished, too, the friendship and nearness of Agnes Fogerty, who was a staunch companion from college days.

'Which reminds me,' she said to her husband. 'I've promised to look out some jumble for the school sale at the end of term. I must do it this weekend.'

Harold passed over the two letters.

'They sound happy enough in Africa, although there seems to be quite a lot of opening doors to find chaps waiting there with pangas at the ready. All in all, I'd sooner be at Thrush Green, wouldn't you?'

'Without a doubt,' responded his wife.

Next door, little Miss Fogerty and Miss Watson were preparing to go across the playground to their school duties.

The breakfast things had been washed, beds made and dusting done, for both ladies were early risers, as schoolteachers need to be, and were quick with their daily routine. Now they were on their way.

'I do so hope that Ray and Kathleen got their card this

morning,' said Dorothy, still glowing with the thought of her forgiving gesture.

'Bound to have done,' Agnes assured her. 'It caught the afternoon post and had a first-class stamp on it.'

George Curdle, aged six, and one of her most promising pupils, now approached and presented her with a splendid posy of sweet peas.

'Why, thank you, George! How lovely! Did your father grow them?'

The child nodded, conscious of Miss Fogerty's sincere pleasure, and the gracious smiles of his headmistress.

'Tell him I am very pleased indeed with them,' said Agnes, passing on.

'Ben Curdle,' observed Dorothy, 'could always do anything.

Took after his dear grandmother, no doubt. I still miss the May Day fair she used to bring here yearly.'

'So do I,' agreed her assistant, 'but it is much more peaceful teaching without it.'

'Well, we should have a peaceful enough day today, Agnes. The children will be able to play outside, and we shall get a little rest.'

It was not to last long.

Later that morning, across the green, the appetising smell of cheese scones scented Jenny's kitchen. They had turned out perfectly, nicely risen and gilded with egg yolk. Jenny admired them as they aired on the wire rack. Richard should enjoy those, she thought. A pity his wife could not sample them too.

After lunch Winnie Bailey fell asleep in her chair, and woke to find it almost three o'clock. Perhaps a good thing to have had a nap, she told herself. Richard's company was always exhausting, no matter how pleased one was to welcome him.

By half past four the trolley was ready in the kitchen, and the kettle was filled. Jenny hovered anxiously, one eye on the clock.

'If he's not here by five,' said Winnie, 'we'll have ours.'

But at ten to the hour, Richard arrived, tea was made, the trolley trundled into the sitting-room, and Winnie awaited the details of his marriage.

He certainly looked very fit. He still had a good head of fair hair when so many of his contemporaries were losing theirs. His blue eyes, behind the spectacles which he had worn since childhood, were as bright as ever. His appetite too was keen, and he demolished five of Jenny's scones before Winnie had started her first.

Winnie had half-hoped that he would make some complimentary remark about the scones which she could have passed on to Jenny, to that lady's pleasure, but he appeared to demolish his tea simply to satisfy the inner man.

'Do you still follow your friend Otto's diet?' asked Winnie, remembering earlier visits when the dining-room table had bristled with Richard's bottles of pills.

'No. I'm afraid he was exposed as something of a charlatan. His pills were mostly sugar with a mild opiate added. If he had been on any medical register he would have been struck off. A great pity about Otto. Quite gifted in some ways.'

Winnie remembered some trenchant remarks of her husband's about Otto and his products, but forbore to tell them to Richard.

'Now, please, I'm all agog. Tell me, when was the wedding?'

'Three weeks ago, Aunt Win. Very quiet affair at our local registry office. We both wanted that.'

'And her name?'

'Fenella. We met about two years ago at a party. She runs an art gallery with a distant cousin of hers. Quite lucrative.'

He helped himself to a slice of fruit cake, and munched busily.

'So will you live in London?'

'Oh yes, when I'm there. There's a flat of sorts over the shop, so to speak. Not very big, but as I'm away such a lot it should do us quite well. Fenella's lived there ever since she started at the gallery.'

'So that's why she couldn't come with you today, I suppose, with the gallery to see to?'

'Well, partly. At the moment she's not too fit.'

'Oh dear,' cried Winnie, envisaging some frail creature lying on a sofa with a severe headache, 'nothing serious, I hope?'

'No, nothing serious,' replied Richard, dusting cake crumbs briskly from his knees to the carpet. 'But our baby's due next month, and she finds the stairs rather trying.'

Winnie, who had been brought up in the days when one's baby did not appear for at least nine months from the wedding day, adjusted herself to this news whilst refilling Richard's cup.

'Which is really why I wanted to come today,' continued Richard.

'I rather hoped you might want to see me,' smiled Winnie.

'Oh well, of course it is always nice to see you,' replied the young man, looking bewildered, 'but it was Fenella I was worrying about. You see, she will be having the baby at our local hospital, but no doubt will be sent out on the third day, if not earlier.'

He paused to take a gulp of tea.

Winnie's heart sank. If she were to be asked to travel to London to look after a nursing mother and new baby, for which she had no qualifications, she would have to refuse. And the stairs sounded daunting too, at her time of life.

'My suggestion is that she comes straight down here, if you could put her up. It's so quiet and peaceful, and the air would do her good.'

'But has she nowhere else to go?' asked Winnie.

'Her mother lives at Wimbledon, but they don't hit it off together awfully well, and in any case she's getting on. She must be well into her fifties.'

'And I'm well into my seventies,' said Winnie, with some asperity. She was about to remonstrate further when Richard spoke again.

'Of course, Timothy might be a problem. He'd have to come with Fenella.'

'Timothy?'

'Yes, he's four now. By Fenella's first husband. Full of life, is Timothy.'

Winnie began to feel slightly dizzy.

'But where will you be, Richard, when this child is born?'

'Oh, that's the point! I have to do a tour of Australia in about three weeks' time, so that's why I'm trying to get things settled before I go. I talked it over with Fenella, and I told her that you had Jenny to help in the house, and John Lovell practically on the premises if anything went wrong, and it all seemed ideal to us.'

Maybe, thought Winnie, with growing astonishment at these plans, but far from ideal for Jenny and for me! How right Donald had been when he described Richard as the most self-centred individual he had ever met! His calm assumption that two elderly ladies would disrupt their lives to accommodate his wife and two children, while he left all his responsibilities behind, astounded her.

She put down her cup very carefully, and took a deep breath. 'Richard, Fenella and the new baby, and the little boy, are your responsibility. You must have known about this situation for months, and should have made plans properly. To my mind, you should have cancelled the Australian trip, and been with them at this time.'

'But that would have been quite impossible, auntie. The contract was signed a year ago. Besides, I wanted to go.'

There speaks Richard, thought Winnie.

'In any case, it is impossible for me to take on your responsibilities. Now that Jenny lives here, we have only one spare bedroom, and really no facilities for coping with a mother and new baby, let alone Timothy.'

'Well,' said Richard, looking much taken aback, 'I really didn't foresee this!'

'Then you should have done. I am in my seventies, and Jenny not much less. I look forward to meeting Fenella and the family before long, but to expect us to cope with the present problem is remarkably naïve of you and – I must say it, Richard – uncommonly selfish, too.'

'Then what am I to do?'

'You must make arrangements for a younger and better qualified woman than I am, to care for your family, if you must go on with this tour, which I consider ill-advised and again extremely selfish. Suppose something goes awry with the birth? How are people to get in touch with you? How will Fenella feel, trying to cope with everything? I'm getting crosser every minute with you, Richard. Have another cup of tea.'

He passed his cup in silence. Winnie found herself breathing heavily. All this was most upsetting. It was against her kindly nature to refuse help at such a time, but the facts were as she stated, and Richard was putting her into an impossible situation.

'So you won't have them?'

'I *can't* have them, and that's top and bottom of it. It would have been more thoughtful of you to have broached this subject months ago. I could have told you then, as I've told you now, that Jenny and I are beyond it, and you would have had more time to make other plans.'

'I'm very disappointed. I shall have to think again.'

'You most certainly will,' agreed Winnie, with some spirit. 'I advise you to try and get someone to live in for a month or so to look after things. No doubt the local district nurse will call as often as she can, but there should be somebody there – you, preferably – to cope with the day-to-day running of the household.'

Richard began to look sulky, reminding Winnie of the time when he had been refused a sixth chocolate biscuit at the age of five. He did not seem to have matured much in some ways.

'You've made things very awkward for me, Aunt Win. I really don't know what to do next.'

'There are plenty of agencies in your part of London,' Winnie told him, 'who will be only too pleased to send you someone who can cope with the nursing and the housework. I remember going to Kensington with my mother years ago when we needed a cook-general.'

'But it will cost money,' protested Richard.

'Naturally,' agreed Winnie. 'If you are expecting skilled and reliable service you must be prepared to pay well. Personally, I should have thought it a small price to pay for help in the circumstances.'

Richard looked at his watch. 'Too late to do anything today, I suppose. I think I'd better get back to town and discuss things with Fenella. I'm afraid she will be as disappointed as I am. I know she was looking forward to a week or two here to recuperate.'

Winnie refused to be browbeaten.

'I'm quite sure she will understand, Richard. Are you driving straight home?'

'Yes, of course. My lecture tomorrow isn't until the evening.'

'Then, in that case, I will pick her some roses. They are particularly fine this year. And you must wait while I write a note to go with them.'

Richard followed her into the garden as she snipped among the rosebeds. He still seemed upset, but Winnie ignored his restless pacing to and fro.

A quarter of an hour later, he was in the car, the roses, beautifully shrouded in tissue paper, on the back seat, and Winnie's letter in his pocket.

'I've no idea how to set about finding a suitable agency,' complained Richard, fastening his seat belt.

'Just look in the Yellow Pages, dear,' advised his aunt, and waved him farewell.

She returned to the kitchen where Jenny was busy washing up the tea things.

'My scones went down well evidently,' she said with satisfaction.

'They did indeed,' her mistress assured her. She went on to explain Richard's mission, and Jenny's eyes grew wider every minute. When, at last, Winnie reached the end of her tale, Jenny summed up the whole proceedings in one word.

'Cheek!' said Jenny.

Nelly Piggott, toiling up the hill from Lulling to Thrush Green after her day at The Fuchsia Bush, noticed Richard's car, which was waiting to enter the busy road to Oxford.

The roses caught her eye first, and then the particularly sulky look on the driver's face.

'Proper nasty tempered, that one,' thought Nelly. 'Wonder what he's doing in these parts? A rep, no doubt, and with them flowers in the back probably no better than he should be.'

She paused to get her breath halfway up the hill, and remembered her faithless Charlie who had so cruelly turned her out of his home when his roving eye had lit upon another woman more to his liking. She dwelt on his infamy with martyred pleasure. The fact that he had taken her in when she had left Albert, her husband, some months earlier, she chose to forget.

All in all, she supposed, both men had treated her fairly well, and Albert had been remarkably amiable when she had returned to him. She would enjoy frying the chops for him which were in her basket. Cooking was the true joy of Nelly's life.

As she reached the top of the hill she could see Edward and Jean Young's fine house beyond the chestnut trees, and recalled the earnest discussion she and Mrs Peters had had that afternoon about veal and ham pie, salmon mousse, roast turkey, spiced beef and a score of other dishes suitable for a particularly select cold buffet. She was going to enjoy getting that lot ready!

Crossing behind the old people's homes, and now mercifully on the flat, Nelly came face to face with her husband's old friend Percy Hodge, who farmed a mile or so northwards off the Nidden road.

'Wotcher, Perce? Nice drop of rain yesterday. Do your crops good.'

'Done the potatoes a bit of good, I suppose, but too late for the wheat and barley. Be a poor yield, I shouldn't wonder.'

'You farmers never stop grumbling,' said Nelly. 'I'm glad I'm not married to one.'

She stopped hastily, remembering the truant Doris. Perhaps she'd said something to upset poor old Perce?

Had she known, he was thinking that Albert did his share of grumbling too, and a fine bonny woman like Nelly might have been better off with a farmer after all.

'Well, I must get on,' said Nelly, somewhat flustered. 'Albert's waiting for his tea.'

'He's a lucky chap to have someone to cook it for him,' replied Percy lugubriously. 'Some of us have to cook our own.'

Nelly felt that the conversation was taking a dangerous turn. Percy Hodge was full of self-pity, and she didn't want any attentions from him. He'd been enough nuisance to that poor Jenny of Mrs Bailey's until she'd boxed his ears.

What a tiresome lot men were, thought Nelly, approaching her door. It made you wonder why they had been put into the world in the first place. If she'd had any hand in arranging matters at the Creation, she would have made sure that there would have been only one sex. Life would have been much simpler.

'And about time!' said Albert, when she closed the door behind her. 'I was getting fair weak with hunger.'

Nelly managed to stay silent, but she banged the frying pan viciously on to the stove to relieve her feelings.

Before Albert's chops were done, an upsetting telephone call came to the school house a few yards away.

Agnes and Dorothy were enjoying the newspapers, and the comfortable thought that it was Friday evening, and the much-blest weekend stretched ahead, when the telephone rang.

Dorothy answered it, and a few stray phrases were heard by Agnes.

'How serious is it? . . . Well, *of course*, we were in school. You must have known, Kathleen! . . . Which hospital? . . . Most inconvenient . . . Yes, of course, I shall go. I shall set off tomorrow morning . . . No, no, don't put yourself to any trouble. I can find a room.'

She came back, pink and flustered.

'Oh, what a kettle of fish! Really, Kathleen gets more impossible yearly! She's complaining because she's tried to ring us twice today, once at ten and then again at two o'clock. *Of course* we were in school, and no one but Kathleen would be so woolly-headed as to forget it.'

'But what's happened?'

'Oh, Ray has had an accident with the car,' said Dorothy, in what to anxious little Miss Fogerty seemed a remarkably off-hand manner.

Her hands fluttered to her face. 'But Dorothy, how dreadful! Is he badly hurt?'

'No, no! Kathleen said he has concussion, and probably a broken arm. The hospital people are keeping him in for a day or two.'

'I heard you say you would visit him. Shall I come with you?'

'No, Agnes. I shall catch the morning coach to London, and then take a taxi. Kathleen offered to put me up if I wanted to stay the night. In rather a *grudging* tone of voice, I thought. But I shall come back during the evening. Really, it is dreadfully annoying. I intended to wash my new cardigan tomorrow.'

'I will do that willingly.'

'It can wait until another day,' said Miss Watson firmly. 'We are not going to get in a flummox over Ray's foolishness.'

'But what happened? Did Kathleen say?'

'I think he swerved into one of those islands with bollards in the middle of the road, but Kathleen didn't say what caused it. Fortunately, no one else was involved.'

'What a blessing!'

'Now one thing I must see to,' said Dorothy, reaching for her handbag. 'Of course, the wretched banks will be closed to-morrow, but I think I have enough money to pay my way. In any case, I can use my Post Office book to withdraw some cash. I must say, my Post Office book is a real friend in need.'

'I have ten pounds put by,' said Agnes, 'in my stocking drawer.'

'Thank you, dear, but there is no need. I shall be all right. I'm meeting Kathleen at the hospital, so I shall know more then.'

'Did she get your card?' Agnes asked.

'She did indeed, and sounded very gratified. In fact, she said if it hadn't been for my kind message she wouldn't have liked to worry me about Ray's accident.'

'Now, isn't that nice!' cried little Miss Fogerty, aglow with noble feelings.

Dorothy gave one of her resounding snorts.

'I'm beginning to wonder,' she said.

5. The Longest Day

Nelly Piggott, hurrying to work on the Saturday morning, remembered that today was the longest day of the year.

'June nearly on its way out,' thought Nelly, 'and them blankets not washed yet for the winter. Not that Albert'd notice.'

As she reached the bottom of the hill she noticed Miss Watson, stick in one hand, and a crocodile-skin handbag in the other, waiting to cross the road. Why was she out so early, wondered Nelly? Looked very smart too. A wedding perhaps?

Although she was not averse to making the occasional derisive remark about her two schoolteacher neighbours, secretly Nelly felt great respect for them. The school which Nelly had attended as a child put discipline at the head of its priorities.

None of the staff could have held a candle to Dotty Harmer's tyrant of a father, but nevertheless due respect to teachers by pupils was expected, and punishment was severe if it was not forthcoming. Nelly herself could remember standing on her chair, a figure of shame before her contemporaries, enduring the while the lash of her teacher's tongue.

'Good morning, Miss Watson,' she said deferentially.

'Ah! Good morning, Mrs Piggott,' replied Dorothy. 'Are we in for a fine day, do you think?'

'I hope so. I only do the morning at The Fuchsia Bush on a Saturday, and I thought I might wash a few blankets this afternoon.'

Dorothy nodded vaguely. She had never washed a blanket in

her life. Surely one would need something bigger than the sink for that? Luckily, the laundry took care of their blankets.

Nelly slackened her pace, to keep in step with her companion.

'Please don't let me hold you up,' said Dorothy. 'I'm rather slow these days.'

'No hurry for me now, we're nearly there,' Nelly assured her.

'I'm catching the coach,' said Dorothy. 'Rather bad news about my brother.'

Nelly was agog. A little drama is always welcome.

'I'm sorry to hear that.'

'A car accident. I don't think he is badly hurt, but I'm going to the hospital to make sure.'

'Oh, of course! Blood's thicker than water, I always say. Have you got far to go?'

'No, it's one of the London hospitals. I can visit any time this afternoon.'

'Then you'll be in nice time,' commented Nelly, wondering why Miss Watson should be making such an early start.

As if reading her thoughts, Dorothy replied. 'I propose to do a little shopping while I'm in town. Selfridge's and John Lewis's are so satisfactory.'

They were now at the coach stop outside The Fuchsia Bush.

'Well, I hope you find your brother pretty well,' said Nelly politely, and departed to her day's work.

Really a very nice woman, thought Dorothy, watching her go. Not many of that calibre about these days. Hardworking, well-mannered, kindly – Albert hardly deserved anyone so worthwhile.

On the other hand, of course, one had heard things about Nelly's moral standards.

But before she could dwell on the baser and more interesting side of Nelly's character, the coach arrived, mercifully half empty, and Miss Watson mounted the steps to choose her seat for the journey.

*

Winnie Bailey had had a troubled night after her encounter with Richard. She did not regret her refusal to take on Fenella and her two children, but she was annoyed with Richard for suggesting it.

And yet she was fond of her nephew, despite his irritating ways, and hoped that he would not have a prolonged fit of the sulks, and cut her out of his life. She was getting too old to cope with harboured grudges, and would like to see Richard, and his wife and family, as she had said.

Well, time would show, she thought philosophically, putting out the milk bottles on the front step.

John Lovell, on his way to morning surgery, hurried across to speak to her.

'Did you ever find that farm, John?' she asked him.

'After a false start or two. The fir tree's gone now, but the house is still there, and the farm buildings, though everything's a bit run down.'

'Who lives there now?'

'At Trotters? Leys Farm, I mean.'

'Yes. Which do they call it, by the way?'

'Leys Farm. Though an old boy on the road knew it as Trotters, as you do.'

'Nice family?'

'Two middle-aged brothers, and a youngster, a nephew, I gathered. It was he who was groggy. Some tummy bug or other. Violent D. and V. but he had responded well to antibiotics when I called again, so I shan't need to make another visit, unless they ring.'

'No women?'

'Not in evidence. They looked a pretty scruffy lot, despite half a dozen expensive-looking cars in the yard. How are things with you?'

'Fine, John.'

She was half-inclined to tell him of Richard's visit, but already a few patients were entering his waiting room, and

Winnie, as a doctor's wife, knew better than to keep him from his work.

She might tell him later, she decided, watching him cross to the surgery. Perhaps she might feel less worried about the affair as time passed.

Downhill at Lulling, the rector decided to take advantage of the sunshine to walk along the towpath of the River Pleshey.

The exercise would do him good, Dimity told him, as she set about preparing a lamb casserole.

'And it might clear my brain,' added Charles. 'Tomorrow's sermon doesn't read very well, I must admit. Perhaps I shall get some flashes of inspiration.'

He always enjoyed this quiet pathway. The willows shimmered their grey green leaves above the water. Their rustling, and the river's rippling, made a tranquil background to the

rector's thoughts, and he walked rather farther than he first intended, until he found himself within sight of the cottage which had once belonged to the water keeper, and now housed his old friend Tom Hardy and his equally ancient dog, Polly.

He decided to call on them, and crossed the wooden footbridge to the house. As was his wont, he went to the back door, and there discovered Tom chopping up wood on the doorstep. Polly was lying nearby in the sun, but came to greet him, tail wagging.

'She remembers you, sir,' said Tom, straightening his back slowly. 'This is a nice surprise, I must say. Come into the kitchen.'

A bench stood against the wall, hard by the back door.

'Let's sit here,' said the rector. 'Too good to go inside.'

The old man sat down heavily with a sigh.

'Who'd have thought choppin' a few sticks would wind you? It does though.'

'Do you need them in this weather?'

'Well, no. I don't light my kitchen stove much come the summer, but I suppose it's going most of the year, and I likes to have plenty of firing put by.'

'It must make quite a bit of work, Tom. Clearing out the ashes and so on.'

'Ah! But it's company. And the kettle's always on, and the oven stays nice and hot. I puts in a chop, or some sausages in a little old tin, and a rice pudden for afters. That cooks lovely that old stove, and in the evening I opens the little door, and Poll and me enjoys the firelight and the warmth on us.'

Charles Henstock recalled the massive black hod which held the fuel for Tom's stove, and wondered how he could lift it nowadays. He had never completely regained his strength after his sojourn in the local hospital, when Polly had been a welcome guest at Lulling Vicarage in her master's absence.

'Do you get anybody to help you in the house?' asked Charles.

'Well, my good neighbour comes now and again, but she's a busy soul. But that reminds me, sir, she brought a form for me to write on to see if I could have a home help once or twice a week.'

'That's a splendid idea.'

'Yes, I s'pose so. But I'm no hand at forms. Would you be so good as to help me with it? It's upstairs.'

'Willingly, Tom. Let's fetch it.'

Tom led the way through the kitchen which Charles always admired for its practicality and bare, but beautiful, simplicity. It was as tidy as ever, the table top scrubbed white, the now cold stove black and shining.

The staircase opened from this room, and Charles watched Tom mount the steep flight with shaky steps. The rope banister against the wall was the only support, and Charles watched his old friend's progress with mounting anxiety.

'Shall I come up, Tom?'

'No, sir,' wheezed Tom, 'I'll bring it down.'

Charles waited at the foot of the staircase, listening to the old man opening drawers and shifting furniture. A print of a moonlight steeplechase hung on the wall, foxed with age and damp, but the intrepid riders in their white night shirts could still be descried, if one peered closely. It seemed to be the only picture in the house, and hanging in such a murky place, it obviously did not gain much attention.

Tom reappeared, letter in hand, and descended carefully.

'Let's spread it out on the kitchen table,' said Charles, and was relieved when the two of them were sitting on sturdy wooden chairs with their task before them.

The rector filled in the data as Tom answered his questions, and in ten minutes the form was ready and signed in Tom's quavering hand.

'I'll post it for you with my letters,' said Charles. 'I have to go to the Post Office this afternoon.'

'Then I'll give you the stamp money,' said the old man,

pulling out the drawer of the table and taking out an old tobacco tin.

'No need for that, Tom.'

The old man looked stubborn. 'I won't be beholden,' he said.

'Very well,' replied the rector amiably. 'If you insist. Second class will do, I'm sure.'

Tom handed over the coins, and gave a great smile.

'That's a weight off my chest. How about some tea?'

'I'd better not, Tom. I've got to eat a meal when I get back. But let's have a few minutes outside in the sun.'

He stayed for half an hour, relishing the old man's company, and the affection displayed by Polly to them both. She and Tom were a devoted pair, and enjoyed each other's tranquil companionship.

On his way back, the rector thought seriously about Tom's future. Here, surely, was an absolutely suitable person for one of Thrush Green's new homes. He would not have to negotiate those dangerous stairs, or chop sticks, or handle that hefty coal hod. He could have a meal brought to him, if need be, and although the rice pudding might not be as good as those he cooked himself, the rector felt sure that Tom would appreciate it in time.

But even if a place were allotted to Tom, would he want to move? He loved his cottage hard by the river, his little garden filled with old-fashioned flowers, pansies, a musk rose and mignonette. And most of all he loved his independence. He could be obstinate. Charles recalled the tight lips and stern eyes when he had attempted to wave aside the stamp money. No, it would not be easy to move Tom should the need arise.

And Polly? What about Polly? He would never leave her, that was certain. They were as close as mother and child, or husband and wife.

Charles stood stock still for a moment, taken aback by this problem. A moorhen, scared at the intrusion, fluttered squawking from the reeds, and crossed the stream with trailing legs that scattered diamond-bright drops.

'We must cross that bridge when we come to it,' Charles told the bird, and continued on his way to attack tomorrow's sermon once more.

Little Miss Fogerty spent the morning doing the usual Saturday chores, the personal washing, including Dorothy's cardigan which received particular care, a thorough dusting and carpet-sweeping which was done sketchily on workdays, and sorting out the bed linen ready for the laundryman on Tuesday.

The evening meal was to be cold chicken and salad, and Agnes went down the garden to pull a fine lettuce and some radishes to wash.

Her college friend Isobel was in her garden next door.

'Agnes dear, could I bring the jumble stuff round this afternoon?'

'Any time, Isobel. I am on my own all day.'

She explained about Dorothy's absence, and knew that her headmistress would not mind Isobel hearing about Ray's accident. Normally, at Thrush Green, one needed to filter one's thoughts before speaking and getting a name for being a gossip, but the two neighbours relied on each other's discretion, and knew that they could discuss matters unguardedly.

'Why don't you come to lunch with Harold and me? Come and take pot luck. We'd love it.'

'I won't, dear, many thanks. I'm having a clearing-up day. But I'll look forward to seeing you with the jumble.'

Agnes partook of a lightly-boiled egg for lunch, and a cup of coffee, had a brief snooze with her feet up on the string stool Dorothy had made at last winter's evening class in Lulling, and was alert when Isobel arrived, and ready for the exchange of news.

As always, Isobel looked pretty in a blue linen frock and white sandals. Agnes secretly admired her unblemished brown bare legs, and thought ruefully of her own heavily veined ones. Ah well! Isobel had not had to stand so many hours before a class, thought Agnes without envy, and it was a pleasure to see how young and healthy she looked, despite being almost exactly her own age.

In the evening, Agnes set the table and then made her way down the hill to meet Dorothy at the London coach stop in the High Street.

It was a golden evening. A glimpse of a cornfield in the distance showed the crop already looking a pale gold in the low rays of the sinking sun. A nearby row of trees had their trunks turned to bronze on their north-west side. It was going to be a spectacular sunset, thought Agnes, and was reminded of a reverberating phrase in her ancient copy of *A Handbook for Teachers*, which exhorted all those who had to teach in dismal towns to 'direct the pupils' attention to the ever-changing panorama of the heavens', if there were nothing else of natural beauty to be seen.

Agnes thought how fortunate she was to have her lot cast at Thrush Green which had such splendid walks suitable for the young. She made a mental note to take her class to see the beauties of the June hedgerows on the road to Nidden. The elder flowers were magnificent at the moment, and the wild roses at their best.

With any luck, they might see a nest, but really it might be wiser not to disclose such treasures. The girls would relish the secret, no doubt, but one really could not trust *all* the boys to be quite so gentle. That youngest Cooke boy, for instance, had a truly barbaric streak in him, sad to say.

By this time, Agnes had reached the coach stop. The High Street was pleasantly quiet, and the lime trees already showing pale flowers. The coach was late, and Agnes found a low wall near The Fuchsia Bush for a comfortable seat. She was observed there by the three Miss Lovelock sisters who peered from time to time from their drawing-room window to make sure that nothing of note escaped them.

Agnes was unaware of their scrutiny, but was turning over in her mind certain plans for her winter wardrobe. Her camel coat should do another season. Such a useful garment, and equally wearable with black or brown. On the other hand, she rather favoured a green hat for formal wear, and wondered if it would go well with her new black suit and the camel colour? Of course, there were always *scarves*, Agnes mused, and at that moment the coach arrived, and Dorothy descended the stairs carefully.

'Agnes, how *nice* of you to come! No, no, I can quite well manage the parcels. They are very light, just a few little things for the winter, though why we should be dwelling on that on this gorgeous summer's day, I really don't know.'

'And how did you find Ray?'

'Very little amiss. But I'll tell you all when we are home. This hill takes all one's breath, doesn't it?'

And Agnes could not help but agree, despite her eagerness to hear Dorothy's news.

After the chicken and salad had been enjoyed, Dorothy kicked off her shoes and settled back on the sofa with a sigh.

'Delicious, Agnes! I feel quite restored. How people can think of a day in London as a *treat* beats me! I find it an endurance test, I must say, although as a girl I really enjoyed pottering round Liberty's or dear old Heal's, and then going to a matinée or an exhibition after that. What resilience we used to have!'

'But Ray?' pressed Agnes. 'How was he?'

'In bed, of course, and he had a bandage round his head which made him look rather worse than he was. His forehead evidently had a nasty gash from the windscreen. It was quite shattered.'

'*His forehead?*' exclaimed Agnes aghast.

'No, no, dear. The windscreen. I heard the whole story in bits and pieces between the two of them.'

'So you met Kathleen there?'

'Yes, as I told you, at two-thirty.'

Agnes forbore to point out that Dorothy had told her nothing of the sort, but awaited enlightenment.

'As a matter of fact, I very much doubt if Ray would have

told me much at all – certainly not about the dog – if Kathleen hadn't blurted it out.'

'The dog? What was its name now?'

'Harrison, of all the stupid names. Called after their butcher or some such whimsical nonsense. I do dislike animals referred to as Miss Poppet or Mr Thompson. One is misled into thinking they are lodgers at first hearing. What's wrong with Rover or Pip or Towser? Though, come to think of it, I haven't come across a Towser for years. My Uncle Tom had a Towser, a most intelligent mongrel.'

'But Ray's accident,' prodded Agnes, who felt that Dorothy's digressions from the main subject were more infuriating than usual.

Miss Watson sat up, and began to look more attentive. 'Well, I met Kathleen as arranged, although, of course, she was ten minutes overdue, as one would expect. She referred again to my anniversary card, and they both gave me a warm welcome which was gratifying.'

'Yes, indeed. Bygones must be bygones.'

'She had brought a great sheaf of irises for Ray, and the nurse looked a bit taken aback, as well she might, for the ward was not very well furnished for bouquets which would have been more suitable in a cathedral. I took three bunches of violets, incidentally.'

'Ray would like those, I'm sure.'

'The first thing he did was to enquire after the dog, which I thought rather absurd, until Kathleen replied that he was recovering well and had eaten some minced beef and four beaten eggs in milk.'

'How *expensive!*' commented frugal little Miss Fogerty.

'Exactly. I asked if the dog were seriously ill, and do you know what Kathleen said?'

'How *could* I know?' answered Agnes reasonably, but with a touch of impatience. Would the story never end? It reminded her of *Tristram Shandy*, read long ago at college.

' "Not seriously ill, but still a little upset by the accident." I ask you!'

'So the dog was in the car too?'

'It was indeed, and it transpires that it was the cause of the accident. Evidently, Ray was driving alone, with the animal sitting in the back, when it saw a cat on the pavement, went berserk, leapt into the front seat and created pandemonium. Just as it did at our tea party, you remember.'

'I do indeed. What a dreadful thing! And so Ray swerved, I suppose?'

'Right into one of those islands, and at some speed. The windscreen shattered, and the side of the car was pushed in. It's a wonder poor Ray wasn't killed. They had to cut part of the car away to get him out.'

'Is he badly cut about?'

'Only his forehead, and he has two cracked ribs and a broken arm. Nothing to worry about,' said Dorothy with sisterly casualness. 'The concussion seems to have been very slight. He should be out in a day or two.'

'Well, it was right to go and see him,' said Agnes. 'And it is a blessing he is not worse, poor fellow. And I'm glad the dog is well. They are so devoted to it.'

'Much *too* devoted, if you ask me,' said Dorothy, with asperity. 'I very nearly told them what I thought of their foolish indulgence of that disgustingly behaved animal, but it didn't seem quite the time and place for a bit of plain speaking. It might have started Kathleen off on one of her hysterical fits, and I didn't think the other patients in the ward should be subjected to that. After all, they all had enough to put up with, Ray included.'

'That was thoughtful of you,' agreed Agnes, who knew how easily her friend was stirred to outspokenness, sometimes with disastrous and embarrassing results.

'Do you know, Agnes, I should really enjoy a cup of coffee. It's been a long day.'

'The longest of the year,' said Agnes, pointing to the calendar. 'Stay there, my dear, and I'll go and make the coffee.'

The two ladies went to bed early. Little Miss Fogerty had also found it a long and tiring day, but was relieved to have Dorothy back safe and sound, and to know that her brother was making steady progress. There was much to be thankful for, she thought, gazing out of her bedroom window across Thrush Green.

It was still light, although the little travelling clock on the bedroom mantelpiece said ten o'clock. The statue of Nathaniel Patten shone in the rosy light of a spectacular sunset, now beginning to fade into shades of pink and mauve.

The air was still. Far away, a distant train hooted at Lulling station, a pigeon clattered homeward, and a small black shadow crossed the road below Miss Fogerty's window. Albert Piggott's cat was about its night time business.

'Time for bed,' yawned little Miss Fogerty.

It really had been an exceptionally long day.

6. The Fuchsia Bush to the Rescue

Throughout July work went on steadily at the old people's homes. The weather was kind, and the outside painting went ahead without disruption. Edward Young was relieved to see such progress, and optimistic about its opening in the autumn.

He said as much to his wife Joan, one breakfast time.

'I only hope the weather will hold up for my lunch party,' she replied. 'I've made plans to hustle everything under cover if need be, but it would be splendid if people could picnic on the lawn.'

'Of course it will stay fine,' Edward said robustly. 'Looks settled for weeks. Mark my words, things will go without a hitch!'

But he was wrong. Later that morning she answered the telephone to find that it was her sister Ruth speaking, sounding much agitated.

'It's mother, Joan. I went in just now to see if she were needing help in dressing, and found her on the floor.'

'Oh no! Heart again?'

'There's no saying. I've got her into bed, but John's on his rounds, of course. I've left a message.'

'I'll come straightaway.'

Molly Curdle was in the kitchen, at her morning duties. She and her husband Ben now lived in the converted stable where Joan and Ruth's mother had lived until recently.

Joan explained briefly what had happened, and left Molly troubled in mind. She had known the Bassetts, Joan's parents, ever since she was a child, and the death of the old man had grieved her. Was his wife to follow him so soon? Ben, now busy at work in Lulling, would be as upset as she was.

Joan found her mother barely conscious, but the old lady managed to smile at the two anxious faces bending over her.

'John's just rung,' whispered Ruth. 'He's coming straight back from Lulling. Miss Pick caught him at the Venables', luckily.'

Mrs Bassett's eyes were now closed, but she seemed to be breathing normally.

Ruth smoothed the bedclothes, nodded to her sister, and the two tiptoed from the room.

Agnes Fogerty, with a straggling crocodile of small children behind her, recognised Joan Young's car outside her sister's. It was nice to see how devoted the two were, she thought fondly. So many sisters did not get on well. Families could be quite sorely divided. Look at Dorothy and Ray, for instance.

'John Todd,' called little Miss Fogerty, temporarily diverted from her musings on the variability of family relationships, 'throw that nettle away, and if I see you tormenting George Curdle again I *shall send you to Miss Watson.*'

This appalling threat succeeded in frightening John Todd, a hardened criminal of six years old, into temporary good behaviour, and the observation of the Thrush Green hedgerows continued.

There was plenty to be seen. On the grass verges the pink trumpets of mallow bloomed. Nearer the edge grew the shorter white yarrow, with its darker foliage and tough stems, and in the dust of the gutter, pink and white striped bindweed showed its trumpets against a mat of flat leaves, as pretty as marsh-mallows, thought Agnes.

Nearby was yellow silverweed with its feathery foliage, almost hidden by a mass of dog daisies, as the children called them. In the sunshine their pungent scent was almost overpowering, but three small brown and orange butterflies were giving the plants their attention, and the children were excited.

'My grandpa,' said John Todd, anxious to reinstate himself in Miss Fogerty's good books, 'has got six drawers in a cabinet, full of butterflies with pins through 'em.'

Some of the girls gave squeaks of disgust, and little Miss Fogerty herself inwardly recoiled from the picture this evoked.

'They're dead all right,' John Todd said hastily. 'He done 'em in in a bottle. Years ago, it was.'

'Very interesting,' commented Agnes primly. One could not always believe John Todd's stories, and even if this one happened to be true, good manners forbade one to criticise the child's grandfather.

'Now we will stop under this tree for a moment,' said Agnes, diverting the children's attention, and remembering 'the ever-changing panorama of the heavens' phrase of long ago. 'You may sit on the grass as it is quite dry, and I want you to notice the lovely creamy flowers hanging down. This is a lime tree, and if you breathe in you can smell the beautiful fragrance of the flowers.'

Some unnecessarily squelchy indrawing of breath made Miss Fogerty clap her hands sharply.

'Perhaps we will have a little nose-blowing first,' she said firmly. 'Hold up your hankies!'

There were times, thought Agnes, trying to recapture the heady bliss of breathing in the perfume of flowering lime, when children were excessively tiresome.

It was a good thing that Miss Fogerty had taken her children on the nature walk when she did, for a rainy spell of weather set in, when mackintoshes were the rule, and many of the fragrant lime flowers fell wetly to the ground beneath the downpour.

The gardeners of Lulling and Thrush Green welcomed the rain. The broad beans plumped out, the raspberries flourished, red flowers burst out on the runner bean plants, and the thirsty flowers everywhere revived.

Joan Young viewed the wet garden with less enthusiasm. In a week's time the buffet lunch was to take place, and that morning before breakfast, she had made a decision. She must ask Mrs Peters of The Fuchsia Bush if she could cope with the waiting on her guests, and with the main bulk of the catering.

Her mother was still in a precarious state, needing to be in bed for most of the day, and Ruth, with two young children, was hard pressed.

Joan and Edward's only child, Paul, was away at school, and Joan was sharing the nursing duties as often as she could, but the extra work of the lunch party was beginning to worry her enormously.

'If The Fuchsia Bush could take it off my shoulders,' she said to Edward, as they dressed, 'it would make it so much easier.

You see, I had planned to collect plates and cutlery from no end of people, and napkins and serving bowls for the salads and trifles and whatnot.'

'What about glasses?' asked Edward, putting first things first.

'Oh, that's simple. The wine people are coping with that anyway. But with Mother as she is, I want to feel I could slip away, if need be, without disrupting anything.'

'You bob down to Lulling, and see Mrs Peters,' advised Edward, fighting his way into his pullover. He tugged it down, and went to look at his latest project through the streaming windowpane.

'They really look splendid, don't they?' he said with satisfaction. 'A great improvement on Charles's ghastly abode.'

'Will this weather hold up the work?'

'Not greatly. There's plenty to finish off inside.'

He put his arm round his wife, and gave her a kiss.

She was glad his work was nearly over. Hers, it seemed, was about to begin.

When Nelly Piggott entered The Fuchsia Bush the next morning, she found Mrs Peters sitting at the vast table in the quiet kitchen. She was busy making a list, and looked up as Nelly entered.

'Such news, Nelly,' she cried. 'Come and sit down.'

Nelly took off her wet mackintosh, hung it in the passage, and flopped down thankfully on the chair opposite her employer.

'I had a visit from Mrs Young last night,' she began. 'She's in rather a state about this lunch party of hers.'

She went on to explain Joan's needs, and her own plans to help her in this emergency. Nelly listened enthralled. Here was a challenge indeed!

'But can we do it?' she asked at length. 'What about getting the food up there? And the plates and dishes? And who's going to look after this place? After all, Saturdays are always busy.'

'I rang Bunnings about transport and they'll ferry everything.

The Wine Bar's coping with the drink and glasses. We can take most of our own crockery and silver, and I intend to ask Mrs Jefferson if she would take charge here until we are back.'

Mrs Jefferson had been at The Fuchsia Bush for many years, but ill health had meant that she now only came part time. But, as Nelly knew, she was quite capable of holding the fort for a day in an emergency. Really, thought Nelly, it was all very exciting!

'How many of us will you need?' she asked.

'Well, you'll be my chief assistant, Nelly, if you feel you can undertake it.'

Nelly beamed. 'I'll thoroughly enjoy myself,' she assured her employer. 'What's the plan of campaign?'

'We'll take up the plates and things on the Friday evening when we're closed. I'm sure I can get all we need in the car. Then the food can go up with Bunning on Saturday morning. People will help themselves. It's just a case of us slicing the meat and the pies and quiches. We'll get the various salads ready here.'

'Just the two of us?' asked Nelly enthusiastically.

'Well, no. I'll see if Gloria and Rosa will come too. We shall want a few more hands, and though they leave much to be desired, at least they can stack plates, and put the dirty cutlery in a bucket to bring back here.'

Nelly thought swiftly. 'So really we'll be busy from Friday night till Saturday night?'

Mrs Peters looked suddenly anxious and careworn, and Nelly's kind heart was stirred.

'Yes, that's about it, Nelly. How do you feel?'

'Dead keen!' that lady told her energetically, and meant it.

Albert Piggott was remarkably docile when Nelly told him the great news.

'As long as I gets my tea as usual, it's all the same to me,' he said, pushing aside the plate which had been filled with oxtail stew ten minutes earlier.

'It might have to be cold that day,' his wife warned him.

'Then make a decent bit of pie,' said Albert. 'That brawn you brought back from the shop hadn't got no staying power in it for a hardworking chap.'

Nelly forbore to comment, but set about clearing the table with her customary energy.

While she was thus engaged a knock came at the door, and Albert, heaving himself from the armchair with a sigh, went to answer it. To his amazement, Percy Hodge stood on the doorstep holding a bunch of roses. Percy himself looked equally taken aback.

'What the hell do you want?' asked Albert of his drinking companion.

'I thought this was your evening over the churchyard,' spluttered Percy.

'Well, it ain't. Young Cooke's wasting his time there tonight.'

He peered at the roses with dislike. Nelly, secretly nettled at this unwanted attention, came forward, drying her hands on a teacloth.

'Good evening, Percy,' she said primly.

'I was wondering,' said Percy, who had been thinking as quickly as his slow brain would allow, 'if Mrs Peters down the shop would like these roses for the tea tables. Maybe you'd be kind enough to take 'em down in the morning.'

'I'm sure she'd be pleased,' said Nelly. 'Won't you come in?'

'Just going next door,' said Percy hastily, thrusting the bouquet into Nelly's arms, to her discomfort. 'You coming for a pint, Albert?'

'No, I ain't,' said Albert grimly, and slammed the door.

'Well,' said Nelly, much flustered, 'I'd better put these in a bucket overnight.'

'Best place for them,' responded Albert sourly, 'is the dustbin. And how long, may I ask, has all this been going on?'

At the village school, end of term was bringing its usual flurry of activity, and Miss Watson and her staff were looking forward to the final day with ever-increasing exhaustion.

'Sometimes I wonder if it is practicable to have Sports Day and the Annual Outing and the Parents' Fête and the Leavers' Service, all in the last month when we are so busy with reports and all these wretched returns to the Office,' sighed Dorothy, as she walked homeward across the playground.

'But we couldn't really arrange things very well for the end of any of the other terms,' pointed out little Miss Fogerty. 'Christmas is hectic as it is, and anyway most of the activities are out of door ones. They must be held in the summer.'

'Yes, dear, I know. But it doesn't make things any easier.'

There was a letter on the door mat which Dorothy picked up.

'Kathleen's writing. Now I wonder what she wants?'

The two ladies made their way to the sitting-room, and sat down with sighs of relief. Agnes closed her eyes, listening to the rustle of Kathleen's letter, as Dorothy read it with an occasional snort.

'Well, it appears that we can expect a visitation from them soon. Ray is getting so bored with being unable to do much, and a neighbour has offered to take them for a drive. Why Kathleen has never had the commonsense to learn to drive, *I do not know*. Scatterbrained, I know she is, and completely lacking in mechanical skills, but sillier people than she drive cars after all, and it would have been a help to Ray now and again.'

'Are they coming soon?'

'It's left to us. I suppose we'd better say they're welcome.' Dorothy's voice sounded anything but welcoming. 'But not until we've broken up,' she said firmly. 'One thing, this neighbour refuses to have the dog in his car, sensible fellow, so we shan't have a repetition of their last disastrous visit.'

She rose from her chair.

'I shall make tea today, Agnes, you look tired. Shall we have Earl Grey for a change? So refreshing.'

'That would be lovely, Dorothy,' replied Agnes.

Nelly Piggott descended the hill the next morning with the roses in her basket.

There had been a few harsh words between herself and Albert after Percy's departure, but nothing seriously amiss. Nelly's conscience was clear, and she told Albert so in plain terms.

Albert, knowing Percy, guessed that for once Nelly was telling the truth about this unwelcome admirer, and after ten minutes of bickering the quarrel petered out.

Nelly was extremely cross with Percy but had no intention of confronting him. Better to tell his sister, Mrs Jenner, with whom she went to Bingo occasionally, and let her pass on the message to silly old Percy.

Nevertheless, it was rather a comfort to Nelly to know that she could still inspire devotion. She had always had admirers, and was romantic by nature. She passed over the roses to Mrs Peters with a twinge of regret.

That lady was far too engrossed with the plans for Joan Young's buffet lunch to do anything but accept them with perfunctory thanks, and Nelly was not called upon to give any explanation of her gift.

The roses were put into a copper pitcher and had pride of place in the front window of The Fuchsia Bush for two days, where they were much admired by the customers.

Meanwhile, preparations proceeded apace. Mrs Peters was a born organiser, Nelly an enthusiastic supporter, and the two waitresses were sufficiently stirred by this change in routine to agree to don clean overalls and welcoming smiles for their part in the project. All that everyone prayed for now was a fine day.

The weather forecast was equivocal. There might be showers, there was a chance of sunshine, it would probably be overcast, temperatures would be normal for the time of year, winds would be light.

The morning dawned grey and still. Joan Young, a bundle of nerves, could only manage a cup of coffee for breakfast, and was soon outside surveying the preparations.

Molly and Ben Curdle had cleared their garage so that the produce stall and the plants could be displayed under cover.

The gipsy caravan, which had once been Ben's grandmother's home, now stood nearby in the orchard, and this today housed the white elephant stall, including some of Ella's handiwork.

The dining-room and drawing-room were given over to the food, to be spread on long tables for the visitors to help themselves. Both rooms had french windows opening to the lawn and it was Joan's earnest hope that the weather would allow her patrons to sit outside, balancing plates and glasses, and dropping crumbs at their will. All the garden chairs which could be mustered were disposed under trees or near the small ornamental pool, and very pretty and welcoming it all looked.

She could do no more. Now it was over to Mrs Peters, as yet untried, and the Wine Bar in whom she had confidence from past experience.

Edward had volunteered to take the money at the gate and to collect the tickets of those who had gallantly bought them beforehand. At twelve o'clock, he was ensconced before his card table, while Mrs Peters, Nelly, Gloria, Rosa, Joan Young and Molly Curdle were hard at it in the kitchen, dining-room and drawing-room.

A hazy sun began to shine and everyone's spirits lifted as the first few friends came up the drive, and were directed to the paddock, today the car park, by Ben Curdle.

They had catered for one hundred guests. All seemed to have excellent appetites, and to intend to eat their three pounds-worth of the delicious offerings set before them. Nelly was gratified to receive compliments on her veal and ham pie, the quiches, the spiced beef and other delicacies. Mrs Peters, flushed and happy, watched the delectable trifles, mousses and flans vanish gardenwards.

A good many people had come from Lulling in a coach organised by Mrs Thurgood, a wealthy widow and a regular churchgoer at St John's.

It was she who had fallen out with poor Charles Henstock, soon after his induction, over the kneelers which she was deter-mined to replace against all opposition. Luckily, the quarrel was in the past, and now she and Charles were the best of friends, the relationship being cemented by the marriage of her daughter Jane to a young man, John Fairbrother, to whom Charles had introduced the girl.

Mrs Thurgood insisted on inspecting the kitchen, much to Joan Young's and Mrs Peters' annoyance, but the lady was renowned for her autocratic ways and allowed to snoop without comment, at least of an audible nature, but meaning glances were exchanged behind the lady's back, and later Joan told Edward just what she thought of such behaviour.

Trade was brisk at the stalls. Ella was delighted to find that almost all her weaving and wickerwork had been bought, and even the wispiest geraniums seemed to be snapped up at the plant stall.

At the end of the day, Edward counted his money, and that taken at the stalls, and added it to the ticket money already banked. To everyone's amazement and gratification it came to nine hundred and seventy-four pounds and a halfpenny.

After paying Mrs Peters and the Wine Bar there would still be a handsome profit.

'Well,' said Joan, when everyone had gone home and she was sitting on the sofa with her shoes off, 'that's a good beginning for the Heart Appeal and the Church Roof Fund.'

It was the beginning of much more, if she had only known.

7. SUMMER VISITORS

Work on the new homes was almost finished, and Edward Young was proud of his work. After the rectory fire, there was much conjecture about possible purchasers of the site. Eventually, an old-established charity, which owned similar sheltered accommodation elsewhere, bought it, and worthy local people were appointed trustees.

The vicar of the parish was one, and as for many years Mrs Thurgood's husband had been a generous benefactor to the foundation, it was thought proper to appoint his widow as another. Justin Venables was another of the trustees.

John Lovell also took a keen interest in the project, for he was one of the trustees who would not only help to select the first lucky residents, but would keep an eye on their health. After much discussion, it had been decided to call the new homes Rectory Cottages.

There would be seven houses to allot, for the end house was reserved for the warden and his, or her, spouse. Applicants for this joint post were to be interviewed very soon, and already some twenty hopeful couples had sent in their application forms. It could be a pleasant job for the right people, but the trustees had agreed from the start that they must look for a couple who were energetic and healthy and particularly sympathetic to the needs of the elderly people in their care.

By the time the closing date had arrived, the trustees met to go through the list in order to whittle it down to four, or possibly five, applicants.

It had not been easy. There were one or two couples who

could be eliminated from the start, either because of age, or because one or other would be of no use in a post which demanded the help of both partners. One likely woman, who had trained as a nurse and had a good deal of experience in old people's welfare, had a husband who almost seemed to boast, on the application form, that he had no idea how to fit a tap washer, mend a fuse, or mow a lawn. He added that he had spent most of his life in India and expected such things to be done for him.

In another case, the man seemed an intelligent handyman, but the wife admitted to prostrating attacks of migraine and crippling arthritis. In the end, the trustees sent out four letters to couples they would like to interview, and seventeen to the unsuccessful applicants.

The plan was to install the wardens first before the residents arrived. It looked now as though all should be in readiness by the first of October when, with any luck, the weather would be pleasant enough to see everybody settled comfortably before the onset of a Cotswold winter.

The rector was particularly interested in one couple who were going to be interviewed. She was the daughter of his old friend Mrs Jenner who lived along the Nidden road, and her husband was an ex-policeman.

The couple had married before Charles Henstock's time, and he had never met them, but Mrs Jenner had often talked about them when he and Dimity had lodged in her comfortable farm-house after the devastating fire which had made them homeless.

He spoke to John Lovell about them after the meeting.

'Well, I never met the girl,' said John, 'but I remember Donald Bailey speaking highly of her when she was nursing at the Cottage Hospital. She became a sister there, and then got this post in Yorkshire where she met her husband. If she's anything like her mother, she'd be ideal.'

'She would indeed,' agreed Charles, remembering the cheerful manner, the down-to-earth commonsense, and the never-failing kindness of his one-time landlady. 'Nevertheless,' he went on, 'one really must try and keep an open mind. We may find that the other couples are even more satisfactory. I must say, some of their qualifications make excellent reading.'

'You can't believe all you see on paper,' observed John. 'I know half a dozen chaps, in my line, with strings of letters after their names. I wouldn't trust 'em with my patients, and that's flat.'

He climbed into his car, hooted cheerfully, and drove home.

The visit of Ray and Kathleen was planned for the last week in August.

'It had better be lunch, I suppose,' said Dorothy resignedly. 'And, of course, the neighbour who is driving them must come too. Cold, do you think, or something in a casserole, Agnes? You know how unpunctual they are. It's hopeless to expect them to arrive on the dot.'

'I think a casserole would be best,' replied Agnes. 'It may be a miserable day, and in any case you don't want to be mixing mayonnaise or white sauce last thing. A casserole is so good-tempered. It won't spoil if they are a little late.'

'Then we'll make a steak and kidney one,' decided Dorothy. 'Men always like that. It was my dear father's favourite dish. And could you make one of your delicious raspberry trifles?'

And so the menu was half settled, and the ladies were prepared when the day came.

It was a morning of drizzle and mist, a foretaste of autumn. Dorothy congratulated herself upon the provision of such a comforting dish as stewed steak and kidney, as Agnes decorated the trifle with a few raspberries.

Much to their surprise, the car arrived promptly at twelve o'clock. Evidently the kind driver was a punctual individual. The two ladies hastily doffed their aprons and hurried to greet their guests.

Ray appeared to be very cheerful, the only visible sign of the accident being the sling supporting his broken arm. But he was rather pale, and Agnes, ever-solicitous, thought he had lost weight.

Kathleen said that the country was looking lovely, but she always suffered with her head, even on the shortest drive, and would they mind if she took one of her pills?

'Not in the least,' said Dorothy briskly. 'Anything to put you right, Kathleen. Would you like a glass of sherry to go with it?'

Kathleen closed her eyes and looked pained.

Dorothy busied herself with pouring drinks, and ignored what she privately designated 'Kathleen's vapours'. The good Samaritan who had driven all the way was called George White, and was a quiet fellow who commended himself to the two ladies by admiring the school house garden, and asking to be shown around it later on.

This they did after the lunch had been enjoyed by all, except Kathleen, who had been obliged to leave most of her helping on the plate, in deference to her headache. Ray managed his lunch most competently, and congratulated his sister on supplying the sort of meal with which a one-armed man could cope easily.

Dorothy led the way round the garden with a man on each side. Agnes followed more slowly with Kathleen, who said that the air might do her good if she could manage to totter a few steps.

'Perhaps you would like to sit down for a minute or two,' said Agnes, pausing by the garden seat.

Kathleen sank down with a sigh. Agnes was greatly perturbed on their guest's account. Surely, she could not be feigning illness? Dorothy was always so *trenchant* in her remarks about Kathleen's health, but Agnes, much softer in heart, felt sure that something must ail the poor woman.

She was somewhat surprised therefore when Kathleen spoke with undue firmness.

'About Ray, Agnes. He needs a change badly. And so do I, for that matter. Nursing is so debilitating.'

'I can quite imagine it is,' agreed Agnes.

'I thought perhaps Dorothy would like to have us here for a

week or so. The air at Thrush Green is so refreshing. It would do us both a world of good.'

'What, now?' squeaked Agnes, envisaging vast trunks already packed in the boot of the neighbour's car. What would Dorothy say? And in any case where could they sleep? There were only two bedrooms at the school house, and one could hardly expect a one-armed invalid to cope with a sleeping bag, even if he had had the forethought to pack one. And the thought of Kathleen in anything less than a luxurious double bed was not to be contemplated.

Recovering quickly from this mental battering Agnes had the sense to answer diplomatically.

'You must discuss it with Dorothy, of course. As you know, term starts very soon and accommodation here is rather limited. Still, I'm sure that a change of some sort would do you both a lot of good. Shall we go and have a look at the vegetable plot?'

The advance party was already admiring the shallots and some splendid feathery carrot tops. Agnes, much agitated, trusted that Kathleen would not choose the present moment to broach the subject of a holiday at the school house. Dorothy's reaction might well be forceful, and it seemed a pity to involve the innocent Mr White in a family fracas.

Luckily, Dorothy herself solved the problem by taking Kathleen's arm in a rare spasm of solicitude and leading her to the end of the garden where a plum tree was displaying a bumper crop of half-grown fruit. Agnes, with remarkable aplomb, swiftly directed the men's attention to some new geraniums, well out of earshot of any possible explosion.

'I really think I shall have to sit down for a moment,' said Ray, as they neared the seat recently vacated by Kathleen and herself. The three sat comfortably, and George White kept up a flow of gentle comment about his surroundings, which allowed Agnes to watch the two distant figures under the plum tree.

They seemed to be in earnest conversation, and Dorothy had ceased to support Kathleen by the arm. However, voices were not raised, no physical assault appeared to be threatening, and Agnes breathed again.

A few spots of rain drove them into the house where Kathleen asked if she could go upstairs for a rest. Two aspirins and half an hour in a darkened room often helped her headache. Not that it cured it completely, mark you, that was too much to expect, but such conditions certainly mitigated the agony a little.

Dorothy led the way with a little too much alacrity to Miss Fogerty's way of thinking, and the rest of the party disposed themselves in the sitting-room, awaiting Dorothy's return.

'Well, that's that!' she remarked cheerfully, rather as if she had just posted an awkward parcel, when she reappeared.

She turned to her brother. 'Kathleen has just told me how much you both need a little break. Of course, if we had more room here, and more time to entertain you, then it would be nice to have you here. However, you know how we are placed, but perhaps The Fleece could put you up. Would you like to ring them while you are here? Or call perhaps to select a room?'

Little Miss Fogerty could not help admiring the masterly way in which Dorothy cut the ground from beneath her adversary's feet, presenting him with a firm ultimatum at the same time. Nevertheless, she felt sorry for poor Ray, who looked completely nonplussed. Had he been in ignorance of his wife's plans, perhaps?

'We certainly had spoken of a little holiday,' he said at last, 'but I don't think Thrush Green was mentioned. My idea was a few days by the sea somewhere. Kathleen has been run off her feet looking after me, and you know how delicate she is.'

'Yes indeed,' agreed Dorothy, with some emphasis. 'Well then, you won't want to bother The Fleece, I take it?'

'Not at the moment.'

George White, who had been looking uncomfortable during this exchange, suggested that a turn about the green, now that the rain had eased, might be a good idea while Kathleen rested, and before they set off for home.

'I should enjoy that,' said Ray, getting to his feet.

'Then we'll see you later,' said Dorothy graciously.

The men's footsteps died away, the gate clanged, and Dorothy exploded.

'Well, of all the nerve! Really, Kathleen is outrageous!'

'Please, please!' whispered Agnes in much agitation, 'she may hear you.'

'I don't know that I worry particularly about that,' replied Dorothy. 'A born trouble-maker, that one. I think she simply wanted to rile me. And in that, I suppose, you could say she's suceeded.'

She plumped up a cushion with excessive vigour, and punched it back into place on the sofa.

'But not another word will I say,' she announced, breathing heavily. 'Let us go and get the tea tray ready for when the men return.'

True to her word, the rest of the visit passed in outward harmony. The visitors were attended to with every courtesy, and Dorothy and Agnes waved farewell from the gate with their faces wreathed in polite smiles.

Agnes, following Dorothy back to the house, waited for the inevitable explosion after so much dangerous repression.

'I really don't know,' began her friend, 'what passes in the minds of some people. Do they never think of anyone but themselves?'

Agnes took this to be a question of the rhetorical kind, and gave a non-committal clearing of the throat.

'Kathleen knows how we are placed *perfectly well*,' went on Dorothy, now in full spate. 'We have no spare room, no spare time, no spare energy, and yet she expects us to take on an invalid and, worse still, herself – a hypochondriac of the first water. It's too much! It really is! Simply because we are lucky enough to live in Thrush Green, she seems to think that we must be available at all times to share our good air and surroundings with all and sundry.'

She paused to take breath in the midst of this tirade, and Agnes managed to insert a gentle word.

'Don't dwell on it, dear. You know she's probably over-anxious on Ray's account, and that's made her thoughtless.'

'Humph!' snorted her headmistress. 'That's as maybe! But we may as well listen to the news, as I see it is time. At least it might act as a counter-irritant.'

And little Miss Fogerty rose to switch on the set.

Across the green, Winnie Bailey was also considering the question of summer visitors to Thrush Green.

Occasionally, she had a twinge of remorse about her refusal to fall in with Richard's plans, although she knew perfectly well that it would have been impossibly difficult to have coped with a strange young mother, a new baby, and an energetic four-year-old.

But she had heard nothing from Richard since his visit, and

had received no thanks from his wife for her letter and the roses. It made her rather sad.

She had seen the announcement of the birth of a daughter in the newspaper, and written a little note of congratulation, but that too had elicited no response.

Well, there it was, thought Winnie, she could do no more, and if Richard was still sulking then there was nothing she could do about it but hope that time would heal the rift.

Meanwhile, she decided to go into the garden and collect some geranium cuttings. They could stand in water overnight, and she would pot them tomorrow. A little work with one's hands could be a great comfort when one was worried. It had been one of Donald's maxims, and Winnie, making her way into the garden, had always recognised its wisdom.

John Lovell too had been gardening that afternoon, and as he was blessedly free from surgery duty that evening, he was studying the paper with his feet up.

His attention was caught by an item concerning car thieves who seemed to be running a lucrative business in London and its suburbs. Only expensive cars were being taken, it appeared, and the police were of the opinion that the cars were stolen to order, disguised in some remote spot, such as a lonely farm with outbuildings, and then fixed up with faked or trade number plates and often shipped abroad.

Dr Lovell lowered the paper and gazed through the window at his garden. In his mind's eye he saw again the yard at Leys Farm on his second visit.

He had called without warning, simply to check that his patient was progressing satisfactorily. The double doors of a barn had been standing open, and two, or possibly three, large cars were visible. The older men seemed to be at work on them, and the doors of the barn had been hurriedly slammed when the doctor had been noticed.

In front of the house a Porsche stood, and the young man whom John had treated, was busily unscrewing a hub cap.

'Now I wonder?' said John to himself. 'What would be the best thing to do?'

The local police superintendent was a friend of his. The magistrates at Lulling court knew them both well.

Well, he could only look a fool, thought John, making for the telephone. Better that than failing to do one's duty as a responsible citizen. He began to dial the number.

Down the hill, in Lulling High Street, one light still burned in The Fuchsia Bush.

Mrs Peters had stayed after the shop shut to make up the accounts, and to check an order for one of her wholesale suppliers.

Despite the fact that the café and shop were always busy, and that home-made cakes, scones and biscuits sold briskly every day, there were times when Mrs Peters wondered how long such a business would survive.

Staff wages were a heavy item in her expenditure. Rates and rent added to the burden. The cost of such basic necessities as flour, butter, sugar, coffee and tea had risen astronomically since she first took over the business, and she did not want to price her excellent produce beyond the purse of her loyal customers. It was becoming something of a headache, and short of dismissing one of the staff, or finding some extra way of adding to her income, the worries seemed likely to become more demanding.

She was still studying the accounts when the telephone rang.

'Ah!' said a woman's voice. It was rather a domineering type of voice, thought Mrs Peters, the sort of voice belonging to someone known as 'a born leader'. Could this caller have found a fly in an Eccles cake, and was now about to threaten The Fuchsia Bush with a visit from the Public Health Office? Poor Mrs Peters quailed.

'So glad I found you at home. I presume you live above the shop?'

'Well, no, I don't, but I stayed late to see to some office work,' replied Mrs Peters. 'Can I help you at all?'

'We met at Joan Young's lunch party. My name is Thurgood.'

Light dawned. This was worse than she imagined. Mrs Thurgood, wealthy and influential, could make life unendurable if she had an excuse for complaint.

'I remember,' said she, her mouth dry with apprehension.

'My little party were all most impressed with the catering,' went on the ringing voice. 'I know at least two people who are going to get in touch with you about arranging something similar. That's why I wanted a word with you about a little affair of my own.'

'How kind,' faltered Mrs Peters.

'We are having a christening at St John's church here in Lulling, in about a month's time. The dear rector will conduct the service, of course. He was instrumental in bringing my daughter and her husband together in the first place, incidentally. We are all *devoted* to him.'

Mrs Peters knew, as did all Lulling, of Mrs Thurgood's initial animosity to poor Charles Henstock. She had been a great admirer of Lulling's handsome vicar, Anthony Bull, and had made his successor's early days very uncomfortable. Mrs Peters had heard too of the battle of the kneelers, which had taken place before the engagement of Mrs Thurgood's daughter, but naturally said nothing.

'A charming man,' she agreed.

'We shall be quite a small party, somewhere in the region of twenty to thirty guests, and I wondered if you could cater for us?'

'I should be delighted.'

'It would be a tea party mainly, and of course I should like you to make the cake. Perhaps a few little savouries to have with the parting glass of wine? Shall I come down one day to make arrangements, and discuss the budget?'

'Please do. Shall we say on Tuesday afternoon?'

'That will suit me perfectly. I will be with you at two-thirty,' said the lady graciously. 'So glad you can take it on. My friend is envisaging a large buffet lunch, rather like Joan Young's, in aid of the Lifeboat Institute, but no doubt you will be hearing from her. The other person is planning a golden wedding celebration, I gather, for her parents. No doubt there will be other claims on your time.'

Mrs Peters renewed her thanks and put down the receiver. Her hands were trembling, but her heart was light.

Could this be the beginning of a new venture, and a boost for the dear old Fuchsia Bush's fortunes?

PART TWO

Moving In

* * *

8. NEW NEIGHBOURS

Thrush Green village school was now well into term time. Tearful newcomers had settled into Miss Fogerty's class and now knew their way to classrooms, lobbies and lavatories, without the guidance of their elders and betters.

Text books and exercise books had been distributed to the older children, desks allotted, monitors appointed, weather charts fixed to the walls and nature tables laden with the produce of a mellow September. Taking it all in all, both Dorothy Watson and her loyal assistant were glad to get back into harness.

It was Agnes who first noticed the removal van outside the wardens' house, at the end of the block of new homes. The name of the firm was emblazoned on the side in a type of Gothic script so fanciful that even little Miss Fogerty, used to all manner of calligraphy, found it impossible to read. But lower down, in large clear Roman capitals, was the word RIPON.

'Ripon,' mused Agnes. 'Yorkshire, surely? And an Abbey or something similar? I must ask Dorothy.'

At that moment, John Todd fell from a low bench, 'meant to be *sat* upon, and not *stood* upon', as his teachers had told him innumerable times, grazed his knee, and set up a hideous howling which drove all geographical conjecture from little Miss Fogerty's mind until later in the day.

Dorothy affirmed that Ripon was indeed in Yorkshire.

'*North* Yorkshire, I think, is the correct postal address. Why we couldn't keep those nice Ridings, heaven alone knows. A charming place, Agnes. I went there as a girl. One day, when we have retired, we must go north again. A coach tour of the Dales should be very pleasant. What put it into your mind?'

Agnes explained about the removal van, and her head-mistress became very animated.

'But this must mean that Mrs Jenner's daughter and her husband have the post of warden. What good news! I wonder why we haven't heard before?'

'Betty Bell has usually left the school before we arrive in the mornings,' pointed out her friend.

'And we have gone when she comes after school on most days,' agreed Dorothy. 'We don't seem to hear as much local news as we did when Mrs Cooke cleaned the school.' She sounded slightly wistful.

'But how much better Betty Bell does her work,' said Agnes robustly. 'And she is so honest and cheerful always. I really wouldn't wish to go back to Mrs Cooke's slatternly ways, would you?'

And Dorothy agreed, with some reluctance.

The advent of the removal van had been noted by many other eyes at Thrush Green. Albert Piggott, who never missed much, commented upon the various items of furniture which he had watched on their way from van to house, when he supped his beer.

'Got a nice bit of carpet, and that'll be in a fine old muck with them paths still treadin' in,' he announced with some relish. 'Needs a bit of drugget over it, I reckon, but folks are too careless to bother with such things these days.'

'I daresay they know their own business best,' said the land-lord.

'It's the Jenners' girl as has got the job,' continued Albert. 'Name of Jane. Used to be a nurse down Lulling hospital years ago. Mrs Jenner told my Nelly about it at Bingo last week.'

'She should be all right then,' said Mr Jones, swabbing down his little sink. 'What's the husband like?'

'Been a policeman,' replied Albert gloomily.

'None the worse for that, surely?'

'Ah, but he was a *Yorkshire* policeman. Not homegrown, as you might say.'

'I've met some jolly nice Yorkshire folk,' said Mr Jones sturdily. 'They tell you themselves they're the salt of the earth.'

'Well, I haven't met one at all. Still, now we'll have our chance, won't we? You'll have to keep to closing hours pretty sharpish, with him living on the doorstep.'

Pleased to have the last word, Albert put down his glass, and departed to his leisurely duties.

Ella Bembridge's front garden was an ideal viewing spot. Winnie Bailey had called with some magazines, and found her friend leaning on the gate, cigarette drooping from her mouth, and eyes fixed upon the activities at the new house.

'Who's moving in, d'you know?' she asked Winnie, as she opened the gate.

'Why, I thought you knew! Jane Jenner that was, and her husband. But there, it's all before your time.'

She stood waiting for Ella to take the magazines and lead the way into the house, but it was obvious that the lady was much too engrossed in watching the removal men negotiating the doorway with a Welsh dresser to attend to Winnie and her offerings.

Resignedly, Winnie sat down on the garden bench, and surveyed a sturdy clump of sedums. They were already changing colour from pale green to pink. Soon, thought Winnie with a pang of regret, they would be a brilliant coral, and autumn would have arrived.

'Ella!' she called. 'Don't you think you might embarrass the newcomers by staring so?'

Ella turned, her face a study of amazement.

'Why on earth? I wouldn't care a fig if people watched me. Come to think of it, they often do. I don't mind.'

Nevertheless, she left the gate, and took her place beside Winnie.

'You know this Jane woman then?'

'Since a child. I'm surprised you hadn't heard she'd been appointed as warden. Mrs Jenner's as pleased as Punch.'

'What's the husband like?'

'A good down-to-earth fellow, I believe. They'll be a first-class pair for the job. I know Charles Henstock was delighted when they were the successful couple.'

'Good! We can do with some fresh blood at Thrush Green. It'll be nice to have more neighbours. I still miss Dim about the house.'

Winnie handed over the magazines at last. She rose to go.

'Don't hurry away, Winnie. You can see things better from here.'

'I'll call when they have settled in,' Winnie told her. 'They've enough to cope with at the moment.'

Ella followed her to the gate.

Winnie looked back before turning into her own home. Ella had rearranged her bulk upon the gate top, and was watching proceedings as avidly as before.

Charles Henstock was indeed delighted with the appointment. He had not met Jane's husband before the interview, but was impressed, first of all, by his magnificent physique, and then by his quiet confidence.

He was the sort of man, Charles surmised, who would keep his head in any situation. Police training may have had something to do with it, but Charles guessed correctly that here was a particularly well-balanced person, intelligent and kindly, who would be as competent in dealing with a burst water main or an old person's heart attack, as he had been with a riot or a car accident.

The choice of those to live in the homes was being much more difficult, and the meeting of the selection committee had been quite stormy.

The list had been whittled down fairly easily at first. People, like Percy Hodge, who already had a home and were relatively young and able-bodied, were firmly rejected. Some hopefuls from far away, and with no connection with, or relatives living in, Thrush Green, were also crossed from the list, but the rest were dauntingly numerous.

A few general rules had been drawn up. One was that the residents should still be active, and that they should face the fact that minor illnesses such as coughs and colds, temporary stomach upsets and the like, could be coped with competently, with the warden's help, in their own homes, but anything needing sustained nursing must inevitably be dealt with by hospital treatment.

Another rule was that no animals could be allowed, and it

was this which Charles did his best to alter. He made no secret of the fact that it was Tom Hardy who was in his mind.

He had broached the subject of a move when he had seen Tom one day, and was surprised to encounter far less opposition to the idea than he had imagined.

'Look at it this way, sir,' the old man said. 'My neighbour's a good sort, and does what she can for me, but I don't like to be beholden, and that's flat. And these meals on wheels I can't eat half the time, and I've had four home helps since you helped me do that form, and not one can I get on with, and that's the truth.'

'You wouldn't miss your garden too badly? And the river?'

'I'm getting past it. It grieves me to see the weeds growing, and the trees needing pruning. And I don't know as the river damp don't make my joints stiffer than they should be. No, taking it all ways, I could up sticks and settle at Thrush Green. I know plenty of folk there, and I'd have Poll.'

The dog looked up and wagged her tail on hearing her name. The rector, the gentlest of men, wondered how best to broach this painful subject.

'At the moment,' he ventured, 'there is a feeling that pets could not be admitted, but I'm hoping to alter that.'

A flush crept up the old man's neck and across his wrinkled face.

'No pets, eh? Well then, that settles it. I ain't agoing anywhere without my Poll.'

And Charles knew, all too well, that there would be no budging him from that decision.

'But if we do it for one,' said Justin Venables, who was chairman of the committee, 'we must do it for all. And suppose someone has an Alsatian, and next door there is a Siamese cat? What then?'

Justin, who was a retired solicitor from Lulling, was a perfect chairman, patient, clear-headed, and cognisant of all the legal difficulties which cropped up. Since his retirement he had, of course, been rather busier than when he was in a full-time profession, but that was only to be expected, and secretly he was rather gratified.

Apart from one day a week in his old office to deal with any aging clients he still served, Justin seemed to spend his time on just such committees as this present one. He felt considerable sympathy for his old friend Charles Henstock, and knew that no one was more deserving of a place than Tom Hardy, but the 'no pets' rule did seem to be a sensible one.

'Worse still,' put in Mrs Thurgood, who was also on the committee, 'would be a cat of *any* sort next door to budgerigars. I really think we must be firm about this.'

Charles began to feel that he was fighting a losing battle, but persisted nevertheless.

'Let's tackle this another way. Select the residents for our seven homes, see if any have pets, and then decide the next step.

I agree that "no pets" is a sensible rule in the long term, but perhaps with these first tenants we might stretch things a bit.'

'I think Mr Henstock has a point there,' said Mrs Thurgood graciously. 'How far have we got?'

'The three doubles are already settled,' said Justin, turning over his papers. 'Mr and Mrs Cross, Mr and Mrs Angell and Captain and Mrs Jermyn. So we are now allotting the four singles, and I think it was generally agreed that old Mrs Bates from the end almshouse at Lulling should be offered one, as that is due to be gutted in readiness for a new laundry room and a store room there. We have her application here. It came in early.'

'So that leaves three?' said Mrs Thurgood.

Justin acknowledged this feat of arithmetic with a kindly nod.

'Let us go on with our selection then, shall we?' he suggested. 'Let's take the case of Miss Fuller, the retired headmistress from Nidden.'

The committee applied themselves to the application forms, among them Miss Fuller's, one from Johnny Enderby, an old gardener, and finally to that of Tom Hardy.

After an hour's hard work the homes were allotted. Now to discover if the lucky ones had pets, and if any arrangements had been made for them.

'Perhaps I could draft a letter,' suggested Justin.

'Why not telephone?' said Charles, who was growing increasingly anxious.

'But there was a note about all this somewhere on the application form,' pronounced Mrs Thurgood, turning over her papers with such energy that half of them fell on the floor.

John Lovell, bending to pick them up, hit his head against hers and the air was full of apologies.

When things were settled again, it was found that there certainly was an insignificant spot on the form asking for information about any pets already kept.

The Jermyns had put in 'One Cat'.

Miss Fuller owned 'Two Love Birds'.

Tom Hardy had one dog.

The rest appeared to be without animals.

Justin Venables began to look relieved, and Charles less strained.

'The Jermyns are at one end of the block, and Miss Fuller's apartment is several homes distant, I see, and Tom Hardy's is some way off. And in any case, one imagines that the birds are accommodated in a cage. Well, ladies and gentlemen, what about it?'

'If I may,' said Charles diffidently, 'I should like to suggest that these first tenants are allowed to bring their present pets, on the clear understanding that they may not be replaced and if they cause problems an alternative home must be found for them. Any tenants who come after must realise that pets are not allowed.'

'I think that's an excellent suggestion,' said John Lovell. 'It means that people such as Tom Hardy will not be penalised for having a pet, and debarring them from the homes they really need, I propose it formally.'

'I'll second it,' said Mrs Thurgood. 'So much fairer to the pets,' she added. 'I know I should *never* consent to be parted from my dear pekes.'

'Those in favour?' asked Justin.

All hands went up, and to Charles's mortification he felt tears prick his eyes.

Letters to the successful applicants were to go out during the week, with the pets' clause clearly stated, but Charles took it upon himself to go beforehand to see Tom. He had left the old man in some turmoil of spirit, he feared, and wanted to calm him.

He had intended to walk to the cottage by the river, relishing the prospect of gentle exercise in the company of moorhens, willow trees, and the pleasant burbling of the River Pleshey, but at breakfast time the heavens opened, the rain came down in a deluge, and Charles, standing at the window, watched the last of the petunias and marigolds being flattened under the on-slaught.

Resignedly, he took out the car, and drove down the main street of Lulling through the downpour. The road was awash, the pavements streaming, and passing vehicles threw up a cloud of spray.

It was still pouring down when he drew up at Tom's cottage, and the rector, collar turned up, hurried across the slippery plank bridge, and gained the shelter of the little porch.

'Why, bless me,' exclaimed Tom, opening the door. 'What brings you out in this weather?'

'Good news, Tom,' said Charles, brushing drops from his jacket.

Polly advanced to meet him, putting up her grey muzzle to be stroked, and wagging her tail.

'You come right in before you tells me more,' said Tom. 'Kettle's hot. Coffee?'

'I'd love some,' said Charles.

He watched the old man moving slowly about his work, taking down a mug from the dresser, reaching for a jar of pow-dered coffee, making his way deliberately to the drawer where he kept the teaspoons. There was no doubt about it, thought Charles, although he could just about manage when things were going normally, there must be times when a kindly war-den would be needed in the future.

'There you are, sir,' said Tom at last, putting the steaming mug before his visitor. 'Get that down you. There's a real autumn nip in the air this morning, and we can't have you ail-ing anything. Good people are scarce, they tell me.'

'This goes down well,' said Charles. 'Now the news!'

'About the little house?'

'That's right.'

'And Poll?'

'She can go there with you.'

Tom's face lit up. 'Well, that's wholly good news, I must say. What made them change their minds? You, sir, I expect!'

'Only in part, Tom. We all thought it out. It seemed wrong to part people like you from their animals, but I think the long-term idea is still "no pets". That will apply, of course, to the residents who come later.' He took a long draught of coffee. 'You will be getting a letter in a day or two, Tom, but I wanted to tell you myself.'

'Any idea when we shall move in?'

'In the early part of October, I think. Can you get someone to help you with the move? If not, I'm sure some of the young fellows at my Youth Club could give a hand.'

'I might be glad of that, sir. Most of my friends are as shaky as I am now. More coffee?'

'No thanks, Tom. I must get back, but I'll call again in a few days' time.'

He bent to pat Polly. 'Coming back to Lulling with me again?' he asked her.

'She would too,' said Tom. 'She's as fond of you as she is of me, and that's the truth. But I wouldn't want to part with her, not even to you, sir.'

'Well, there'll be no parting now, Tom. You and Poll can soldier on together. Many thanks for the drink.'

He wrung his old friend's hand, and set forth again into the wild wet world.

9 . SOME MALEFACTORS

John Lovell's telephone call to the police superintendent had set loose a stream of local activity. He learnt a little from his friend when they met.

'By the time we went to Leys Farm the birds had flown, as you might expect, but we found a few clues, tyre marks, paint scrapings, bits of cloth and so on, which the forensic boys are working on. However, I think these are the chaps directly involved, and it was bright of you to spot them.'

'Not bright enough to twig earlier,' said John ruefully. 'And as for recalling the makes of the cars and colours, not to mention numbers, I'm afraid I'm a broken reed. All I had in mind, of course, was how my patient was reacting to my prescription. He'd had a pretty bad go of sickness and was seriously dehydrated when I first saw him.'

'He must have been in a very poor state for the others to have called you in. I bet that was the last thing they wanted – a visitor to the premises. Obviously, they hid the cars away when you were expected, but were caught on the hop when you turned up unexpectedly.'

'Have you any leads at all?'

'Well, all the other areas have been notified, and we're keeping a sharp watch on the ports which have car ferries, but no doubt they'll lie low for a bit. One thing in our favour, it isn't easy to hide a car. A small packet of heroin can be tucked away quite successfully. A thumping great Rolls isn't so simple.' He rose to go. 'Anyway, you did a good job by getting in touch. I hope we'll be able to see you in court as a prime witness before long.'

'Heaven help you!' exclaimed the doctor. 'I've always lived in dread of someone asking me where I was on the night of October the fourth three years earlier.'

'Who hasn't?' laughed his friend.

Naturally, John Lovell had said nothing about the affair. All that Jonn had allowed himself was a brief word to Ruth who, as a doctor's wife, was the soul of discretion. Nevertheless, it was soon common knowledge in Thrush Green and Lulling that something delightfully wicked and illegal seemed to have been happening at Leys Farm over the past year.

Betty Bell was agog with news and conjecture when she went to clean at Harold and Isobel Shoosmiths'.

'Never knew such a carry-on,' she puffed, dusting Harold's study energetically. 'My cousin Alf opened the door, not three days since, to find Constable Darwin on the step with one of them little notebooks. Well, to tell the truth, he's not my *real* cousin, not like Willie Bond, I mean, but Alf's mum and mine used to work up the vicarage when they was young, and they was always good friends even after they got married.'

This sounded to Harold, busy trying to fill in a form for an insurance company which was incapable, it seemed, of expressing its needs in plain English, as a slur on marriage. Did it mean that early friendships usually foundered after a spouse had been acquired?

'So, of course, I always called her Auntie Gert,' went on Betty, knocking an antique paperweight to the ground, 'and Alf was a sort of cousin. When he was born, I mean.'

Harold said he understood that, and watched Betty retrieve the paperweight, luckily unharmed.

'Well, Alf had been ploughing just behind Trotters after they'd harvested the barley, and the police wanted to know if he'd seen anything funny.'

'Funny?'

'Funny unusual, I mean. Suspicious like. Men with stockings over their faces, holding machine guns. That sort of thing, Alf thought.'

'But surely,' expostulated Harold, setting aside the form for quieter times, 'they wouldn't be got up like that if they were *living* in the place?'

'Who's to say?' said Betty airily, flicking her duster dangerously across a row of miniature ornaments of Indian silver much prized by her employer.

'Anyway, Alf hadn't seen nothin' much, just an odd car or two being put in the barn. That PC Darwin kep' all on about what colour and what make and when was it and that, until Alf said he was fair mazed, and as his dinner was just on the table he told young Darwin one car was red and another was blue just to get rid of him. Alf reckons he'd have been there still if he hadn't told him something.'

'But that is definitely hindering the course of justice!' Harold exclaimed, much alarmed at such behaviour. 'It was very wrong of your cousin to mislead the police like that. For two pins I'd ring the station now and tell them what you have just told me.'

'Oh, I shouldn't bother,' replied Betty. 'Ten to one that Darwin never wrote it down. He's not much of a scholar, they tell me.'

She whisked from the room, leaving Harold confronting his form with severely heightened blood pressure.

At The Two Pheasants the subject was aired with more drama than accuracy.

Percy Hodge said that the way the police handled things was a crying scandal, and it was a wonder more decent people weren't murdered in their beds when you heard how long these Trotters chaps had been up to a bit of no good. What did we pay our rates for, he wanted to know?

Albert Piggott opined that you could earn more by being

dishonest these days, than by sweating day in and day out, as he did, at his own back-breaking job.

And an old man in the corner, toothless and shaky with age, said that no good ever came out of Trotters. It had always had a bad name, and that fellow Archie Something who farmed there before the war – the first war, he meant – had three daughters who all went to the bad, and the local lads was warned about them by the vicar at that time. Not that it stopped 'em, of course.

He would have continued with his reminiscences to the great pleasure of his hearers, but Mr Jones, the landlord, spoiled everything by rapping on the counter and ordering his clients to drink up sharpish.

Even little Miss Fogerty heard something of the affair, for John Todd, capering about in the playground with his hand extended pistol-fashion, yelled that he was a car robber from Trotters and that he was spraying his unconcerned playmates with real bullets, and they ought to be lying dead.

On relating this to Miss Watson later, her headmistress replied: 'Yes, dear, I did hear something about it. Trust John Todd to pick up such news! That boy is not as green as he's cabbage-looking.'

With which statement her colleague agreed.

Nelly Piggott was one of the few inhabitants who managed to ignore the excitement at Leys – or Trotters – Farm.

The truth was that she had a great many other excitements to think about. The first, and most pressing one, was the christening party at Mrs Thurgood's, due to take place in just over a week's time.

She told her friend Mrs Jenner about it as they walked down the hill to a Bingo session in Lulling. The two women had struck up a firm friendship. Mrs Jenner, a lifelong resident at Thrush Green, and sister to Percy Hodge, recognised the good qualities in Albert's wife which far too many local people ignored.

It was true that Nelly was somewhat flighty. She was occasionally vulgar in speech. She dressed rather too flashily for Thrush Green's taste. Nevertheless, she was hard-working, good-tempered, and coped splendidly with Albert's moodiness and bouts of drinking. Altogether, Mrs Jenner approved of Nelly Piggott, and enjoyed their weekly trip to the Bingo hall.

'Mrs Peters gets a bit worked up,' said Nelly confidentially. 'Well, I suppose she's a lot to lose if anything goes wrong, and say what you like, that Mrs Thurgood is proper bossy. All teeth and breeches, my father used to say. Tough as they come. She did her best to beat down the price per head when she came to work things out, but give Mrs Peters her due she stuck to her guns, and we've got a fair price, I reckon.'

'She seems to rely on you quite a bit,' responded Mrs Jenner.

'I don't know about that,' replied Nelly, sounding surprised, 'but I don't get in a flap about things, so maybe she talks to me to calm herself. After all, I haven't got the same responsibilities that she has. Stands to reason she worries more.'

'You've got your livelihood to get, and to lose,' pointed out her friend.

'I suppose so,' reflected Nelly, 'but I could turn my hand to pretty well anything, if need be. After all, I did a good spell of cleaning at The Drovers' Arms, and thoroughly enjoyed it. I don't mind a nice bit of scrubbing.'

And that, thought Mrs Jenner, as they approached the hall, was one of Nelly's virtues. She was game to take on anything, even Albert Piggott.

It said much for her courage.

On the way home, Nelly was invited for the first time to have a cup of coffee at her friend's house along the road to Nidden.

'There's nobody in obviously,' said Mrs Jenner, as the two women surveyed the Piggott establishment which had no glimmer of light in the windows.

Next door The Two Pheasants was glowing with lights, and

it did not need much thinking to surmise where Albert was spending the evening.

'Just for a few minutes then,' agreed Nelly, pleasantly surprised by the invitation, and a quarter of an hour later she was ensconced in Mrs Jenner's farmhouse kitchen with a steaming cup in front of her.

She looked about the great square room with approval. The solid-fuel stove gave out a comfortable warmth. From the beams overhead hung nets of onions and shallots, bunches of drying herbs, and some ancient pieces of copper. A blue and white checked cloth was spread cornerwise on the scrubbed kitchen table, and a thriving Busy Lizzie was set squarely in the middle.

'My! I could do with a kitchen like this,' said Nelly enviously. She thought of the small room at Albert's where she cooked, cleaned and lived.

'Come any time you like,' invited Mrs Jenner. 'I like a bit of company, and although Jane and Bill are only down the road now, I don't suppose they'll have much spare time for a bit.'

'How do they like being wardens?'

'Very much. Mind you, they've only got one couple in at the moment, so things are easy. But they're a good pair, though I says it as shouldn't, and to my mind those old people are lucky to have them.'

'So I've heard,' said Nelly, 'and from several people too.'

Mrs Jenner looked gratified. 'Of course, how things will work out when all the houses are taken remains to be seen.'

'They'll shake down all right, I'm sure,' said Nelly.

'That I don't know,' answered her friend. 'I've had a lot to do with old people in my life, and it's my opinion that they can be downright awkward. Worse than children sometimes.'

Later, Nelly was to remember those prophetic words.

During the next two weeks, the new residents began to filter into the homes allotted to them.

Captain Eric Jermyn and his wife Carlotta had been the first to move in. Theirs was one of the larger homes at the farther end of the block. Jane and Bill Cartwright, the wardens, were now comfortably settled at the other end, and were glad to be welcoming the first of their neighbours.

Mrs Jermyn had been an actress before marrying her husband at the beginning of the Second World War. Remnants of youthful prettiness remained, but arthritis had distorted her hands and feet, and the pain made her querulous at times.

Her husband was considerably older than she was, thin, rather shaky, but still very straight-backed and dapper. They had lived in Lulling for some years since the war, and both given a great deal of service to the town.

Their means were small for their savings had vanished when an overseas bank had collapsed. They had lived in army quarters, and later in rented accommodation, and were grateful when they were allotted this present home in their old age.

Their black and white cat Monty was named after the late Field Marshal Montgomery, who was greatly revered by Monty's owner. He was a portly animal of much dignity, and protested loudly at being shut in a basket for several hours while the move was in progress.

The next day little Mrs Bates from the Lulling almshouses moved in, and two days after that Miss Fuller, who had been headmistress of the tiny school at Nidden, took up her abode next door to Mrs Bates. The latter had no pets to add to the usual confusion of moving day, but Miss Fuller's two lovebirds were carried in first thing, their cage heavily draped in an old bedspread.

A week later George and Mary Cross moved into the second double apartment, and Jack and Sybil Angell soon followed them.

Two single homes remained. Johnny Enderby, a retired gardener, was due to move in, and Tom Hardy and Polly the day after.

The rector still worried about uprooting his old friend from the riverside cottage, but when the day came, all was well.

It was one of those translucent October days when the distant hills seemed to have moved ten miles nearer. The sun shone from a cloudless sky, and the vivid gold of the horse chestnut trees vied with the pale lemon of the acacias in the Youngs' garden. It was heart-lifting weather, and the rector was sincerely thankful.

There had been no need to call on the Youth Club members for help.

With surprising efficiency, Tom had organised the move, parcelling up a few treasures, putting out the detritus of years of hoarding for dustmen, the local scrap merchant and the Cubs' jumble sale. It almost seemed, Charles thought, as if he welcomed this new start, despite his age and infirmities.

Polly looked upon the upheaval with a mild eye, seeking out a sunny place in the garden while the turmoil spread around her. As long as she was with her master, it was plain to see, she had no fears.

The last of the residents was safely ensconced by mid-afternoon. Polly explored her new home, found the familiar rag rug, and settled down on it with a sigh of pleasure.

Tom filled the kettle in his tiny bright kitchen, and switched on, marvelling at the speed with which it began to murmur. This was better than the old kitchen hob!

He sat down, his feet beside Poll on the rug, and gazed approvingly at his new abode.

In the end house, Jane and Bill Cartwright were also enjoying a cup of tea. Now all their charges were in residence, and the real job began.

Both were tired, but relieved that the moving in was over, and that, so far, no real problems had arisen.

Jane was perhaps more apprehensive than her sturdy husband.

'I can't help wondering if the hot water system is going to stand up to the demands made on it. Do you think we ought to give a gentle warning to the residents about running their hot taps? After all, Tom Hardy and Johnny Enderby have never coped with hot water straight from the tap. And we must make sure that the emergency bells work in each house. It would be terrible if anything happened, and we knew nothing about it.'

Bill Cartwright smiled at his wife's agitation. 'The bells have been tested time and time again, and everyone here can cope with the hot water taps. None of them's a fool. You just calm down, and see how easily things will run. Before it gets dark we'll go together to make sure they have all they want.'

Jane smiled back. 'You're right, as usual. Well, it's good to have our family around us. Let's hope they all get on well together.'

'I expect they'll turn out like any other family,' replied Bill, pouring a second cup. 'A good deal of affection spiced with bouts of in-fighting. We'll see soon enough.'

*

Edward Young, as architect, took a keen interest in the residents' reactions to his work, and on the whole was gratified. All agreed that the houses were light, warm, well-planned and easy to run.

The main objection came from John Lovell one day when he met his brother-in-law, by chance, as he returned from a visit to the Cartwrights.

'All going well there, Edward?'

'No great problems so far,' said the architect.

'There will be,' replied John.

Edward looked taken aback. 'How d'you mean?'

'Well, those outside steps, for instance. You've been extra careful to have no steps inside, but that flight outside could be a menace, particularly in slippery weather.'

'I don't see,' said Edward frostily, 'how you can overcome a natural incline except by steps – and these are particularly shallow ones – or a ramp. As it happens, I've provided both. And an adequate handrail.'

'No need to get stuffy!'

'I'm not getting stuffy,' retorted Edward, 'but I do dislike outsiders criticising something they don't understand. You don't seem to realise the difficulties that confronted us when facing the problems that this site gave us.'

'I'm not such an outsider that I can't see what a mistake you made with those steps—'

'*Mistake?* What rubbish! You stick to your job, John, and leave me to mine.'

'Unfortunately, I shall have to patch up the results of your mistakes! Mark my words, a few slippery leaves, or later on some snow and ice, and I shall have some old people in my surgery with sprains and breaks. It could all have been avoided with proper planning.'

'Are you suggesting that I'm a bad architect?'

'Not always. But to design an old people's home with a hazard like that, is not only stupid, it's downright criminal.'

By this time, both men were flushed with anger. They took

their work seriously, and were sensitive to criticism. The fact that normally the two brothers-in-law got along very peaceably made this present exchange particularly acrimonious.

'The steps are perfectly safe,' said Edward, with considerable emphasis. 'You're getting a proper old woman, John, seeing danger where there is none. I shan't come criticising your healing methods, though I gather that some of them leave much to be desired, so I'd be obliged if you left well alone in my field.'

He strode off across the green to his home, leaving John fuming.

'Pompous ass!' said John to the retreating back. 'You wait till I get my first casualty from the homes! I shan't let you forget it!'

As was to be expected, the new residents soon had visitors. Sons and daughters, grandchildren, and old friends called to see how they had settled into their new quarters.

Miss Watson and Miss Fogerty were greatly intrigued by the comings and goings, and agreed that it would be right and proper to invite Miss Fuller, whom they knew slightly through their teaching activities, to have tea with them.

'I always liked her,' said Agnes warmly, as they carried the tea things into the sitting room. 'She was always so good with the mothers.'

'Sometimes a little too good,' responded Dorothy, arranging tomato sandwiches neatly. 'I think a headmistress should keep her distance with the parents.'

She began to set out the best cups on the tea tray.

'Such a pretty tea set,' commented Agnes, anxious to turn to a safer subject.

Her friend sighed. 'Mother left a very fine Wedgwood tea service to Kathleen in her will, although she must have known that I'd always hoped for it. But there you are, Kathleen did her wheedling to good effect, and I have to make do with this.'

'And very nice too,' Agnes assured her, as she added teaspoons to the saucers. But privately she pondered on the unhappy results following the distribution of the worldly goods of the recently dead.

These melancholy thoughts were interrupted by the ringing of the front door bell, and she hurriedly joined Dorothy in welcoming their guest.

10. Settling Down

October, drawing to its close, saw Lulling and Thrush Green in their most vivid colours.

The horse chestnut avenue outside the Youngs' house glowed a bright gold, and the glossy conkers were fast being snatched up from beneath them by the village school's pupils.

Scarlet berries beaded the pyracantha growing over The Two Pheasants, and the Virginia creeper clothing Winnie Bailey's house was the rich colour of red wine. The hedges along the Nidden road were spangled with scarlet hips and crimson haws, while a few late blackberries, glossy as jet, waited for the birds' attentions.

In Miss Fogerty's classroom, sprays of cape gooseberries brightened the corner by the weather chart, and such seasonal joys as collecting hazelnuts and mushrooms enlivened the children's days.

Miss Fogerty gave her usual autumn handiwork lesson on the making of chairs for a dolls' house from horse chestnuts, pins and wool. This involved four pins for the legs, five for the back, and simple weaving of the wool, in and out of the latter, to form a comfortable back rest for the diminutive occupants.

This operation was always accompanied by heavy breathing, enormous concentration and ultimate rapture. Agnes Fogerty enjoyed this annual instruction in the art of miniature furniture making, and felt great satisfaction in watching the children bearing home the results of their labours.

'I suppose,' she commented to Dorothy, over tea that afternoon, 'that they get so much more satisfaction from making a three-dimensional object. I mean, one would far rather have a cat than a *picture* of a cat.'

'Although, of course, a *picture* would be less bother,' observed her headmistress, after due thought.

The tiff between John and Edward still made itself felt. The two couples frequently had an evening together playing cards, but when Joan broached the subject to her husband she was surprised at his response.

'Oh, skip it for a bit! John's in one of his awkward moods. Let him simmer.'

'How do you mean?'

'Oh, he was rather offensive to me the other day.'

'John? Offensive? I can't believe it.'

Edward began to fidget up and down the room. 'Nothing too personal, I suppose, but he was throwing his weight about over the steps at the old people's place.'

'Well, he may be right. Mr Jones mentioned them to me the other morning. He hoped the residents there wouldn't slip on them.'

'Oh, don't you start! There's absolutely nothing wrong with those steps,' exploded Edward. 'The point is I don't particularly want to spend a whole evening in John's company at the moment.'

'Well, calm down,' begged Joan, taken aback at such unaccustomed heat. 'You'll have a seizure if you get into such a state, over such a silly little thing.'

'It isn't a silly little thing to me,' almost shouted her incensed husband. 'It's a criticism of my work, and I'm not standing for it.'

At that Joan shrugged her shoulders, and went out, without comment, to do her shopping.

Ruth Lovell, Joan's sister, was also perplexed by her husband's moodiness. She knew from experience that he took everything seriously. It was one of his qualities which his patients appreciated. He was willing to give time, as well as his medical expertise, to their troubles, and this they warmly appreciated.

Such dedication frequently exhausted him, and Ruth did her best to provide a relaxing atmosphere in their home. Their occasional evenings at the Youngs, or in their house, at the card table, were one of John's few outside pleasures.

But he too, it seemed, did not want to spend an evening with his brother-in-law, but said less about his reasons than the voluble Edward.

'Perhaps later on,' he said when Ruth suggested a card-playing evening. 'I'm rather tired these days, and Edward can be a bit overpowering, I find.'

'Just as you like,' answered Ruth. 'And if you're feeling tired, what about a dose or two of that tonic you make up for the patients?'

'That stuff?' exclaimed her husband. 'Not likely! It tastes appalling.'

Ella Bembridge, looking with approval at the bright October landscape, decided to take a pot of newly-made plum jam to Dotty Harmer, and to collect her goat's milk on the same errand.

The air was fresh and invigorating. Three dogs who had escaped from their owners were playing a mad game of 'He' on the green, observed at a safe distance by Albert Piggott's cat sitting on the churchyard wall.

Albert himself, cigarette dangling from his lip, was supporting himself on a hoe, as Ella went by.

'Lovely day,' shouted Ella.

'Ah!' agreed Albert.

'Busy?'

'Always plenty to do,' growled Albert, prodding in a desultory way at a dandelion root.

'That's what keeps you in such good trim,' said Ella bracingly.

She passed on her way, leaving Albert more than usually disgruntled by this exchange.

'*In good trim,*' repeated Albert disgustedly, flinging his cigarette stub over the wall. 'That's a laugh, I must say.'

But Ella was well out of earshot, and by now was traversing the narrow path by the Piggotts' cottage which led to Lulling Woods and Dotty's house.

She found Dotty sitting on the sofa surrounded by various woollen garments which she was busily unravelling.

'Connie and Kit are at the end of the garden,' she said, 'having a bonfire. They'll be here in a minute. How nice to see you.'

'Too good to stay in, so I thought I'd bring you a pot of plum jam.'

'Lovely! I really miss jam making, but Connie won't let me stand for too long, and last time I put in rather too much sugar, and burnt the saucepan. The stove was rather messy too.'

Ella could well imagine it, but forbore to comment.

'And what are you doing with all that wool?'

'It's for a knitting bee in Lulling. Everyone's going to knit squares, for blankets, you know. I thought these old jumpers would do very well to supply some of the wool.'

Ella, who deplored things made from old materials in this way, nobly took hold of a dilapidated scarf and began to un-ravel it, only to find that innumerable moth holes resulted in lengths of wool not much more than a yard long.

'Better throw this away,' she said after some examination of the material.

'No, no!' protested Dotty. 'Just go on rolling it up, dear, and the knitters can quite well cope with it.'

Luckily, at this moment, Connie and Kit, flushed with ex-ercise and smelling exceedingly autumnal from the bonfire smoke, arrived to take over, and Ella could sit back and enjoy the rest of her visit.

'And how are your new neighbours settling in?' enquired Connie.

'Pretty well, I gather from the Cartwrights. I bobbed over to see dear old Tom Hardy and his dog yesterday. He's as pleased as Punch with the house. Great relief for Dimity and Charles, who were beginning to worry about getting him to uproot him-self.'

'I was going to call there yesterday,' said Kit, 'but had to go to the dentist instead.'

'Bad luck! Why is it one always dreads the dentist more than the doctor? After all, there's a lot more to go wrong in the doctor's section.'

'I'm thankful to say,' said Dotty, wrenching madly at a jumper sleeve, 'that I haven't a tooth left in my head.'

'Neither shall I have, at this rate,' observed Kit. 'I must say though, he seems a quiet decent sort of chap. I once had a dentist who had music in the background. I suppose he thought it might soothe his patients.'

'What an idea!' said Connie.

'Exactly! I felt like shouting: "Switch that row off, and attend to your job, man!" But, of course, with all the ironmongery in my mouth at the time, I was helpless!'

'I had a dentist once,' mused Connie, 'who had a tank of tropical fish in one's eyeline. Far from soothing, I found it. I kept worrying about the air flow, and one particularly terrified fish that kept hiding behind some water weed.'

'I heard of one,' said Ella, adding her mite, 'who kept bees in his surgery.'

'In a skep? Surely not?'

'No, in a glass observation case. They had an opening to get out to fly for honey. Quite fascinating really, if you were in any mood to enjoy practical demonstrations.'

'All I can say is,' said Dotty, 'at least you are not shown the tooth he's just extracted, all bloody at one end, as our dentist used to do when we were children.'

'How gruesome!' said Connie.

'He was a friend of my father's,' went on Dotty, dropping half a dozen balls of wool on the floor, much to Flossie's delight. 'They both felt that children should learn to face up to life.'

'And death too, I should think,' said Kit shortly, 'at that rate. Here, what about a cup of tea?'

'An excellent idea,' replied Dotty. 'And we could have some of Ella's plum jam. Unless, of course, you would like to try mine?'

'Yours, dearest aunt, is now making excellent compost,' said Connie gently, 'so we'll settle for Ella's today.'

Although Ella had assured her friends that all was going well at the old people's homes, that was not quite true.

To be sure, the residents had enjoyed a little party arranged by Jane and Bill after all their charges had arrived.

Here introductions were made, a glass of wine or orange juice taken, and invitations given to each other's abodes. The atmosphere was cordial. All were thankful to have been among the lucky applicants, and anxious to make friends with those who shared their environment.

Jane and Bill were greatly relieved to see how well their charges settled down, but they did not deceive themselves by thinking that such halcyon conditions would continue for ever. There were bound to be differences of opinion, little complaints, and perhaps ill health to face, but at least, they comforted themselves, the party had gone well and everyone appeared amicably disposed.

The animals, whose inclusion at the homes had so concerned the trustees, gave no trouble at all. The Jermyns' cat Monty, large and placid, was content to sun himself in the angle of a wall at his end of the row. At night time he fraternised with Albert Piggott's cat and the two explored Thrush Green in great contentment. Tom Hardy's Polly they simply ignored.

Polly was equally content. She had Tom, her adored master. The house was warm, her food arrived regularly, and she was getting too old to bother about taking much exercise. A gentle amble about the green, or a leisurely walk at her master's heels along Lulling High Street, suited the old lady very well. She soon forgot the river sounds and smells which had once meant so much to her in her earlier years.

As for Miss Fuller's lovebirds, they twittered together in their cage set in the window, and behaved exactly as they had done for years. If anything they seemed more animated, and according to their doting mistress their appetites had improved since the move.

But although the animals had soon settled in, it was their human companions who seemed more restless. This, of course, was natural as the first euphoria wore off. People were bound to begin to make comparisons with the homes they had left. Some found a lack of cupboard space. Some found the hot water system inadequate. Some complained that, despite Edward Young's care in sound-proofing, they could hear the next door's television.

Jane and Bill did their best to mitigate these little upsets. They were genuinely sympathetic to these elderly people. They persuaded those who complained about the lack of storage space to look again at their possessions and perhaps part with some of them. They suggested certain rearrangements, and put in a lot of time and energy in sorting out a great many articles. Some were much-loved old friends, and it was clear that to part with, say, an ancient corner cupboard, or an occasional table inherited from a grandmother, was going to be a wrench which their owners could not face. Jane was wonderfully diplomatic in these matters, and knew when to stop her suggestions, before agitation took over. But she was successful in helping several of her charges with problems of this kind.

The hot water system was soon remedied by means of a midday boost. The question of noise from neighbouring houses was not so simply answered. Some of the tentants were getting deaf, and automatically set their radios and television sets to a high volume. The fine weather meant that windows, and sometimes doors, were open, and Jane paid several visits to those offenders who were annoying their neighbours in all innocence.

It was soon apparent that the most difficult resident was going to be Carlotta Jermyn. She was a woman who had always demanded attention, and though, as a small-time actress, she had never received national acclaim, she had expected a certain amount of limelight among her fellow artists and even more admiration from the public. As a pretty child and young woman, she had been spoilt, and her husband had continued the process throughout their married life. It was soon common knowledge that her husband took tea to her every morning in bed, and that it took her over an hour to dress and make up her face, before she was ready for the day. Such behaviour occasioned disapproval among one or two of the neighbours, particularly in the case of Miss Fuller, who as a hard-working teacher had always been up betimes, cooked her own breakfast, and never had a meal in bed in her life, except when confined to hospital with broken ribs.

However, all this could have been born if Carlotta had not taken to calling on her neighbours at the most awkward times. In truth, the poor woman was increasingly bored and missed the daily routine of her life in the little town of Lulling. There she had enjoyed the company of a next-door neighbour whose husband had also been in the army. As his rank had been higher than Carlotta's husband's, a certain amount of deference was shown, and Carlotta was gratified to have the friendship of a senior officer's wife and to exchange confidences over the garden hedge.

She still met her friend in The Fuchsia Bush now and again, and the two couples exchanged visits. But naturally Carlotta was thrown more upon her own resources, and very soon began to turn to her neighbours for company.

As it was usually midday before she began to pay her social calls, several of her victims found them annoying. It was true that she did not bother Tom Hardy or old Johnny Enderby, guessing that they would not provide the light chit-chat which she so missed since moving from Lulling, but Mrs Bates and Miss Fuller were early among her prey, and very exasperating they found her attentions.

Both these ladies, and the single old men for that matter, were used to having their main meal at twelve or soon after, making do with a snack in the evening and sometimes a bed-time drink.

Carlotta was accustomed to preparing an evening meal, and

the Jermyns were quite happy with a bowl of soup, cheese and biscuits and fruit at midday. This meant, of course, that Mrs Jermyn, once her lengthy toilet was completed, was at leisure to call somewhere between half past eleven and twelve upon her neighbours just when they were at a crucial stage of their cooking arrangements, either stirring gravy, prodding potatoes, setting the table, or putting on the sprouts.

Mrs Bates, a humble soul who had spent her active years as a first-rate maid, was flattered at first to be called upon, and was inclined to call Carlotta 'Madam', which pleased her visitor exceedingly. But after three visits in four days, on the last of which poor Mrs Bates had been in the middle of eating shepherd's pie when the imperious knock came at the door, she quite firmly said that it would be more convenient if calls could be made around three in the afternoon when she was not so busy.

Miss Fuller, less impressed with Carlotta's social graces, made it clear on the occasion of the lady's second visit, that she had her lunch promptly at twelve-fifteen, having got used to this over the years of eating school dinners.

Carlotta had laughed merrily in a patronising way and had commented: 'Oh dear! What a dreadful time to have to face a meal! When do you fit in your little drinkie? I'm usually looking forward to a spot of gin about then.'

'I don't drink,' Miss Fuller had replied shortly, shutting the door smartly upon her visitor.

The Cross pair, George and Mary, and Jack and Sybil Angell had not been hounded quite so severely, possibly because they seemed to be out quite a lot, and also had a number of friends who dropped in.

Jane Cartwright soon became aware of Carlotta's nuisance value and wondered if she should drop a hint.

'A hint?' said Bill, when the matter was discussed. 'Carlotta Jermyn wouldn't know what a hint was! No, my love, just let things sort themselves out. She'll twig before long that her attentions aren't welcome. Our Miss Fuller will make that plain, and if she doesn't, then I'll have a word with the Captain. He's got plenty of horse sense.'

Most of the residents were more than satisfied with their new circumstances, and Tom and Johnny, who had met before on various Lulling occasions, were fast becoming firm friends.

Each little house had a small garden at the back, and a slip of a garden beneath the front windows.

The two old men were soon busy planting their crops in the little plots. Johnny Enderby shared a bundle of fine wallflower plants with his neighbour, and their two front gardens were the first to be prepared, ready for a bright and fragrant show the next spring.

They took to walking along the Nidden road together on fine afternoons, Polly at their heels, and sometimes called at The Two Pheasants of an evening for a pint of ale. It was plain to the Cartwrights that here were two model tenants.

The Thrush Green residents took a great interest in their new neighbours. Winnie Bailey knew most of them from the old days when her husband had been in practice. Ella Bembridge and Mrs Bates were old acquaintances, and Sybil Angell had been to the same craftwork evening classes as Ella.

George and Mary Cross knew the Shoosmiths, and soon there was a good deal of visiting, and being visited, by old and new inhabitants of Thrush Green. Miss Watson and Miss Fogerty's first tea party for Miss Fuller was soon followed by other modest invitations, and the Cartwrights found themselves as busy as their charges in various hospitable engagements around Thrush Green.

'Seem to have settled down lovely, don't they?' said Percy Hodge to the landlord, when Johnny and Tom had departed to their homes across the darkening green.

'Ah! Lovely! Lovelily, I mean,' agreed Mr Jones, twirling a snowy cloth in a glass. He stopped suddenly. Somehow, that last word sounded wrong.

He resumed his polishing more slowly, still puzzled. Say

what you like, he mused, English was a deuce of a language to get right. It got worse the more you thought about it.

'Nearly time, gentlemen,' he said, putting the gleaming glass on a shelf.

That was plain English anyway.

11. PREPARING FOR BONFIRE NIGHT

During the last few days of October, the large heap on Thrush Green of inflammable material such as wood, cardboard boxes and paper sacks full of dried leaves, grew daily as November the fifth approached.

Miss Watson's class had made a splendid Guy Fawkes stuffed with straw, and dressed in some trousers which once belonged to Ben Curdle, a jacket of Albert Piggott's which Nelly had handed over secretly, much to her husband's rage, and some Wellington boots contributed by Ella Bembridge and destined to smell appallingly when the fire got going.

The guy was crowned, somewhat incongruously, by a solar topee which Harold Shoosmith had once sported in his working colonial days. As Isobel had pointed out, the sun in Thrush Green, even at its best, hardly warranted keeping such a piece of head gear.

Once the guy was completed, it had been decided by Miss Watson that such a great man-sized object would be best stored in her garden shed. This decision, however, caused such agitation and even some tears in the classroom that she relented, and the figure hung from a hook on the back of the schoolroom door, and seriously impeded anyone going in and out.

It also frightened several of Miss Fogerty's infants who had been sent with messages to Miss Watson, and one particularly timid child had suffered night terrors as a result.

'It really makes one rather cross,' commented Miss Watson, handing over the letter from the child's irate mother to Agnes, 'when one sees the sort of horrors they watch on the telly. Why, our guy looks positively *benign*!'

Privately, it was not how little Miss Fogerty would have described it. In her opinion, there was something decidedly gruesome in the figure suspended from its hook. Visions of desperate offenders taking their lives in prison cells hovered before her, and she had every sympathy with the young child who had been so affected by the sinister guy.

'Well, it won't be long before we burn it,' she replied diplomatically. 'Frankly, I dread the fireworks far more than the bonfire. At least Thrush Green people seem to have the sense to keep their poor animals indoors.'

'Albert Piggott didn't keep his cat indoors last year,' responded Dorothy Watson somewhat tartly. 'I saw it myself.'

'Oh dear!' cried Agnes. 'The poor thing! Where was it?'

'Sitting by the bonfire washing its face,' replied Dorothy. 'Quite unaffected by the noise.'

'Isn't that just like a cat!' commented Agnes, much relieved.

The celebration of Guy Fawkes's attempt to blow up the Houses of Parliament in 1605 was always a communal affair at Thrush Green.

The schoolchildren helped to build the bonfire and to supply the guy. Fireworks were given by various people who still enjoyed such things, and Harold Shoosmith and his friend Frank Hurst were among the most generous donors.

Percy Hodge always gave a sack of large potatoes which the Boy Scouts baked in the ashes of the bonfire for everybody, and Mr Jones of The Two Pheasants brought out glasses of beer and mugs of cocoa for the assembled throng.

The day before Bonfire Night turned out dank and drizzly, much to the dismay of the children. Would the bonfire light? Would it be too damp? Should they rush over to it and shroud it in a tarpaulin? Percy Hodge'd have one for sure. Could they buy a can of paraffin to make sure it would go? From school funds, say? Or what about firelighters?

Miss Watson dealt with all these anxious enquiries until she saw that a whole hour of arithmetic and geography teaching had somehow vanished, when she became extremely stern and threatened the entire class with Mental-Arithmetic-All-Through-Playtime, which somewhat sobered her pupils.

Over at Rectory Cottages Jane Cartwright decided to put on her raincoat and remind her charges that they were invited to the party on the green at six-thirty on the morrow. The new steps and paths were slippery in this moist weather, and wet leaves lay like bright pennies wherever one looked.

She completed her tour successfully, and was touched to see how pleased everyone was at the invitation.

'Second childhood, it seems,' thought Jane indulgently, hurrying back to put on the sprouts for lunch.

But they were never to be cooked. Jane's feet went from under her on the top step, and she landed with a sickening crunch.

Lying dazed, Jane's nursing knowledge still functioned.

'The femur,' murmured poor Jane, closing her eyes.

While Jane was still engaged on her rounds that fateful morning, Joan Young and her sister Ruth were enjoying a cup of coffee together, and discussing the odd behaviour of their respective husbands.

'They really are a couple of sillies,' said Joan. 'What grandmother used to term "mardy babies". What on earth is the matter with them?'

'I'm always anxious about John,' admitted Ruth. 'He works far too hard, and I think this police business is worrying him.'

'What police business?'

Ruth explained about the robberies and John's involvement with Leys Farm.

'Funnily enough,' said Joan, 'Betty Bell said something about it, but I had no idea John was mixed up in it.'

'Well, he's not exactly "mixed up in it" as you say, but the young man whom John treated has been sighted evidently, and if the police can pick him up it means that John will probably have to identify him. I'm sure that's one of his worries at the moment.'

'Poor old boy! Luckily, Edward hasn't anything like that hanging over him, but he's remarkably short-tempered lately. I blame it on a job he's just undertaken near Cirencester. It's an old vicarage which they want Edward to convert into eight flats, and according to him it will only make six. There's a pretty ferocious battle going on at the moment, I know.'

'Never mind. It makes no difference to us,' replied Ruth comfortingly. 'They'll get over it no doubt, and we'll be able to have our card parties again.'

'Maybe they'll be more amenable at the firework party to-morrow,' agreed Joan. 'It's good that it coincides with Paul's half-term this year. He's bringing home a school friend, and Jeremy Hurst has his half term at the same time, so the house will be cheerful.'

'Will Edward be able to stand it?'

'He'll have to,' replied Joan lightly. 'Anyway, I notice that he has an enormous box of fireworks in his study, so that augurs well for all concerned.'

'That's good. Well, I must get back. It's John's half day, and there's lunch to get ready. He comes in straight from his morning round.'

'Not too busy, I hope, with this mild autumn?'

'No, touch wood! It's after Christmas that the trouble begins.'

The sisters kissed affectionately and parted.

Down at The Fuchsia Bush in Lulling High Street Nelly Piggott had been summoned to Mrs Peters' little office.

It was a quarter to twelve. Morning coffee was practically over, and the midday lunch was well ahead, being supervised by Nelly's two competent kitchen maids.

What could this be about, she wondered, taking off her

overall? It wasn't like Mrs Peters to interrupt kitchen activities at such a time, unless something urgent had cropped up.

'Sit down, Nelly,' said her employer. 'I won't keep you many minutes, but I thought you ought to know Mrs Jefferson called last night, and she's definitely giving up. The doctor insists, so that's that. You can guess how sorry I am. We've soldiered on here together for many years, and I'm going to miss her.'

'So am I,' said Nelly, with feeling. 'She's one in a thousand. What will you do?'

'That's the question. I shall have to advertise for someone experienced, but the two girls are doing well under you, and can take a certain amount of responsibility.'

She began to fidget with papers on her desk, and Nelly began to wonder what the future would hold for herself.

'If you want me to do more,' she offered, 'I think I could arrange things. Albert's no bother, and you know I enjoy working here.'

Mrs Peters nodded abstractedly. 'Yes, thank you, Nelly. You've been an enormous help, and it's due to you that we're building up this home catering side so successfully. It's plain to me, Nelly, that that's where our living's going to be in the future. That christening party of Mrs Thurgood's has sparked off six, and probably, eight more functions. I'm thinking of investing in a van of our own.'

'Well now, isn't that good news!' exclaimed Nelly. Things must be going better than she had thought. A year ago Mrs Peters had been worrying about the state of the business. Now, it seemed, the outlook was brighter.

As if reading her thoughts, Mrs Peters began to explain.

'We're not suddenly rich, Nelly, or anything like that, but business is certainly looking up and I was left a house last Christmas by an old aunt of mine. It's way up north, at a little town called Alnwick, and as I shall never use it I put it on the market and have a little over twenty thousand from the sale.'

'That must be a great relief to you,' said Nelly warmly.

'It certainly is. But what I wanted to tell you is something I've had in mind for some time. Poor Mrs Jefferson's retirement has brought it to a head.'

She resumed her fidgeting, and Nelly began to wonder if the apple crumble was getting overdone.

'If I get a van and do more of this catering on the spot, I shall need someone who can take complete charge at this end. Would you consider becoming a partner in the firm, and doing that?'

Nelly, for once, was flummoxed.

'Heavens alive! *Partner*? But I could take charge here as I am, couldn't I? I mean, to be a *partner*—'

Words failed her.

'Nelly, I want someone who has the interests of this place at heart. And you have shown that you are proud of The Fuchsia Bush, and willing to turn your hand to anything. All the girls respect you. If you feel you can take this on, I shall be very much relieved. Naturally, your income would be greater.'

She named a sum which to Nelly sounded colossal, and she was about to remonstrate.

'Say nothing,' urged Mrs Peters. 'Think it over. Talk to Albert about it, and let me know before the end of the week.'

She rose and patted Nelly's massive shoulder.

'I'm fair bowled over,' said that lady. 'But it's a wonderful offer, and I'm proud.'

'Off you go then,' said Mrs Peters. 'Something smells good in the kitchen.'

'Well-done apple crumble, I shouldn't wonder,' replied Nelly, making towards her own domain.

The first person to reach Jane Cartwright lying prone on the damp steps was Carlotta Jermyn. She had just emerged from her home and was bound for the Crosses on one of her morning calls.

She was surprisingly calm and competent in this emergency, and knelt down beside Jane, murmuring reassuring words and ignoring the dampness which stained her knees.

'Don't move, my dear,' she said. 'I'll get someone to you immediately.'

But Bill had already arrived and taken charge. Heads emerged from doorways. Faces were stricken, and lamentation loud.

'If you could go to Dr Lovell's,' said Bill, supporting his wife's head, 'it would be a great help.'

Carlotta hurried across the green, leaving Bill to comfort his wife, and organise a rug and cushions to ease her position. He was not short of helpers. Everyone, it seemed, was anxious to render first aid.

Within five minutes one of Dr Lovell's young partners arrived.

'Dr Lovell's not on duty at the moment,' he explained, as he examined his patient, who was now able to talk to him and to the throng around her. He made a makeshift splint and he and Bill carefully carried Jane to her own sofa.

'I'll get an ambulance straight away. She'll be taken to St

Richard's, of course. As far as I can see, it's a straightforward break, but the X-rays will show up everything.' He began to dial. 'Those damn steps are a menace in this weather,' he remarked conversationally, as he waited for the hospital to reply.

'So it seems,' said Bill, holding his poor wife's hand.

Excitement was running high at the village school, so high indeed that Agnes Fogerty decided to put aside her idea of an autumn collage for the classroom wall that handiwork session, and to substitute the theme of Bonfire Night with plenty of well-sharpened red and yellow crayons.

Her class worked industriously. There was rather more chattering than Agnes normally allowed, but occasionally, she told herself, one must give a little licence to young children. The thought of Christmas so soon to be upon them, with all its accompanying trappings of paper chains, calendars, blotters, Christmas cards and rather terrible ornaments made from pine cones, all manufactured in this very classroom, was one to be shelved, at least until this present excitement had gone.

She wandered around the tables admiring guys suspended, black and spider-like, among flaring fires. The red and yellow crayons were working overtime, and Agnes made a mental note to get a few in reserve from the stock cupboard. Red ones always ran out early when Father Christmas hove in sight. And, come to think of it, black ones would be needed urgently, after all these guys, for Father Christmas's boots.

It might be as well, mused Agnes as she nodded encouragingly at the upheld masterpieces, to look out that well-tried bookmarker pattern from *The Teachers' World*. A tassel made of bright wool, hanging from the pointed end, would be a useful exercise for young fingers, and would use up the remains of some scarlet four-ply left over from knitting mittens for the church bazaar. Looking ahead has always been one of the attributes of a good teacher, and earnest little Miss Fogerty was one of the very best.

Across the playground, in the top class, peace reigned. Miss Watson, made of sterner stuff than her assistant, had quelled the chattering and the insatiable need, it seemed, to stand up to see if the unlit bonfire was still safely established on the green.

Here handiwork on a more sophisticated scale was being done. Embroidery, knitting, single section book-making and paper models were keeping fingers busy, and the most competent reader – and the worst knitter – was sitting in front of the class regaling the rest with a passage from *Three Men in a Boat*.

Dorothy Watson, between marking some deplorable mental arithmetic tests and watching over her charges, was also thinking about Christmas preparations, but in a negative way.

No nativity play, was her first definite decision. Far too much preparation, and really the costumes alone were a headache, despite the help of the parents. If Thrush Green school possessed a proper stage it would be a different kettle of fish, of course, but the heaving about of school furniture was a sore trial. No, a nativity play was definitely out.

And the usual boisterous Christmas tea party seemed rather daunting. Perhaps a simple celebration with carols and some readings would fit the bill? It might be combined with a cup of tea and a slice of Christmas cake for parents and the school's friends after the performance. Something really *simple*, she repeated to herself. She supposed that the cake should really have been made by now. She must ask Nelly Piggott if The Fuchsia Bush had any on sale. Perhaps it could be suitably iced for the school's festivities?

It began to grow murky in the classroom, and the school clock showed that it was nearly home time. She could hear the cries of the infants as they tumbled across the playground to the bliss of freedom.

'Pack up your work, children,' said Miss Watson. 'Thank you for reading to us, dear, but do remember that "Harris" begins with an aitch. All stand, eyes closed. *Closed*, Pat Carter!

'*Keep us, O Lord, in Thy care, and safe from any dangers of the night.*'

'Amen!' said the children with unnecessary vigour. Would school never end?

They streamed out to the lobby, collected coats and scarves, and rushed joyously homeward.

'I shall be glad when tomorrow's over,' said Dorothy to Agnes. 'Guy Fawkes has a lot to answer for.'

While Jane and Bill Cartwright waited for the ambulance to arrive, the elderly folk were persuaded to return to their homes. In this undertaking Carlotta and her husband showed signs of tactful leadership which Bill recognised with much admiration.

As soon as he could see that all were being safely shepherded, he made another telephone call. This time it was to Jane's mother, some half a mile or so away along the road to Nidden. Listening to the bell ringing in Mrs Jenner's hall, Bill wondered if he would find her in. Probably she had finished lunch by now. He hoped that she had not gone to her bedroom for an afternoon snooze, as sometimes she did.

At length, he heard her voice.

'Mother,' said Billy urgently, 'don't get alarmed, but I've some rather bad news. Are you sitting down?'

'Good heavens, man! Of course I'm not sitting down! There's no room for a chair in this passage. In any case, I'd sooner stand up to bad news. Quickly, what is it?'

He told her briefly.

'Jane says you're not to worry. The ambulance is on its way. Come and see her in Dickie's, she says.'

'Oh, the poor girl!' cried Mrs Jenner. 'That sounds like a long job to me. How will you manage?'

'I was wondering,' began Bill hesitantly, 'if you could see your way clear to coming down here for a day or two?'

'I'll be with you in twenty minutes,' said that noble woman, and hung up.

'Your mother,' said Bill huskily to Jane, 'is an angel. A proper angel!'

'You don't have to tell me that,' said her daughter, as the ambulance swished up to the door.

12. THE FIFTH OF NOVEMBER

A clammy mist engulfed Thrush Green at daybreak on November the fifth. The waiting bonfire glistened damply. The hedges were heavy with droplets, the trees' gold had slipped to their feet, and the leaves lay thick and sticky in the wet grass.

It was uncannily silent. Distant sounds were muted. Footsteps, and even the noise of car tyres, were muffled by the fallen leaves and muddy roads. It was a chastened assembly that met at the village school, but Miss Watson did her best to cheer them by saying that the weatherman had promised a finer afternoon.

'But do 'e *know?*' asked one infant anxiously.

And all that Miss Watson could say in reply was that presumably he knew better than most.

She hoped it was true.

Across the green, Dr Lovell heard for the first time about the accident at the old people's homes, and was magnanimous enough not to make any comment about Edward Young's steps in front of his partners. Nevertheless, he felt a certain satisfaction in hearing that his fears were not groundless, although he had every sympathy for poor Jane Cartwright's mishap.

'I hope all the old dears over there will hold tight to the hand rail,' was his only remark, when he was told the news, but he said more to Ruth when he went home at lunch time.

'Well, that's the first casualty at Edward's famous edifice. And won't be the last, as far as I can see!'

'What's happened?' asked Ruth, soup spoon suspended in mid-air.

'Jane Cartwright's broken a leg on those idiotic steps. Asking for trouble to put steps like that where there are old people. I told Edward so months ago.'

'But Jane isn't old,' protested Ruth.

'Oh, don't quibble!' snapped her husband. 'I know she's not! All I'm pointing out is that those steps are a hazard, and one which any sane architect would have omitted from his plan from the start.'

Ruth continued to sip her soup in silence. When John was so short-tempered it hardly seemed possible to conduct a civilised conversation. However, by the time the apple tart stage had been reached, Ruth spoke.

'I'm taking Mary to watch the bonfire just after six. Paul's home and Jeremy Hurst's going to be there as well. Joan suggests we have a drink with them, before or after, just which suits you best.'

'I suppose Edward is attending this bean feast?'

'Naturally.'

'Well, I'll come along for a little while to the bonfire, but don't accept for me later. I'm on surgery duty tonight.'

'Fair enough. We won't be late back. Mary will be tired out with all the excitement.'

'You'll be a lot tireder, I surmise,' said John with a smile.

He pushed back his chair, kissed his wife, and went back to his duties.

Well, he seemed to have cheered up, thought Ruth, clearing the table. But if only he would try some of his own tonic!

The weatherman must have known something after all, for by midday a watery sun was trying to disperse the mist.

Winnie Bailey, taking a turn in her garden in the hope of finding a few flowers for the house, was cheered to see the sunshine. She dreaded the winter even more keenly now that Donald had gone. It was not so much the piercing cold of the Cotswold winters, as the short murky days which she found hardest to bear.

She realised, with a shock, that this was the first time she had been outdoors for three days. The rain and dismal weather had turned her attention to a multitude of little tasks indoors. She decided that she would get some exercise during the afternoon by taking some magazines to Dotty, and hearing the news from her old friend.

Meanwhile, she collected four somewhat battered late roses, a few sprigs of hardy fuchsias and two nerines which struggled for existence in the unwelcoming cold of this area, and realised that these were all the flowers to be gathered here in November. It was true that the pyracantha tree which she and Donald had planted years ago was ablaze with scarlet berries, but their prickly stems discouraged any picking, and in any case the berries would soon wither indoors. Better to admire them from the garden, thought Winnie, carrying her rag-taggle posy inside.

Later she set off across the green, admiring the bonfire as she did so. Nathaniel Patten on his plinth seemed to smile benignly on the peaceful scene. Before school ended, as Winnie knew from earlier years, the children would carry the guy across and put him on the top of the pyre, where carefully crossed twigs made a chair for him.

To her surprise, she found Dotty in the garden, throwing weeds over the top of the chicken run to an appreciative bevy of Rhode Island Red hens.

'Should you be out in this damp weather, Dotty?'

'Oh, yes, dear, it's perfectly all right, Connie and Kit are down in Lulling. Do come in.'

She began to wipe muddy hands down her skirt, eyes beaming behind her spectacles.

'Dear things,' she said affectionately to the scrabbling hens. 'You see, I know Connie is most conscientious in feeding them night and morning, but I feel that they miss fresh greenstuff.

Now I have just given them dandelion leaves, groundsel, shepherds' purse and some dock leaves. A wonderfully healthy mixture of essential minerals. Have you ever read Gerard's *Herball*?'

'Well, no, Dotty. But I know that Donald had a copy and read it with much enjoyment. He often said that the old boy knew what he was talking about.'

'He was quite right. Dandelion and dock in particular he understood, and I'm sure he would approve of the hens having plenty of them.'

'I must say they seem to appreciate your largesse,' observed Winnie, 'but don't you think you should come in now? Your slippers are soaked.'

She ushered her hostess into the house, and was relieved to see her settled by the fire. Dotty took off her slippers, displaying a pink big toe emerging through a hole in her stocking, and Winnie put them in the hearth to dry. What a time Connie must have looking after this eccentric old aunt!

'Now you must tell me all the news from Thrush Green,' said Dotty, arranging her legs on the sofa. 'Has Mrs Bassett quite recovered? And have you heard about Richard's baby? And is Percy Hodge still courting your Jenny? And how are Agnes Fogerty and Dorothy? And are you going to the Guy Fawkes' party? I believe Ella is.'

For one supposed to be out of the swim of village affairs, thought Winnie, Dotty seemed remarkably up to date.

'Mrs Bassett's much better, but Joan and Ruth watch her like hawks, I believe. No, no news of Richard, and as far as I know Jenny is free from Percy's attentions. In fact, I gather he has transferred them to Albert Piggott's wife.'

'That won't please Albert, will it?' exclaimed Dotty with much pleasure. 'Go on, dear.'

'The village school is in a state of great excitement, Molly Curdle told me. George can't wait for tonight when they light the fire. And no, I don't think I shall go, even if Ella does. Jenny and I get an excellent view from the house and it gets rather too boisterous for me with all those fireworks. Donald used to love it.'

'I never did. The poor frightened animals, you know. Which reminds me, Kit and Connie are making plans to go to Venice.'

'What's the connection, Dotty dear?'

'Why, the animals! I went once as a girl and was quite shaken by the callousness of some of the inhabitants, to the cats, in particular. But I'm much relieved to hear that things are greatly improved. Still a lot to be done though, according to the Anglo-Italian Society for Animal Protection. Their report came yesterday. You must borrow it.'

'Thank you. And when are Kit and Connie off?'

'Oh, as soon as possible,' said Dotty somewhat vaguely. 'I tell them Venice gets foggy about now, but I don't think they mind about that. And I have warned them about being taken hostage on these aeroplanes, and advised them to pack a lemon or two to add to the drinking water if they are held up at some rather uncomfortable place like Beirut.'

'It doesn't happen often,' Winnie pointed out.

Dotty gave a little shriek, lowered her legs from the sofa and snatched up the poker.

'Look, dear, a poor earwig on that log on the fire! Can you reach it? Let me get a shovel.'

Winnie followed her gaze, and bent to the rescue with her hostess. Not until the insect was safely deposited outside on the fence was Dotty able to relax again.

'What a mishap! I've always been devoted to earwigs. As children we used to chant a rhyme:

> *Marco Polo, Marco Polo*
> *His mother was an earwig*
> *His father was a whale.*

'Now, I wonder what the derivation of that was?'

'I've no idea,' confessed Winnie, her head beginning to spin, as it so often did in Dotty's company. 'But I did hear some children chanting much more topically this morning:

> *Please to remember*
> *The fifth of November*
> *Gunpowder, treason and plot.*
> *I see no reason*
> *Why gunpowder, treason,*
> *Should ever be forgot.*'

'And were they begging? With a guy I mean?'

'No, not this time. I wonder what they would expect these days? A penny for the guy wouldn't go very far, would it?'

'A pound probably,' said Dotty. 'Ah! I think I hear the wanderers returning. Stay for tea.'

Nelly Piggott, busy in the kitchen of The Fuchsia Bush, was still unsure about the answer to be given to Mrs Peters. Her employer was out, chasing up some supplies which a tardy wholesaler had failed to deliver, and Nelly had not had a chance to put one or two queries to her.

Her first, and most overwhelming desire, was to accept the offer with all the delight she felt, but Albert had put one doubt in her head. To be sure, he had not been much help in discussing this momentous news, when he had returned from the public house next door rather more befuddled than usual.

Nelly insisted on his drinking a cup of black coffee before she told him about Mrs Peters' offer, but she doubted if it did much to clear her spouse's brain.

'Partner?' exclaimed Albert. 'And what pay does that give you?'

Nelly told him.

Albert continued to peer sourly into his coffee cup. 'She won't be givin' you that much for nothin',' was his comment.

'What d'you mean? It's a fair offer, isn't it? I'll be working harder, that's all.'

'You don't reckon to be a partner unless you puts something into it.'

'Well, I am! My work, my experience, my know-how! And all that,' ended Nelly weakly.

Albert snorted, pushed away the cup, and began to lurch towards the stairs.

'You mark my words, gal, she'll want money before you're taken on as a partner. *Partner indeed*! Don't make me laugh! I'm off to bed, so come up quiet when you do.'

Nelly washed up the cup. Tears joined the water in the washing-up bowl. She did not believe Albert's words, but it had been a long hard day, and what she had needed was some support and comfort in this crisis.

Well, Albert was Albert! Half his trouble was jealousy, she told herself, mopping her eyes. He acually resented her success, that was part of it, the mean-spirited old toss-pot! She had been a fool to expect anything helpful from that source.

She went to bed in the little back bedroom, and lay awake listening to Albert's snoring next door, and wondering if, just possibly, he was right about having to contribute money to a firm if you were made a partner. She must get things straight with Mrs Peters before she accepted.

If only there were someone to ask! She supposed that she could consult someone like Mr Venables, but that would look as though she did not trust Mrs Peters, and anyway it would cost money.

Suddenly, she thought of her new friend, Mrs Jenner. The very person! Sensible about business affairs, and fair-minded. Tomorrow evening she would walk up the Nidden road, and have a good talk with her!

She had no idea, of course, that her friend was much nearer at hand, sleeping in the spare bedroom of the wardens' house, with the alarm clock set at six-thirty ready for her new duties on the morrow.

A light breeze sprang up round about five o'clock on Guy Fawkes' day, and the children rejoiced. Now the bonfire should blaze merrily, and the guy catch fire without recourse to unseemly proddings with paraffin-soaked rags and such demeaning aids to combustion.

It sat upon its funeral pyre looking splendidly remote. Harold Shoosmith's topee had tilted a little on its way to the summit, and gave the guy a slightly rakish appearance, but all agreed that it was one of the best efforts of Thrush Green school.

At six-thirty sharp the scoutmaster thrust a flaming torch into the base of the pyre and within minutes yellow and orange flames leapt skyward. Cheers went up from the spectators, and the boxes of fireworks began to be sorted out by those in charge, ready for the display.

The scoutmaster, freed from his chief duty, now began to

supervise the positioning of the scrubbed potatoes in the bonfire base with the vociferous help of his charges.

What with the shouts of excited children, the crackling of the bonfire, and the sharp reports of a few premature fireworks, it was almost impossible to carry on a conversation, as John Lovell found, when at last he made his way from the surgery to join his family.

Mary was jumping up and down in a frenzy of ecstasy, her face scorched with the heat and her tongue wagging non-stop. Her cousin Paul and his friends were equally excited. It was plain that they would be a long time getting to sleep after such jollifications.

'Marvellous sight!' shouted John to Edward. 'Luckily, I had a short surgery tonight. All my patients are here, I reckon!'

He beamed across at a bevy of old people from the new homes, the Jermyns, Mrs Bates, and the Crosses.

Edward followed his gaze. 'You've got one in hospital, I hear,' he said.

John glanced at him. 'Yes. But I'm not going to say "I told you so", if that's what's in your mind.'

'I should hope not,' snapped Edward, and moved away.

Pompous ass, thought John, turning away from the heat of the blaze. Edward was getting stuffier with every year that passed, the irritating fellow.

At that moment, the first rocket of the evening whooshed skyward, and sent down a cascade of pink and violet stars.

'Ah!' sighed the crowd in great contentment.

'Where's the next?' shouted one wag.

And, as if in answer, the second streaked away towards a black velvet sky.

It was Albert who told Nelly where to find Mrs Jenner that evening. He had heard all the news during the day at The Two Pheasants, and a very pleasurable time he had had discussing morosely where the blame lay for the accident, and how long Jane Cartwright could expect to remain in hospital.

'It's not so much the surgeon's knifework,' he told his unimpressed listeners, 'as what the shock does to your system. I mean, all them muscles and glands and tubes, they must get in a fine old muddle when the knife goes in, and it's bound to take time to get 'em to join up again.' He took a gulp of beer. 'That's if they ever do. Did I ever tell you about my operation?'

'Time and again,' said one.

'Too often, Albie! Don't start that again!'

The landlord interposed. 'Jane Cartwright will soon be back. Plenty of spunk there, and a nice healthy woman, like her ma.'

'She's over there now, I'm told, holding the fort.'

'That's right,' said Mr Jones. 'Knows when she's needed, and never been afraid of hard work.'

He looked pointedly at Albert who, by rights, should have been at his duties. Albert chose to ignore the hint until closing time.

The bonfire was at its peak of glory as Nelly crossed the green. As she stepped along the path to the wardens' house, a great cry arose from the watchers round the fire, and she was just in time to see the guy crash through the flames to the inferno below.

'Lot of babies!' was her private comment as she rang the bell.

Mrs Jenner looked tired, but her smile was as welcoming as ever as she invited Nelly to take a seat.

'Bill's just gone along to St Richard's to see poor old Jane,' she said. 'One thing, my duties are pretty light this evening as about half the people are at the beano on the green.'

She told Nelly more about Jane's misfortune and made light of her own help.

'Oh, it's a good thing to be able to turn your hand to what crops up,' she said cheerfully. 'Keeps you on your toes, you know. Now, Nelly, what brings you here?'

Nelly began her tale, diffidently at first, but gradually gaining confidence from her listener's calm attention.

'And so I just wondered if Albert might be right. What do you think?'

'I should say that Albert is hardly *ever* right,' said Mrs Jenner robustly. 'Obviously, you'll want to get things absolutely straight with Mrs Peters now this doubt has crept in, but I'm sure she would have said something about it from the start, if that's what she had in mind.'

'That's what I think,' cried Nelly, much relieved. 'She's absolutely straight, I'm sure of that, and I can't think of anyone I'd sooner work for.'

'Work *with*!' corrected Mrs Jenner. 'You see, Nelly, she realises that you are willing to try your hand at anything. She's had plenty long enough to watch the way you go about things, and believe me, she wouldn't have offered you this if she had any doubts about you being able to cope with it.'

'That never occurred to me,' confessed Nelly.

'You go ahead and accept. You have to look after yourself in this life, even if you are a married woman. And to be frank, Nelly, your Albert's rather more trouble than he's worth, if you'll pardon my saying so.'

Nelly laughed, slapping her hands on her knees.

'You never spoke a truer word,' she replied. 'Thank you, my dear, you've put my mind at rest. I'll be off now.'

'Not before you have a cup of coffee,' said her friend. 'I've still got to find my way around this place, but I found the teapot and the coffee pot before I'd been here five minutes.'

The embers of the bonfire still glowed red when Winnie Bailey undressed for bed.

She and Jenny had watched from the house for an hour or so, enjoying the children's caperings silhouetted against the bright flames. They watched until the last rocket had blazed its way skyward, and the last Catherine wheel had whirled itself to darkness. The sound of firecrackers went on, and small children waved sparklers until they too had gone and they were herded, protesting, to their beds.

It was very peaceful after the din. Winnie leant from her window to survey the scene. There was a moon showing between silver-edged clouds. It was almost full, and lit Thrush Green with a gentle light.

Nathaniel Patten's statue gleamed opposite, and wet branches glistened as the moonbeams caught them. An owl hooted from Lulling Woods and, high above, the lights of an aeroplane winked rhythmically.

Little drifts of smoke wavered across on the air, bringing that most poignant of autumn scents from the bonfire's remains. Tomorrow morning, a ring of white ash and a few cinders would be all that would remain of the past hours' splendour. The children would scuffle among the debris, hoping for a stray burnt potato, or the gnarled metal of a firework component to treasure. Miss Watson and Miss Fogerty would deplore the state of pupils' shoes, and the yawns which would be the outcome of an evening's heady bliss.

They won't mind, thought Winnie fondly. They've had their fun, and nothing can take away those thrilling memories.

How Donald would have loved it, she thought with a pang, as she climbed into bed.

13 . OLD PEOPLE'S FEARS

The murky weather continued. By now the clocks had been put back, and it was time to draw the curtains at around four or five o'clock.

As Jenny remarked to Winnie Bailey: 'No sooner were you up and about than it seemed you were getting ready for bed.'

At the village school the lights were on all day, and Mr Jones' bar lamps, with their red shades, did their best to cheer the gloom.

In Lulling High Street the shops were already beginning to show signs of Christmas looming ever nearer. A large poster in the Post Office window exhorted customers to post early for overseas' mail, and agitated passers-by realised that yet again they had missed surface mail to New Zealand and Australia and would have to send to distant aunts and brothers by air mail. They went on their way toying distractedly with such gifts as silk scarves, handker-chieves and tights – anything, in fact, which could be weighed in grammes rather than pounds, and even then, they thought mournfully, the cost of postage would be devastating.

At The Fuchsia Bush a discreet notice stood in the corner of the window reminding customers that the last orders for Christmas cakes, mince pies and puddings must be put in immediately. The florists nearby requested early orders for holly wreaths and crosses, and the coal merchant's window had a large card saying sternly, 'Order now for Christmas'.

The three Misses Lovelock, Ada, Bertha and Violet, had resolutely set their faces against preparations for Christmas until the beginning of December. They had taken up this stance some years earlier, their reasons being that early December was quite time enough to start thinking about preparations, and there were plenty of jobs to be attended to in November anyway.

'But what about your pudding,' said Dimity, 'and sending off presents to people abroad?'

'We don't eat Christmas pudding,' came the austere reply. 'And we don't send any presents to people who live overseas.'

There seemed to be little to say after this, and Dimity, who had called about contributions to a Christmas bazaar, retired without daring to mention the subject. One Lovelock was intimidating enough. In triplicate they were formidable.

On this particularly dismal November morning, Charles was in some anxiety.

'It seems, my dear,' he said to Dimity, as he ruffled the leaves of his pocket diary, 'that I have promised to go to the old people's Christmas party at Thrush Green, at the same time as the preview of pictures at Janet Thurgood's gallery. Janet *Fairbrother*, I should say now.'

'Just ring one of them and explain,' advised Dimity, who frequently had to cope with such errors.

'But this morning,' went on Charles, becoming even more agitated, 'I had an invitation – well, more of a summons – from the bishop, and that too is for the same afternoon.'

'Then the bishop's must take precedence,' said Dimity, 'and you must telephone to the others. Now, stand away from the table, Charles, while I roll out this pastry, or you will be looking like a miller.'

Charles sat down obediently in a corner of the kitchen, still looking worried.

'I think I shall take a walk up to Thrush Green to see Bill Cartwright and explain. Poor Jane is still in hospital, I hear, but no doubt he and Mrs Jenner are going ahead with Christmas arrangements.'

'A good idea,' responded Dimity, sprinkling flour energetically. She sometimes wondered what her dear husband would feel if she sat down in his study while he was writing his sermons. He probably would not notice, she thought, and would certainly not feel as irritable as she did when he invaded her work room.

'I want to see Mrs Bates in any case. She's offered to clean the church silver at St Andrew's, and it seems a kind gesture. She did all of it here, you remember, and I suppose she misses it.'

'I thought the Bassetts always did it.'

'Mrs Bassett hasn't been able to for some time, and I believe Ruth and Joan have carried on as it was largely given to the church by their great-grandfather. I must call on them and see what they think.'

'Well, dear,' said Dimity, attacking the pastry again with her rolling pin, 'you go and sort out things up there, and I'll see you at lunch time.'

Charles rose with a sigh.

'I do seem to get myself in a pickle with my dates. What should I do without you?'

He kissed her forehead and made for the door. There was flour on his black lapel, but Dimity forbore to comment. The dear man had quite enough to worry him already.

While Charles Henstock was making his way to Thrush Green, Dr Lovell was just finishing surgery and checking his bag before setting out on his rounds.

The telephone rang. It was the police superintendent.

'I think we may have your man here,' he said. 'Could you get down to an identity parade?'

'What now? No hope!'

'No, probably late tomorrow afternoon. The chief inspector, who is independent of this enquiry, of course, will organise everything. He has to collect several chaps who are fairly similar in looks. It shouldn't be too difficult. Our fellow has no beard, or bright red hair, or anything too outlandish.'

'What happens?'

'We put these chaps in a row, and then invite the suspect to take his place, wherever he likes, among them. Then you – who have been kept away from all this obviously – are brought in and hopefully can touch the right man on the shoulder.'

'It sounds straightforward enough, but I can't tell you how I dread it. Suppose I pick the wrong chap?'

The superintendent laughed. 'It doesn't often happen, so take heart. You are still quite willing to help us?'

'Yes, indeed. When shall I come?'

'Say, five o'clock? If there's any difficulty I will ring you.'

John put the telephone down. His hands were trembling. He picked up his bag and went through the little office towards his car, pausing to tell Miss Pick, the secretary, about the appointment at the police station.

'What have you been up to?' she wanted to know banteringly.

'Nothing yet,' replied John, 'but I might make the most awful hash of things, I can see.'

He left Miss Pick, who looked at the closing door with some perturbation. It wasn't like the doctor to get so anxious about things. Come to think of it, he hadn't looked really fit for some time now. Overwork, she supposed. A dose or two of his own tonic might do him good.

Charles Henstock found Bill Cartwright just about to go shopping in his car. After enquiring about Jane, Charles told him, with genuine distress, about his dilemma.

'Never fear,' replied Bill with a forgiving smile. 'It happens to all of us now and again. You go and see Mother. She's getting a pie ready.'

Charles obeyed, and said he was glad to hear that Jane was making good progress.

'She should be home next week,' said her mother, 'but of course she'll be on sticks for a bit. I'm going to stay on to lend a hand.'

'A sad business,' said Charles.

'And the old people have taken it hard,' added Mrs Jenner.

'They were just settling in nicely, and this accident seems to have upset them.'

'In what way?'

'Well, for one thing they seem to use the steps with quite unnecessary caution, and some will only go down now by the ramp which was really made for cars and vans to use. Then some of them seem very touchy, although I think that's because of Mrs Jermyn, who will interfere with everyone. Bill's had a word with her husband, but it doesn't seem to make much difference. The Crosses were very friendly with them, but since Monty has taken to using their front flower bed as his personal lavatory, things have been a bit strained.'

'Oh dear! Can I help at all?'

'Well, a visit from you is always appreciated,' said Mrs Jenner.

'Actually, I'm going to see Mrs Bates first,' he said, and explained about the silver cleaning.

'That's a good idea. I think she feels a bit useless, and Mrs Young's got enough to do without adding the weekly silver cleaning to her chores. I know the church silver has always been kept at their house as they have a safe, but I expect it could be brought to Mrs Bates on Sunday evenings and she could take it to the Youngs' when she had done it. Or maybe she could call there?'

'We'll sort out something,' promised Charles. 'There isn't a great deal of it – not like the splendid old collection we have at St John's – but there is a fine ebony cross with silver decorations, as you know, and the pair of Victorian silver vases, which flank it, are very heavy, if perhaps a little florid for today's taste, and a nice old chalice which I always enjoy handling.'

'Well, I'm sure Mrs Bates will like that little job,' Mrs Jenner assured him. 'Now, can I give you some refreshment before you call on her?'

'No indeed, many thanks. I'll go immediately. I expect you are busy preparing lunch. I left Dimity rolling pastry.'

'And that's just what I was doing,' Mrs Jenner told him, nodding towards the kitchen door, 'when you called.'

'Apple tart?' asked the rector, now on his way.

'What else, after this season's crop?' said Mrs Jenner, waving him off.

After his visit to Mrs Bates, the good rector called on her neighbours. He spent most of his time with Tom and Polly, but was lucky to find Johnny Enderby there, too. The two old men seemed fit enough, but were very serious when the question of Jane's accident cropped up.

Only the Angells were out, so that Charles saw practically all the new residents that morning, and was struck by the anxiety and downright nervousness, in some cases, which he had not noticed before. It grieved him too, to hear the bitterness with which the Crosses spoke of the Jermyns next door. Monty had a lot to answer for, thought the rector. It began to look as though the 'no pets' rule was certainly going to be needed in the future.

He was relieved to enter the peaceful drawing-room of the Youngs' house. Joan was grateful for Mrs Bates' offer, and promised to go over that afternoon to make arrangements which would suit her.

'Do you think she'd like to come over here to clean the things? We'd love to have her, and it might make a change for her.'

'I'll leave it to you,' said Charles, and set off, more cheerfully now, to his vicarage.

But for the rest of the day, Charles was uneasy. What was amiss at the old people's homes? The residents had settled in so well, had seemed so thankful to be there, so grateful for all the Cartwrights were doing for them. He recalled the happiness at that first party when the new neighbours were warm in their praise of everything, and glad to make friends with each other.

He supposed that a number of things contributed to the

present malaise. Certainly, Jane's accident had left them in a state of shock. After all, she was their mother-figure, someone to turn to with their problems, 'a very present help in trouble'. The fact that she had fallen on the ground that they daily traversed was also cause for fear. If she, so comparatively young and nimble, had come a cropper, what might happen to those older and shakier?

And, of course, the first excitement of their new abodes had worn thin. The relatives and friends who had visited them in the first few weeks now came less often. They had seen the old people happily ensconced, and felt that all would be well with them. The coming of short dark days and the onset of winter ills, also meant fewer visitors, and it was easy for some of these old people to give way to self-pity, the most insidious foe of all.

He thought of Mrs Bates. Perhaps she provided the clue to the future happiness of her neighbours. It seemed to Charles that the old people needed to feel part of the life of Thrush Green. Mrs Bates was doing something to be of service, and by doing so was making herself useful in the community. Could the others find help in this way?

The old residents of Thrush Green had been outstandingly welcoming, and he knew that there were real friendships be-tween individuals such as Ella and Tom Hardy and Johnny Enderby who had their love of gardening in common, and Miss Fuller and the teachers at the school who shared many interests, but perhaps more could be done.

But what?

Charles knew how keenly the old people valued their inde-pendence, and he himself would have disliked any sort of hearty community activities imposed from outside. No, it would have to be most delicately done, and the residents themselves must show the way. Mrs Bates' initiative might well be the inspira-tion.

Well, it would be best to wait until Jane was back and strong enough to help him with the problem, decided Charles. For there was a problem here, and one which could grow and cause much unhappiness unless it could be solved with tact and sympathy.

One thing, both Jane and Bill had plenty of those two qualities.

After her talk with Mrs Jenner on Bonfire Night, Nelly had gone to see her employer with an easier mind.

To her relief, all final fears were swept away by Mrs Peters' reassurances. There had been no thought of Nelly putting money into the firm. What she needed, she reiterated, was Nelly's support, expertise, ideas and loyalty.

Nelly threw herself energetically into her new role as one of the partners at The Fuchsia Bush. She revelled in her new-found position, and welcomed the Friday night sessions when she stayed at the office to go through the books with her partner.

Although Nelly always claimed she was no good at sums, she was well able to look after her own financial affairs. There had been periods in Nelly's life when she had been hard pressed for money, but she had always managed to evade debt or complete penury. She was a saver, too, by nature and, as Mrs Peters learnt, she soon saw how certain methods would bring profit to the shop. To her mind, there were some of the wholesalers whose business ploys were suspect. She suggested to Mrs Peters that they should try others, and in this Nelly's hunches had proved correct.

The home-catering side was steadily growing. The van was already on order, and both partners could see that there was a bright future in that side of the business. But it was Nelly who suggested that fresh rolls with attractive fillings such as ham and tomato, egg and lettuce, cheese and watercress, would find a ready market with many of the office girls and shop assistants who worked so close at hand in Lulling High Street.

'They can't afford the time or the money for a proper sit-down lunch in here,' pointed out Nelly. 'In any case, the single ones are probably going home to something cooked by mum about six o'clock, and the married ones will have something cooking in a casserole to go home to, or a few chops or sausages ready in their baskets. Let's try it for a week anyway. The girls in the kitchen are quick workers and I'll give a hand before putting on the lunches.'

It was a great innovation, and after a week's trial, Mrs Peters agreed it should become a regular service.

'And if need be,' she added when she and Nelly had totted up the books one dreary November Friday, 'we could think of employing a girl part-time, simply to get rolls ready.'

Hope had already replaced her former apprehension, and affairs at The Fuchsia Bush brightened daily.

A week later, John Lovell bumped into the superintendent in Lulling High Street.

'I hear you didn't have much bother in identifying our friend,' said the latter.

'I was lucky. When I was first called to see that fellow, I noticed an old scar over his right eyebrow, and I remember thinking that he should have had it stitched at the time. It had healed well, but would have been less noticeable. I'd forgotten about it until I saw it at the identity parade.'

'Well, there's no doubt he's our man. He swore he was innocent for quite a time, and said he knew nothing about the other two chaps, but he changed his mind after a bit, and now we're looking up north for his buddies. We should get them pretty soon.'

'And what will happen?'

'Oh, they'll go up to Crown Court without a doubt, with the sort of offences they're charged with. It's been going on a long time, and a great deal of money is involved.'

'I'll be needed as a witness, I suppose?'

'Afraid so. You must hold yourself in readiness.'

'Well, it'll make a change from looking at chickenpox spots,' smiled John.

'Much about then?'

'Quite an epidemic. Nidden School is half empty.'

'I *think* I've had it,' said the superintendent thoughtfully.

'If you had any sense,' responded the doctor, 'you'd have put it behind you before your tenth birthday.'

They parted to their particular duties.

Jane Cartwright arrived home from hospital in good spirits, but woefully wobbly. The old people were touching in their welcome, and Bill had to be particularly tactful in restraining their visits in the early days.

'She's being killed with kindness,' he confided to his mother-in-law, when he had ushered out Miss Fuller who had brought a hyacinth bulb in a glass vase to distract the patient's attention from her ills.

'You'll have to be firm,' Mrs Jenner told him. 'I've said that she has a rest every afternoon, and that's that. I know they all mean well, and Jane's grateful to them, but it's going to be some weeks before she's really fit again.'

'You're quite right, Mother,' said Bill, 'but it's difficult when they arrive with bunches of flowers, and little cakes and books, and then beg to see her. I think I'll pass them over to you.'

'You do just that,' said Mrs Jenner firmly. 'I can be quite a dragon if need be.'

One of Jane's early visitors was Joan Young. She gave her news of Mrs Bates and the church silver.

'She comes over to us either on Friday or Saturday afternoon, and stays for tea. She seems to enjoy coming, and we look forward to her visits. Incidentally, the silver has never looked so splendid, and we hear all the news from here as she gets to work.'

'Good news, I hope?' said Jane. 'I think all our people have settled in pretty well. It's a big upheaval for some of them.'

'Oh, I'm sure they all seem very glad to be here,' Joan assured her. 'Molly Curdle usually comes over when Mrs Bates comes, and she gets on with some ironing while the silver's being done. She hears more than I do, I think. They certainly have a hilarious time together and baby Anne gets thoroughly spoilt.'

When Joan had gone, and Jane was alone resting, she turned over Joan's comments in her mind.

Were the old people really as happily settled as she said? Jane was very much aware of all that was going on, and had sensed, since her return from hospital, that some of their charges were a little discontented. The occasional remark had been dropped by her visitors, about the shortcomings of neighbours. Monty's reprehensible sanitary arrangements had been mentioned once or twice. The perennial problem of too-loud radios had cropped up. Someone's refrigerator made a bang every now and again in the night. The lavatory flushings were unduly noisy.

And, of course, the paths were slippery, as poor Jane knew only too well.

She supposed it was inevitable, thought Jane, to have these teething troubles. Her mother had often said that old people were worse than children to deal with, and she and Bill had known this from the start. But somehow, there seemed to be more behind these little worries – a general discontent which could not be blamed on the weather, the reaction to initial euphoria, or any other reasons.

Perhaps, she told herself, she was exaggerating things. Her present low state might have something to do with it. How she longed to be up and about again!

Meanwhile, she must count her blessings. Bill and her mother together were coping splendidly with the job, and she was getting stronger and more mobile daily.

Time enough to worry when she had thrown aside her stick, and could scurry about as nimbly as she did before Fate had stricken her down, she told herself.

14. VISITORS

To everyone's relief the first few days of December became beguilingly mild and sunny. The last of the apples glowed on the bare branches. The hedges were still beaded with hips and haws, and a few hardy fuchsia bushes dangled bright tassels in defiance of the calendar.

In the gardens at Thrush Green there was great activity as the sodden masses of leaves were raked into piles and late bonfires coped with the outcome.

People who had not been able to face the torrential rain in the latter part of November, now hurried to Lulling High Street to catch up with neglected Christmas shopping, and to purchase Christmas air letters to send to all the people overseas who had been forgotten earlier.

At The Fuchsia Bush a spate of orders came in, not only for cakes and puddings, but also for catering arrangements for local office parties. Nelly and Mrs Peters worked happily overtime.

In the infants' room Miss Fogerty picked her way over mounds of paper chains which overflowed from the desks, and deplored the way that so many of the links broke, sending down cascades of coloured paper upon the delighted children below. Certainly paste was not what it used to be, thought Agnes, as she repaired the damage. There was a lot to be said for good old-fashioned paste made by hand in a pudding basin with strong plain flour. And it would work out at a quarter the price!

*

Across the green, Winnie Bailey was inspecting the bowls of hyacinths which she had planted at the beginning of September. They were destined to be Christmas presents for neighbours such as Phyllida Hurst, Ella and Dotty, but at this rate, she thought, they would be nowhere near ready.

Certainly, dear reliable Innocence bulbs were doing well, and Lady Derby too, but why was the bowl of Ostara taking so long? She carried them into the kitchen, and decided to give them all more warmth.

Jenny had just put two lamb chops in the grill pan, and was prodding the potatoes. They always lunched together in the kitchen, unless Winnie had one of her increasingly rare lunch parties.

Winnie was just setting the last of the bowls on the wide window sill, when the front door bell rang.

She hurried to answer it, and to her amazement found Richard on the doorstep.

'Well, what a surprise! Do come in, Richard dear. Are you alone?'

A vision of two lamb chops floated before her. Something would have to be rustled up quickly, especially if Fenella and the children were hard by.

'Quite alone, Aunt Win. I'm on my way to Bath, and saw a familiar signpost, and thought I'd drop in.'

'You'll stay for lunch?'

'Yes, please. I should like that.'

'Then I shall give you a glass of sherry, and leave you for a minute to tell Jenny. Then I want to hear all the news.'

She poured her nephew a glass and left him reading the newspaper.

Jenny was equal to the emergency.

'Plenty of rashers here, and a few sausages. And there are eggs and tomatoes, so we can make a mixed grill. But what about pudding?'

'There are lots of apples in the fruit bowl, and cheese and

biscuits to spare. He's lucky to get that,' said Richard's aunt, 'if he can't be bothered to ring up beforehand.'

'Shall I set the table in the dining-room?'

'Lord, no, Jenny! He can have it here with us.'

She was about to return to the sitting-room when she put her head round the door again.

'And he has *my chop*, Jenny, not yours! That's an order.'

'Now tell me about the family,' said Winnie. 'How's the baby?'

'Growing. Cries rather a lot. Especially at night.'

'It's a way babies have. And Fenella?'

'Quite busy with the gallery. There's an exhibition of paint-ings on glass at the moment. Ready for Christmas, you know.'

'How does she find time with two young children?'

'Actually, Timothy goes to play school three mornings a

week, and of course Roger is mainly in charge of the exhibition.'

'Roger?'

'Fenella's cousin. I think it's five times removed. Something like that. I believe their great-grandfathers were first cousins, but I can never work out those things.'

'Nor me,' confessed Winnie. 'And where does he live?'

'Roger has a flat just round the corner. At least, his wife has. I'm afraid they are not on speaking terms just now, and he quite often sleeps in the gallery.'

'It doesn't sound very comfortable,' said Winnie.

'Oh, he has a sleeping bag,' replied Richard, helping himself unasked to another glass of sherry. 'And the floor of the gallery is carpeted. Can I fill your glass?'

'No thank you, dear.'

At that moment, Jenny came in to say that all was ready, and Richard carried his glass with him to the kitchen table.

Winnie noted, with approval, that Jenny had opened a large tin of baked beans to augment the rations. Richard rubbed his hands gleefully.

'What a spread! Do you always eat so splendidly?'

'Only sometimes,' said Winnie, catching Jenny's eye.

'I'm very glad I didn't drop into a pub,' announced Richard. 'It did cross my mind, but I thought it would be so much nicer to see you both and have a snack with you.'

'And I suppose you will spend Christmas in London?' said Winnie, as they set to.

'Fenella will. I shall be on my way back from China.'

'China? At Christmas? But it's the baby's first one, and surely Timothy will be just the right age to love it all!'

'Yes, it's rather a pity, I suppose, but I was asked to go when I was on the earlier lecture tour, and it's so well paid I felt I really couldn't turn it down.'

'Does Fenella agree?'

'She was a bit miffed at first, but she hasn't said anything since, so I suppose she's got over it.'

It all sounded remarkably unsatisfactory to Winnie, but she felt that she could not continue to cross-question a grown man, even if he were her nephew, about his domestic arrangements, and the subject was changed to Thrush Green's news and the doings of old friends.

Later, aunt and nephew walked around the garden. The sun still shone bravely although the shadows were as long at two-thirty this bright December day, as if it were nine o'clock of a summer evening.

Winnie plucked a few late apples from a tree which she and Donald had planted so long ago.

'Take them with you in the car,' she said. 'They're a lovely flavour, and I think they are so beautiful.'

She held the golden globes towards him, and for once Richard seemed aware of something other than his own affairs. He looked closely at the tawny beauty, striped in red and gold, in his hand and sniffed at it appreciatively.

'Ah! That takes me back to my childhood,' he exclaimed. He looked around the garden, the dewy grass marked with their dark footsteps, and a collared dove sipping from the bird bath.

'Do you know, Aunt Win, I should dearly like to live in Thrush Green. I've always felt at home here.'

'Well, Richard, it would certainly be a splendid place to bring up a family, but property's rather expensive. People can get quite quickly now to the motorway, and it has pushed up the price of houses.'

'I suppose so. And Fenella might not like the country. She seems to enjoy the gallery, and of course she owns it, which means we live very cheaply. I couldn't afford to live as we do if we had to pay rent, or we were buying a house.'

'Then you are lucky to be so well provided for,' remarked Winnie, with a touch of impatience. When she had married, it was the man who expected to provide the home, but times had changed, certainly for Richard, it seemed.

He glanced at his watch. 'I must be off. Thank you for the

lunch and those lovely apples. They will remind me of Thrush Green all the way to Bath.'

Occasionally, thought Winnie, as she waved him goodbye, just occasionally, there was a nice side to dear Richard.

But what a pity he was not more of a family man!

One golden afternoon in the following week, Charles Henstock went to visit some of his house-bound parishioners at Thrush Green.

He had dropped Dimity at Ella's, leaving the two friends in animated conversation and an aura of blue tobacco smoke from Ella's pungent cigarettes.

His first call was at Ruth Lovell's house where he found Mrs Bassett sitting up in bed, looking very frail but pretty in a shell-pink bedjacket. She was obviously delighted to see him, and Ruth left them alone together.

Later, he came through to the kitchen where she was ironing and commented on the improvement in her mother.

'Marvellous, isn't it? John's so pleased too. As a matter of fact, it's John I'm worrying about at the moment. He's terribly touchy, and he and Edward are being so silly about some tiff they had about the old people's steps.'

Charles said it was the first he'd heard of it.

'I shouldn't think about it,' he advised her. 'It'll blow over. They're too fond of each other to let a little bit of nonsense like that rankle.'

'Well, I hope so. There's such a lot of illness about, particularly this wretched chickenpox which I'm sure Mary will get just in time for Christmas, and John's run off his feet.'

Charles patted her shoulder comfortingly. 'Well, give him my love, or regards perhaps? Anyway, wish him well from me. Now I'm off to see Dotty.'

'Don't eat anything!' warned Ruth with a laugh.

Dotty too, was in bed, but not looking as elegant as Mrs Bassett. She had dragged a dilapidated dark grey cardigan over her sensible thick nightgown. There was a hole in one elbow, and the cuffs were fraying.

She must have seen Charles looking at the cardigan's condition for she said cheerfully: 'Connie puts a shawl round me, you know, but it falls off when I'm busy, so I sneak out and get this favourite woolly from the drawer when she's not looking. Violet Lovelock knitted it for me years ago. Such good wool! Sheep seemed to have better fleece in those days. I suppose the grass was purer – none of these horrid pesticides and fertilisers to poison everything.'

'You look very well,' commented Charles. 'Now tell me all the news.'

'Well, the chickens are laying quite nicely for the time of year, and Mrs Jenner has promised me a sitting of duck eggs for one of my broodies later on. Dulcie seems a bit off colour, but goats often do in the winter, I find, and I think Connie forgets to put out the rock salt. Flossie, of course, is in splendid fettle, and is out with Connie and Kit at the moment.'

Charles noted, with amusement, that it was the animals' welfare, rather than her relatives' which concerned his old friend.

'As a matter of fact,' continued Dotty, fishing in the holey sleeve for a ragged handkerchief, 'I think Connie has too much to do with the house and the garden and the animals. The workmen should be gone before Christmas, or *so they say*, but there'll be a terrible mess to clear up. And then, you see, Kit's no gardener, except for manly things like cutting off branches and burning rubbish and chopping down trees – all *destructive*, if you know what I mean. You never see him *tending* anything, putting in stakes for wobbly plants, or pricking out seedlings. That sort of *positive* gardening.'

Charles remembered Albert Piggott's unaccountable passion for Dulcie the goat.

'Do you think Albert would come regularly to take the animals over?' he suggested. 'Would Connie like that? You know how marvellously he looked after Dulcie whenever you were away, and I hear he's handy with chickens too.'

'A good idea, Charles! I shall mention it to Connie when she gets back. Would that fat wife of his let him come?'

Charles explained about Nelly's new commitments, much to Dotty's interest, and went farther.

'What's more, I think she'd be glad of anything which kept him out of the pub, even if only for an hour or so.'

'Well, I can always supply him with a glass or two of my home-made wine. So much better for him than that gassy stuff from The Two Pheasants.'

Charles, knowing the catastrophic results of imbibing Dotty's potions, thought that Albert should be warned, if he decided to pay regular visits, but that, he felt sure, could be left in Connie's capable hands.

'Now, I must be off, Dotty. But before I go can I bring you anything? Shall I make you a cup of tea and bring it up?'

'No, no, dear boy! Connie and Kit will be back soon, but do make a cup for yourself. Or better still, help yourself to a glass of my cowslip wine. The bottle's on the kitchen dresser. And please take half a dozen eggs for dear Dimity. They're in a wicker basket Ella gave me last Christmas. The one that's coming unravelled.'

Charles thanked her sincerely and went below, helping himself, as invited, to six splendid brown eggs for his wife, but prudently abstaining from helping himself from the bottle hard by.

He set off across the meadow behind Dotty's house to Lulling Woods, and on his way met first Flossie, Dotty's spaniel, who greeted him rapturously, followed by Kit and Connie looking pink with fresh air and exercise.

'Come back with us,' they begged. But Charles explained that he was bound for an ailing couple who lived in a cottage by The Drovers' Arms.

'And I must get back to pick up Dimity. It gets dark so early.'

'And what did you think of Dotty?'

'Looking very well,' replied Charles. He wondered if he should mention their conversation about Albert, and decided to be bold.

Connie considered the suggestion thoughtfully. 'You know, it might work out very well. Dotty and Albert have always got on like a house on fire. I'll talk to her about it. Thank you, Charles.'

They parted company, and the rector went on to his duties.

It was dark when he emerged from the cottage. There was a nip in the air already, which presaged a frost before morning. Charles turned up his coat collar, and thrust his hands deep into his pockets for warmth.

The path through Lulling Woods was fairly wide and carpeted with dead leaves and pine needles, so that his progress was quiet. There was no need to brush against outstretched branches or clinging brambles, and his footsteps were muffled in the thick covering below.

Although the woods were as familiar to Charles as Thrush

Green itself, yet in this sudden darkness he found himself apprehensive. One could quite understand primitive man's fear of forests, and the legends which grew up about the gods and spirits who frequented woodland. There certainly seemed to be a presence here, and not altogether a benign one, thought Charles, quickening his pace.

The trees seemed to press nearer the path than he remembered, like a hostile crowd approaching an unwary traveller. Occasionally, a twig snapped with a report like a gun going off, probably triggered by some small nocturnal animal setting off to look for supper. When a screech owl shattered the stillness with its harsh cry, Charles almost broke into a run.

He was glad to emerge into the open meadow. The lights of Dotty's cottage glowed reassuringly on his right, and in a few minutes he had traversed the alleyway by Albert Piggott's cottage, crossed the road by St Andrew's church, and stood for a moment to take breath.

There were all the familiar shapes he knew and loved. There were lights in the windows of friends' houses, the Youngs, Winnie Bailey's, the Hursts, Harold and Isobel's. There were even lights shining in the village school where, no doubt, Betty Bell was busy sweeping up. The Two Pheasants was still in darkness, but a light was on at Albert's next door, and in the gloaming Charles could see the little black cat on the doorstep waiting for its mistress to arrive with bounty from The Fuchsia Bush kitchen.

Calmer now, Charles turned to walk across to Ella's. For a moment, some trick of the light gave him the impression that he was looking at the outline of his old vanished rectory hard by. He thought that he could see the steep roof, the front door, the tall narrow windows that faced the bitter north-east winds.

A great wave of grief for things past swept over the rector. He remembered his study, its high ceiling, its bare look which had secretly pleased him. He saw again the beautiful silver and ivory crucifix which hung on the wall until it had been reduced to a small misshapen lump by the devastating fire. That little pathetic lump was still treasured in his desk drawer at Lulling Vicarage.

And in his heart, thought Charles blinking away a tear, there was still treasured a knot of dear memories of a house much beloved long ago.

The vision faded, and he found himself gazing at the low outline of the new homes, and farther still the lights of Ella's house shone, beckoning him back to the present where Dimity and everyday comfort awaited him.

PART THREE

Getting Settled

* * *

15. CHRISTMAS

End of term was now in sight, and Agnes and Dorothy were in the throes of rehearsing the children for a concert, in rooms bedizened with paper chains, bells, friezes showing Santa Claus, reindeer, and lots of artificial snow made from pellets of cotton wool which fell from windows, as well as the mural frieze, and was squashed everywhere underfoot.

Miss Watson's children were attempting two carols played by the few who had recorders. The noise produced was excruciating, and Dorothy sometimes had difficulty in distinguishing 'Hark, The Herald Angels Sing' from 'O Come All Ye Faithful'. At times, she despaired. Perhaps straightforward singing would be more rewarding? On the other hand it was only right that the young musicians should be encouraged, and the parents would be gratified to see the expensive recorders being used.

The lower juniors, in charge of a young probationer on the other side of the partition, were being rehearsed endlessly, it seemed to Miss Watson, in some hearty mid-European dances which involved a lot of stamping and clapping. As the stamping and clapping never seemed completely co-ordinated, the resultant racket was hard to bear, but the young teacher, to give her her due, was persistent, and it was to be hoped that all would be well before the great day.

Little Miss Fogerty, with years of experience behind her, opted for two simple songs with actions which she had first tried out with success at several Christmas concerts in the past, blessing the ancient copy of *Child Education*, held together with Scotch tape, which supplied the subject matter.

As always, the children were over-excited and belligerent. Agnes sometimes wondered if the expression 'the season of goodwill' was wholly correct. There was some acrimony between infants fighting over the brightest colours when making paper chains, harsh and wounding criticisms were made about desk-fellows' portrayal of Christmas trees, Christmas fairies, carol-singers and other seasonal matters. Two ferocious little girls, having a tug of war with a strip of tinsel, had to have their wounds dressed before being sent home, and poor Miss Fogerty's head ached with the unusual clamour in her classroom.

On the other hand, as Agnes reminded herself, quite a few children were absent as the chickenpox epidemic took its toll. George Curdle was among the invalids, a dear little boy who gave no trouble, thought Agnes. Now, John Todd, a sore trial and possessed of a voice like a fog-horn, flourished like a green bay tree, and a great nuisance he was. Still, it was an ill wind that blew nobody any good, she quoted to herself, surveying the six or seven empty desks, and certainly there was more room to move about in the bustle of Christmas preparations.

The two teachers were thankful to get back to the peace of the school house at the end of the day.

'I'm amazed at the presents the children are hoping to get,' said Dorothy, removing her shoes, and putting up her aching legs on the sofa. 'I let them make lists this afternoon – a little spelling practice really – and I find they are asking for things like cassette players and adding machines and some computer games of which I'd never heard. They cost pounds, I gather. How parents with more than one child can cope, I cannot think.'

'I don't suppose they'll get all they ask for,' pointed out Agnes.

'I hope not. More fool their parents if they do,' said Dorothy trenchantly. 'At home, we used to be delighted with simple things like jigsaw puzzles, and furniture for the dolls' house, and sweets and a tangerine in the toe of our stocking, and lots of books. Mind you, I did get a pinafore every Christmas from one particular aunt, and that rather rankled, I remember, and Ray used to get a pair of woollen gloves which he detested, saying they were slippery and put his teeth on edge, but on the whole we were well content.'

'I always had a doll,' said Agnes. 'Every Christmas my parents gave me one, and it was usually a dear little thing with a red stuffed body and china head and legs and arms. Usually, my mother had made its clothes. Once it had an evening cloak too.'

Little Miss Fogerty's eyes behind her thick spectacles sparkled at the remembrance.

'And of course, a tangerine like yours, and some sweets, and best of all a sheet of transfers which you stuck on the back of your hand and wetted, and then carefully peeled off the paper backing, and had a beautifully decorated hand – ships and bells and lovely animals! I was never allowed to have them during the year, but at Christmas my parents relented, and I really think those transfers gave me more pleasure than anything!'

'Yes, we were pleased with little things,' agreed Dorothy. 'What games we used to play with natural things, do you remember? The boys always had their conkers, of course, but I was thinking of our girls' games. Blowing dandelion clocks, for instance, and smiting the head off another child's plantain.'

'And holding a buttercup under your chin to see if you liked butter,' said Agnes, 'and making daisy chains, and dear little pipes from acorn cups. Weren't we lucky to live where such things grew?'

Dorothy sighed nostalgically. ' "Where are the something-or-other of yesteryear?" ' she quoted. 'What a comfort poetry is, Agnes dear, even if you can't remember it!'

In the week before Christmas, Lulling High Street was chock-a-block with cars, vans delivering extra goods, children on holiday, frantic shoppers and a local brass band which played carols at irregular intervals and with less than perfect notation.

Nelly Piggott enjoyed it all immensely. This was life as she liked it – plenty of noise, colour and movement. Trade was brisk, the till bell tinkled incessantly, and exhausted shoppers queued for cups of refreshing coffee. The savoury rolls seemed to be snapped up earlier each morning by the local office workers and the van drivers, who had soon got to hear of this welcome service and had become regular customers on their way through the town.

Nelly thoroughly enjoyed being in charge, and her exuberance seemed to be infectious. Even Gloria and Rosa wilted less, and almost hurried about the café, and sometimes even managed to smile at the customers.

Mrs Peters was kept busy, running the splendid new van to local business premises where office parties were in full swing. The change in fortune of The Fuchsia Bush was so welcome, that she was too excited to feel tired during the day, but when at last she fell into bed, she realised how close she was to exhaustion.

At Thrush Green, Winnie Bailey and Ella shared their annual task of setting up the crib in St Andrew's church. To the delight of the ladies who decorated the place for Christmas, Tom Hardy and Johnny Enderby had offered to pick holly and ivy on their afternoon rambles, and had supplied them with generous armfuls.

Jane Cartwright, now making steady progress with only one stick for support, was glad to see this interest. If only more of her charges would follow suit, she thought! There seemed to be some slight lessening of discontent with the approach of Christmas, but would it last?

The members of the Lulling Rotary Club, and other good-hearted folk, were busy arranging shopping expeditions for the elderly and disabled, and Christmas parcels were delivered to each of the old people's homes at Thrush Green. These kindnesses were much appreciated, Jane noted, except for some slight bridling by Carlotta Jermyn who muttered something, in Jane's presence, about having no need for charity, and being perfectly well able to buy a Christmas pudding of her own.

Jane, whose hip was giving her some twinges at the time, said that part of the joy of Christmas was the giving and receiving of gifts, and that to be graciously grateful for presents so generously bestowed should be within everyone's power.

At this rebuke Carlotta's face turned pink, and she walked away.

'Perhaps it was wrong of me,' Jane said to Bill later, 'but it really riled me.'

'A bit of plain speaking won't hurt that one,' Bill replied cheerfully.

On Christmas Day St Andrew's church was full, much to the rector's delight. Holly and Christmas roses stood in the two silver vases on the altar. Mrs Bates had surpassed herself, and everywhere the silver gleamed and glinted with the reflected light of candles and a ray or two of winter sunshine.

The flower ladies had dressed a stand by the chancel steps with red and white carnations and hanging trails of ivy, and the brass lectern was similarly festooned. Everyone agreed that the church looked absolutely splendid and as young Cooke, a little befuddled with pre-Christmas drinks, had taken it upon himself to put twice as much coke in the boiler as usual, a pleasant warmth suffused the old building.

Charles Henstock and Dimity had been invited to Christmas dinner at Winnie Bailey's, as the rector was due at the tiny church at Nidden at three-thirty for evensong.

'It's a great problem trying to arrange services for all four parishes,' remarked Charles, neatly cutting his goose into mouth-sized portions. 'I feel quite envious of my predecessors who had numerous curates and lay preachers to help them at such busy times.'

'But you know you enjoy it, Charles,' put in Dimity, passing some extra sage and onion stuffing to him.

The rector nodded slowly. 'Of course I do. I am greatly privileged to serve so many people, and they give me back far more than I can ever give them.'

Winnie, looking after her guests, did not agree with Charles's words, but said nothing. But she thought, as she had so many times, how lucky Lulling and Thrush Green were to have this humble but great-hearted man to look after them.

At three o'clock they listened to the Queen's speech, and then Charles hastened away to his duties, leaving Winnie and Dimity to doze by the log fire.

Dimity, replete with the Christmas feast, fell fast asleep, occasionally emitting a small lady-like snore, but Winnie simply lay back in the armchair, her knitting lying neglected in her lap, while her thoughts ranged over past Christmases shared with Donald.

Mrs Bates had said to her only that morning: 'Christmas is the time of remembering, isn't it?' At that moment, Winnie had construed this as something to do with the giving of cards and presents, but now, in the quiet of the firelit room, she realised that the old lady was probably thinking of Christmases shared with a husband long-dead, or with children now far away. There was an element of sadness in this type of remembering, without doubt, but in fact it was all part and parcel of the renewing of ties between family and friends, and should be considered as something specially dear as one recalled, with gratitude, the days gone by. Nothing, after all, would take those memories away, and they grew more dearly cherished as the years passed.

To say that she still missed Donald was understating things to the point of banality. She still felt that something vital had gone from her, as if an arm or leg had been amputated, and she would never be whole again. But he would have grieved to see her incapable of recovery, and certainly she had been lucky in her home, her friends and Thrush Green itself, to help her through the darkest of the days.

One of her New Year resolutions, she promised, was to give as much comfort to others as she had received. She had much to be thankful for, and self-pity was not going to be allowed to creep in. About that she was adamant.

Her knitting slipped unregarded to the floor. Her head fell forward, and she joined her old friend in a refreshing snooze.

Most of the younger generation at Thrush Green were taking advantage of the dry roads and had set off walking, hoping that the exercise would help their over-taxed digestions.

Edward Young, Joan, Paul and his friends took the path to Lulling Woods. The young ones raced ahead, shouting excitedly, their breath forming little clouds in the chilly air.

Joan was wrapped in her new sheepskin coat, Edward's Christmas present, and chattered cheerfully. As they approached the stile into the woods she took Edward's arm.

'Oh, don't!' he yelped. 'I'm horribly sore!'

Joan looked at him in surprise. 'Have you pulled a muscle or something?'

'No, no. Nothing like that. Must be fibrositis, I think. I've got a sort of itchy burning pain in my right shoulder and back.'

'Too much Christmas pud, I expect,' laughed Joan. 'Would you like to go back?'

'No, I'll be all right,' said Edward, but he certainly looked rather wretched, thought Joan, and she purposely slowed her pace. It was so unusual for any of the Young family to be under the weather that Edward's obvious discomfort was worrying.

The children by now were far ahead, and Joan and Edward stopped to lean over a farm gate and survey the wintry scene. It was very quiet, and in the middle distance they could see eight plump French partridges, standing immobile, their dappled breasts shading to the red feathers above their legs. They were obviously aware of the two scrutinising them, and had frozen into stillness, but as Edward moved along the gate they suddenly took flight, and whirred away across the field.

Already the valley was filling with ghostly white mist, and distant treetops floated as if on water.

'Getting chilly,' remarked Edward with a shiver.

'Yes. We'll be getting back,' agreed Joan, solicitous for his welfare. 'I'll yell for the children.'

There were answering cries from the distance, and soon all the party began to make their way homeward through the early dusk.

'It might be as well to pop over to see John when surgery starts again,' said Joan.

Edward shrugged impatiently. 'Oh, there's nothing really wrong. I'm not going to bother him over Christmas. Probably be gone by morning anyway.'

And with that Joan had to be content.

Mrs Jenner spent Christmas Day with Jane and Bill. There were very few of the old people in their homes. Most had been collected by relatives to spend the day with them, and it was very peaceful in the wardens' new home.

Jane could now get about with much more confidence, often

without a stick for support, but to her mother's solicitous eye she still looked pale and drawn.

'Well, I don't get the fresh air and exercise I'm used to,' agreed Jane, 'but that will change when the spring comes, you'll see.'

'I had a visit from Kit Armitage the other morning,' said her mother. 'They've fixed up for a holiday in Venice, but they want someone to live in with their aunt.'

'It's a bit late isn't it, to find someone now? I heard that they were off in a fortnight.'

'They've been let down by the nurse they got through an agency. They asked if I could see my way clear to help out, but frankly I can't face it. She's an amazing old girl for her age, but to live with her for a fortnight is asking too much.'

Jane laughed.

'And you'd have to watch your diet down there, Mum! So what did you say?'

'I said I would try and find somebody reliable, and I thought of Vi Bailey. She nursed with you at the Cottage Hospital, remember?'

'Just the one, if she'd come.'

'Have you got her address? I might sound her out. I believe she went to live in one of the London suburbs when she married, but I don't remember her married name.'

By this time, Jane had hobbled to her bureau and found the address book.

'Here we are! Violet Ellis, and she's on the phone. Ring her now.'

'No, no! Not on Christmas Day, but I will tomorrow, Jane, and I do hope she'll be free. I know the pay will be exceptionally generous. Kit and Connie know they are asking a lot of whoever takes on Dotty, but they really do need a break, and I'm so fond of them.'

Bill now appeared from going his rounds, and from sanding the treacherous steps and paths which had caused his wife's present condition.

'No cups of tea for the world's workers?' he cried. 'Stay there, you girls, and I'll put on the kettle.'

Darkness came early to Thrush Green on Christmas Day. The mist had thickened as night fell, and wreathed eerily about the statue of Nathaniel Patten and the bare branches of the horse chestnut avenue. It was dank and chilly, the birds had gone to roost before five o'clock, and most of the human animals were equally comatose, toasting their toes by the fire, with curtains drawn and lamps lit.

But about seven o'clock the bedroom lights went on at the school house, as Agnes and Dorothy went aloft to change their dresses ready for a visit next door.

Isobel and Harold had invited them, and their old friends Frank and Phyllida Hurst, to Christmas dinner that evening, and the two maiden ladies were looking forward to a rare evening out.

Little Miss Fogerty surveyed herself in the mirror. She had on her best deep blue woollen frock with a silver locket of her mother's at her neck. The frock was now three years old, but had not been worn more than a dozen times. Her shoes were new, and very daring Agnes felt as she put them on, for they were of grey suede with a splendid cut-steel buckle across the front. She had never owned such dashing shoes in her life, but Dorothy had been present when they were bought, and had egged on her old friend to make the purchase.

It would have been nice, Agnes thought, to have an elegant cape or something really luxurious as a coat, but her everyday camel one would have to do, and she donned it cheerfully. The new blue silk scarf which had been Dorothy's Christmas present was tied over her head. The new gloves, sent by Ray and Kathleen, were put on, and little Miss Fogerty went downstairs to await Dorothy's appearance.

As befitted a headmistress, and one more sophisticated in dress, Dorothy descended the stairs looking quite regal in a bronze silk dress with a matching jacket. A string of amber beads added to the general ambience, and her brown court shoes looked extremely elegant.

'You look truly beautiful, Dorothy,' exclaimed Agnes. 'I just wonder – do you think we should carry our shoes and go in our Wellingtons? It might be rather muddy.'

'Good heavens, no! It's only a few steps, and Isobel has a stout doormat. Shall we go?'

The clammy night air chilled their faces as they emerged from the school house. Near at hand the light glowed a welcome from the Shoosmiths' porch, but it was impossible to see across the green, and even Nathaniel Patten was a ghostly figure in the swirling fog.

'It really is a most unpleasant night,' commented Dorothy. 'I'm sorry for people who have long journeys.'

'Never mind,' replied Agnes. 'Just think, the shortest day is behind us, and soon it will be spring.'

By this time they had rung the bell and were waiting in the porch, admiring Isobel's Christmas wreath hanging on the front door.

Dorothy, touched by Agnes's resolute cheerfulness, forbore to point out that January, February, and probably March stood between Christmas and the hoped-for spring. But no doubt it would come eventually, and here was Isobel at the door, arms wide in welcome, with Harold behind her, looking handsomer than ever.

'Happy Christmas!' they cried. 'And we hope you are hungry. The turkey is twice the size we ordered, and only just fitted into the oven!'

Later that evening, Bill Cartwright ran his mother-in-law home, and saw her safely into the farmhouse.

She looked tired, he thought, and he hoped that her spell of helping him whilst Jane had been in hospital was not the cause.

'I'm glad you didn't agree to staying with Dotty Harmer,' he said impulsively. 'It would have knocked you up completely. I feel we asked too much of you with our own troubles.'

Mrs Jenner looked surprised. 'It was nothing, Bill. I enjoyed it, and would do the same again, but I suppose I must face the fact that I'm getting old. If only Vi Bailey – I mean, Ellis – will be able to come, I shan't feel so guilty. I shall give her a ring in the morning. If she can't manage it, I really don't know who to suggest.'

'Well, don't offer yourself,' said Bill. 'Some people's hearts rule their heads, and you're one of them.'

He kissed her affectionately, and went out into the mist.

16. Winter Discomforts

The bellringers at Lulling rang out the Old Year, and rang in the New, on the famous peal of St John's church. The night was still and frosty, and the clamour was heard across the fields and woods, in a dozen little villages within a few miles.

The vicarage hummed and trembled with the noise, but it was a joyous sound, and Charles rejoiced. This year, he promised himself, as the hands of the clock stood at five minutes past midnight, he would work harder, be more patient, and give more attention to dear Dimity who was far too selfless.

There were a number of people making good resolutions at much the same time, but Edward Young was not among them.

He, poor fellow, was being driven to distraction by the pain in his right shoulder. It seemed to have spread to his neck and down the right side of his back.

Joan, over the last week, had applied calamine lotion, witch hazel, petroleum jelly, and had even contemplated using a sinister looking ointment concocted by Dotty, but did not take this final drastic step. Nothing seemed to alleviate the torment, and Edward grew more fractious daily.

When, at last, some nasty little spots began to appear, and he had spent the last night of the year sitting up in bed and holding his pyjama jacket away from his afflictions, Joan put her foot down.

'I'm calling John in to have a look at you,' she said firmly.

'Oh, don't fuss! Anyway, I suppose I'd better go to the surgery, if I must see him.'

'Not with those spots. You may have something infectious.'

'Thanks. Very reassuring, I must say. What's your guess? Leprosy?'

'Don't be childish. You'll stay there in the morning, and I shall ask John to come after surgery. No arguing now. You need some expert treatment.'

Edward grunted, but forbore to argue. He knew when he was beaten, but it was clear to his wife that he was still reluctant to be obliged to his brother-in-law.

The distant bells had woken Connie. She and Kit had gone to bed at their usual time, both ready for sleep, but Connie was secretly worrying about Dotty's welfare while they were away.

Mrs Jenner had been as good as her word, and Mrs Ellis was to come on New Year's Day to see the cottage, meet Dotty, and decide if she would take on the job.

Connie had no doubt that she would be a most competent person, particularly if Mrs Jenner and Jane recommended her, but would she want the responsibility of such an eccentric person as dear Dotty? The nearer the time came to going to Venice, the more agitated Connie became. For two pins she would throw over the whole idea, but she knew that Kit was longing to go, Dotty was adamant that she would be perfectly safe on her own, let alone with a companion, and Connie herself realised that she was desperately in need of a break.

Looking after the house and Dotty was a full-time job, and the fact that the new addition to the cottage was still not completed was another complication. It was true that the worst was over, but now the finishing touches had to be done inside, which involved a great deal of to-ing and fro-ing through the house when the weather could be at its worst.

Sometimes Connie had a twinge of nostalgia for the life she had left behind. Then she lived alone, in a fairly remote house, looking after a couple of ponies, ducks and hens, three cats and a dog, and quite often old friends who came to stay for a few days, and whose company she relished. But she enjoyed her solitary life. Any decision she made she could make alone, and stand or fall by the result without too much heart-burning.

Now she had to consider Kit and Dotty, and to wonder if she were doing the right thing. Love them dearly, as she truly did, it certainly made for a more complicated life, mused Connie.

The bells ceased suddenly. Well, tomorrow she must face the interview with Jane Cartwright's fellow-nurse. Meanwhile all her cares must be put aside for a few hours. She slid down the bed, tucked the bedclothes round her neck, and settled down to sleep.

She suddenly remembered an anecdote about Winston Churchill, who was asked, during the war, if he worried much at night.

'No,' answered the old warrior. 'I think: "To hell with everybody!" and I go to sleep.'

And very sound advice to follow, thought Connie, turning her face towards the pillow.

Not far away, Winnie Bailey too was ready for sleep, but a thought struck her before she dropped off. There had been no word from Richard this Christmas. There was usually a card, true an aggressively non-Christian one usually, such as an abstract painting which looked the same either way up, but this time nothing had arrived.

Of course, she remembered, he had said something about travelling back from China about Christmas time. That must explain it. Still, it would have been nice to have had a word from him. She was fond of Richard, despite his off-hand ways. Perhaps he would bring his family down for the day soon.

With such comfortable thoughts Winnie slipped into oblivion.

Under the same roof, Jenny was looking forward to the New Year. Life at Thrush Green held all the happiness that she needed. She thought of her early years at the orphanage where, despite good management, adequate food and a great deal of kindness, life had contrived to be bleak.

The years spent as a foster child with an elderly couple, had been better in many ways, but the work had increased as her foster parents grew more infirm. She mourned them sincerely when they died, but Winnie's offer of a flat in her house, the companionship of her employer, and the pleasant surroundings, were a source of constant joy. It was wonderful to have a real home of her own, she told herself, savouring the warmth of the bed and the luxurious scent of Winnie's Christmas present of expensive soap from the nearby wash basin.

If the year ahead proved to be as happy as the last, then Jenny was well content.

Vi Ellis arrived punctually at Dotty Harmer's cottage on New Year's Day.

She and her husband had driven down, and the plan was for her to stay overnight with her old friend Jane Cartwright, while her husband took the car on to Lechlade, where he was going to visit an old school friend, recently made a widower. He would pick up Vi on his way home.

She was a small plump woman with dark curly hair and the brightest eyes Connie had ever seen. She seemed lively, willing, and above all, kind. Dotty appeared to take to her, and after coffee, she was shown round the house by Connie.

'I must make it quite clear,' said Connie, when they were out of range of Dotty's hearing, 'that my aunt is pretty self-willed, and often does something rather unpredictable like popping down in the night to see if the chickens are safely locked up. I'm a light sleeper myself, so I usually manage to head her back to bed.'

Mrs Ellis laughed. 'Don't worry. I've dealt with lots of old people in my time, and I promise you I shall be alert.'

'As a matter of fact, I think my aunt will probably be more tranquil about the animals as we have a neighbour, Albert Piggott, coming to look after them, and Dotty has rather more confidence in him than she has in me.'

Connie took her into the spare bedroom which was next

door to Dotty's own, and Vi Ellis stood looking with admiration at the view across to Lulling Woods.

'One day,' she said, 'when Ted's retired, I hope we'll be able to come and live in the country. We both miss it badly.'

They sat down and Connie told her about the wages offered, the doctor's treatment, Betty Bell's help in the house, and other relevant matters. Vi Ellis seemed happy with all the arrangements, and it was really now just a matter of finding out how Dotty felt about this possible companion, thought Connie.

As if reading her mind, Vi asked if she might go and walk round the garden for a few minutes and get a breath of real country air. While she was so disposed, Connie returned to the sitting-room and went across to Dotty.

'She'll do!' said that lady before anything was said, much to Connie and Kit's relief.

'I'm glad you like her,' replied Connie. 'I do too.'

'Then you'd better fetch her in,' said Dotty, 'before she freezes to death.'

Joan Young had been as good as her word, and soon after Christmas John Lovell had called to see his brother-in-law.

'Let's have a look at this rash,' said the doctor, helping Edward off with his shirt.

He surveyed the spots in silence, whilst the patient awaited the worst.

'Well,' he said at last. 'You know what you've got, I expect?'

'Far from it! That's why you're here!'

'Shingles. I don't think it will be too bad a dose, but it's a beast of a complaint.'

'I'll endorse that,' said Edward. 'I wonder where I got it?'

'Lots of chickenpox about. It's connected, you know. Have you been in contact with anyone particularly?'

Edward thought, as he did up his shirt buttons.

'Young George Curdle's got it, of course, and I've visited him now and again. Playing snakes and ladders and draughts and other thrilling games.'

'Sounds as though that's it.'

'Am I infectious?'

'No, no! It's one of those things that we think lies dormant, and can flare up if the patient has been under strain or run down. Or, of course, in contact with chickenpox.'

'Well, to tell the truth, John, I am having a devil of a time with a contract in Cirencester. Have had for weeks now. Might be that partly.'

'Quite likely.' He smiled at his patient. 'We all worry too much,' he went on. 'I've had a few guilty twinges about ticking you off about those steps. No business of mine really.'

'Oh, forget it, John,' said Edward. 'Can you give me something to stop this plaguey itching?'

'Yes. I'll write you a prescription for a lotion and some tablets. And off work for a week at least. Lots of drink – not spirits, old boy – nice healthy stuff like water and orange juice!'

'Thanks a lot!'

'An evening's card-playing might help. Take your mind off your troubles. Come to us on Thursday. It's my evening off surgery.'

Within five minutes he had gone, leaving Edward to try and decipher the hieroglyphics of his prescriptions.

'Why do doctors have such terrible handwriting?' he asked the cat, who had wandered in.

But, rather naturally, there was no reply.

The chickenpox epidemic still raged in Lulling and Thrush Green, and when term began almost a quarter of Miss Watson's pupils were absentees. It certainly made for more manageable classes, and Miss Watson and the young probationer took the opportunity to do a little extra coaching of slow readers.

Little Miss Fogerty always aimed at sending her top infants to the junior school with the ability to read. But, of course, there were some who were slow, and some practically incapable of reading at all, and always would be.

'There seem to be more these days,' she remarked to Dorothy

when the matter was under discussion. 'I can't make it out. It can't be only television. Perhaps I am losing my touch.'

'Rubbish!' said her friend. 'I think perhaps we are all trying to do too many things in school time, and the reading gets a little neglected. I intend to have a real blitz this term. After all, the older the child the harder it finds learning to read. We must just put our backs into it for a bit.'

It was while she was doing just this one chilly January morning that Miss Fuller walked in, somewhat timidly, clutching a large envelope.

'Do hope I'm not interrupting,' she said, surveying the half-dozen children clustered round Miss Watson's desk, forefingers clamped to a line in their readers.

'Not at all,' said Dorothy graciously. 'Go to your desks, children, and carry on quietly.'

'I thought that you might find a use for these Christmas cards,' said Miss Fuller, proffering the envelope.

'Now, that is most kind of you,' said Dorothy, turning over the angels, reindeer, wise men, cats and dogs, all in happy medley. 'With these dreadful cuts in expenditure, it's a very welcome present, believe me. We can make all sorts of good things.'

Miss Fuller flushed with pleasure.

'I must admit, it's lovely to be back in the classroom again, if only for a few minutes. What were you doing with that little group when I came in?'

Miss Watson explained about the backward readers.

'I was rather hoping to get some remedial work when I'd settled,' responded Miss Fuller. 'Just part-time, you know.'

Miss Watson thought quickly, and replied with her usual frankness.

'As things are, I can't see the Office expending any more money on extra staff, but we could certainly do with a hand at the moment with this reading effort.'

'Oh, I had no thought of payment,' said Miss Fuller, not quite truthfully. 'But if you really think I could help them I should be more than happy to come for an hour or so during the week.'

'It's a splendid offer,' said Dorothy, and her response was wholly truthful. 'I'll talk it over with the others, and call on you, if I may.'

The ladies parted with expressions of gratitude. Miss Fuller looked quite bright-eyed as she waved at the door, and Dorothy returned to her desk with much to consider.

She must inform the Office of Miss Fuller's suggestion, she felt, and then have a word at playtime with her two colleagues. Not that they would have any objection, she felt sure, to such an experienced teacher as Miss Fuller giving them a brief respite from the efforts of backward readers.

Who would, thought Dorothy, beckoning to the group with a sinking heart?

'There's just one thing,' ventured Agnes that evening. 'Much as I respect Muriel Fuller, I do feel that she can be a trifle – er – perhaps just a little—'

'Bossy?' said Dorothy. 'I've thought of that. She's not going to tell me how to run my school, just because she's been a headmistress. In any case, there were less than twenty on roll at one time at Nidden.'

'How well you sum up things!'

'She could have the staff room for her reading sessions. Five children for half an hour, I thought. If she's willing to give us two hours a week, say, it should fit in very well.'

'Which days does she want to come?'

'I'll have to discuss it with her, but if it fits in with her own plans, I suggest Tuesdays and Thursdays, after morning play. She can have her coffee with us, and then carry on when we've gone back to our classrooms.'

'It sounds splendid.'

'Well, time alone will tell,' said Dorothy. 'But it was most kind of her to bring her Christmas cards. I think we'll ask the children in assembly tomorrow morning to bring theirs too.

What a lot we can do with such bounty! It's really rather depressing to have to eke out the painting paper and gummed squares in such a Scrooge-like fashion. Now, we can turn our attention to scrap books and wall pictures, and perhaps a screen. I've always wanted to make a screen!'

Agnes smiled indulgently at such enthusiasm. Really, Dorothy was quite a child at heart. Perhaps all teachers of young children were, she thought, with a flash of insight?

By mid-January the weather had deteriorated into bitterly cold conditions, with an icy north-easter and an overcast sky presaging snow to come.

The last few shrivelled leaves were ripped from the bare branches and skittered about the frozen roads and icy puddles. The birds flocked round the back doors and bird tables, hungry for any largesse that was going.

The hips and haws, the berries of the pyracanthas and cotoneaster were now being attacked ruthlessly, and the half-coconut hanging outside in the playground seemed to have a little posse of tits on it all through the day.

Winter ills now descended upon young and old alike, as well as the wretched chickenpox. Isobel and Harold Shoosmith took to their beds with influenza, managing to stagger in turns to heat soup or milk for each other while the plague lasted.

Jenny had a raging sore throat which John Lovell shook his head over, and spoke darkly about having her tonsils out before long. And Dimity and Charles Henstock found themselves suffering from chilblains, which neither had endured since childhood. They were now stuffing themselves with calcium lactate tablets, and rubbing their afflicted fingers and toes with ointment.

'No good taking calcium lactate now,' their kind friends assured them. 'You should have been taking a course all through the summer.'

'How people do enjoy others' misfortunes,' mused Charles to Dimity, when the third person that day had told them of the uselessness of expecting calcium lactate to work a miracle cure. 'It doesn't give one much hope, does it?'

'Never mind,' said Dimity. 'It makes them feel comfortably superior, and it really makes no difference to us. To be honest, I'm *quite sure* I'm better since we started the tablets.'

'Perhaps it's faith healing,' said Charles.

'And what's wrong with that?' cried Dimity triumphantly. 'You know it is *right* to have faith. And in any case, I don't mind *what* sort of healing it is as long as the chilblains go.'

Ada and Bertha Lovelock were in bed with bronchitis, and Violet did her best to provide rather thin soup, and a succession of depressing 'Cold shapes' which were a Lovelock dessert speciality, for the invalids. Luckily, the Lulling doctor, surveying his patients' emaciated frames, suggested that suitable meals might be sent in from The Fuchsia Bush next door.

This, he told Violet, was to ensure that she herself did not succumb, but his advice was taken, and once a day a tray of succulent, but easily digested, dishes appeared, and was borne aloft by Gloria or Rosa to the two old ladies.

'Perishing cold it is in there, too,' they remarked to Nelly. 'All they've got in the bedrooms is a one-bar electric fire, and a stone hot water bottle apiece.'

Nevertheless, the good food, and their own indomitable constitutions, helped them to recover, in record time.

At the old people's homes, the only real casualty was Tom Hardy who also went down with bronchitis, but Jane insisted that he stayed in bed, supplied him with an extra-thick cardigan of Bill's to wear as a bed-jacket, and generally cosseted the old man.

His chief worry was Polly. Was she getting her walk regularly? Was she having the tablets the vet recommended? Had anyone brushed her coat? The ruff round her neck was inclined to tangle.

John Enderby undertook these duties cheerfully, and kept his neighbour company, teaching him to play chess and keeping him informed about all the news of Thrush Green.

He himself had offered to give Ella Bembridge a hand in her garden, and gladly had she accepted.

'Not that there's much to do at the moment,' he told Tom one bitterly cold afternoon, 'but I did the rose pruning for her, and I'm going to spread the muck from the compost on her vegetable patch. She does well enough, for a woman, but don't dig as deep as she should. I'll soon get the place to rights.'

Jane Cartwright had seen this development with the greatest satisfaction. This was what was needed to settle her charges. Mrs Bates was as happy as a sandboy with her little weekly silver cleaning, Miss Fuller had found herself a couple of hours' teaching at the school, and now Johnny was doing something which used his skills and, even more important, made him feel needed. It looked as if things were looking up at Rectory Cottages after earlier teething troubles, and Jane felt mightily relieved.

*

The day of Kit and Connie's departure was as cold as ever, but mercifully clear and bright, and the flight was due to go at the time announced, much to their relief.

Harold had offered to take them to the airport, but was still suffering from influenza. As it was a Saturday, Ben Curdle offered to take his place, and Harold knew that he would take even more care of his car than he would himself, and agreed gratefully.

'Well, you're lucky to be going to the sunshine,' said Ben, whose idea of anywhere abroad was of coral beaches, palm trees and continuous sunlight.

'It should be warmer than this,' agreed Kit, 'but we'll be lucky to see much sun in Venice at this time of year. Still, it's such a beautiful city, and with dozens of lovely buildings and pictures to look at, we shall have plenty to do.'

It did not sound much of a holiday to Ben, but people had their own ideas of fun. Look at all those people who went skiing in deep snow and ended up, more often than not, with their legs in plaster. Give him a deckchair on the beach with an ice cream cornet, thought Ben, taking the turning to Heathrow.

The place was a seething mass of agitated people, piles of luggage and a formidable block of traffic.

Kit took charge with his usual calm authority.

'I'll get a trolley, Ben, if you could get the cases out of the boot. Connie dear, just mind the hand luggage and stay here by this door. I want Ben to get away as quickly as possible with Harold's car. I can't imagine anything worse than getting it damaged before we set off.'

He hurried away and Ben went to the rear of the car.

Connie gazed despairingly at the throng of people. What an unnerving sight! If only she could go back with Ben to the peace of Thrush Green!

'Oh, Ben,' she cried, 'you will let us know if anything goes wrong at home, won't you? I'm really horribly worried about my aunt. She's not quite – not quite—' she faltered.

'Miss Harmer will be as right as rain,' said Ben, with his slow sweet smile. 'We'll *all* be looking after her, don't you fret.'

Calmed and relieved, Connie returned his smile. One could quite see why Molly had married him. Ben would be a tower of strength in any crisis.

'Here we are!' called Kit triumphantly, piling cases on a trolley. 'Practically there!'

'Yes, they went off all right,' he said to Molly on his return. 'She was a bit panicky at the last minute about Dotty, but I told her she'd be fine.'

'I think she will,' said Molly slowly, 'but I wouldn't want to be in that Mrs Ellis's shoes, not for all the tea in China.'

17. NELLY PIGGOTT MEETS THE PAST

Connie need not have had any fears, for the two ladies settled down very well together. It was true that Dotty, with her usual forthrightness, had taken it upon herself to put certain matters straight, but after a day or two's adjustment, harmony reigned.

The first clash had come when Vi, slipping back into hospital language, had said, as she tucked a shawl round her charge's shoulders: 'There, dear, we don't want to get a chill, do we?'

Dotty looked at her with some hauteur. 'When you use the word "we", are you using it in the editorial, or royal, sense? Or are you simply referring to the two of us – you and me?'

After that, Vi was more careful.

She was touched too to get a telephone call from Connie on the night of their arrival in Venice. Although she privately considered it overwhelmingly extravagant, she was proud and pleased to get Connie's appreciation of her services.

Dotty had her own conversation with Connie once the preliminaries were over.

'Oh, we're doing splendidly, dear. So glad the flight was satisfactory and the plane wasn't hi-jacked. It must be so tiresome when that happens, and if people are firing off guns in such a confined space, the noise must be indescribable. Yes, dear, Mrs Ellis is unpicking my Florentine stitch cushion cover, and I'm doing the crossword. Do you know the anagram of DAIRYCATS? Of course, CARYATIDS! That will help a lot. We're having poached eggs for supper. Goodbye, dear, and my fondest love to you both.'

She smiled across at her companion.

'Now, wasn't that thoughtful of her?'

'It was indeed. It's good to know that they arrived safely.'

Dotty suddenly looked agitated. 'Oh dear! I believe I said we were to have *poached* eggs for supper, but now I come to think of it, I think you suggested *scrambled*.'

'I can cook whichever you prefer,' said Vi.

'Then let's make it poached eggs. You see, I shouldn't like Connie to be imagining us eating poached if we were actually eating scrambled eggs. I should feel rather dishonourable.'

'Then we'll certainly poach the eggs,' said Vi kindly, 'if you would feel happier about it.'

'I would indeed, Mrs Ellis. Incidentally, would you be offended if I called you Vi?'

'I should like it.'

'Then you may call me "Dotty". Most of my friends seem to think it a very suitable name for me, though I can't think why.'

Vi did not enlighten her.

The bitter winds brought a roaring blizzard during the next few days, and considerably added to the usual winter miseries.

The only people to enjoy this weather were the children. Screaming with joy, they rushed about, mouths open to catch the snowflakes, faces scarlet and eyes shining. Those with sledges found themselves unusually popular with their schoolmates, and after school little bands of children hurried to the slopes behind Harold Shoosmith's garden, and set off on their toboggans on the run down to Lulling Woods.

Only when darkness fell and hunger became acute, did they go reluctantly home, praying that this miraculous weather would hold.

Miss Fogerty and Miss Watson, in company with the other adults in the neighbourhood, were less ecstatic about the weather conditions.

'What a blessing we invested in a freezer,' said Dorothy one evening. 'At least we don't have to go shopping every day. I feel really sorry for people struggling up and down the hill. Willie Marchant said it was like glass when he brought the post this morning.'

'You must be extra careful,' said Agnes solicitously, 'with that hip of yours. They do say that a pair of socks over one's shoes is a great help in slippery weather.'

'You did warn the children, I take it, about the dangers of making slides in the playground?'

'I certainly did.'

'I only ask, dear, because that wretched Todd boy was starting to make one near the lavatories. Just where it wouldn't be seen from the school windows.'

'He really is a *dreadful* child! I fear he will become a delinquent.'

'He's that already,' said her headmistress firmly. 'Mark my words, that boy will either end up in prison, or go on to win the VC if we have another war, which heaven forbid! He's that sort of character, I'm afraid.'

'I shall speak to him tomorrow morning,' said Agnes, looking almost ferocious. 'I can't say that I shall be sorry to see him leave the infants' class, except that he will be one step nearer your own class.'

'You need not worry about that,' replied Dorothy robustly. 'I've sorted out many a John Todd in my time, and I don't think I've lost my touch.'

Winnie Bailey was sorely troubled about Jenny, who seemed to take a long time to recover from her tonsilitis. Jenny fretted at the delay, and was impatient of the restrictions put upon her by Dr Lovell and her employer.

'I don't like the idea of you going out in this weather,' she croaked to Winnie.

'I'm not going out anywhere,' said Winnie calmly. 'The baker, the milkman and the butcher are calling, bless them, and we are managing very well. We've enough provisions in the house to withstand a month's siege, thanks to you, Jenny, so just sit back and relax. You won't get better if you worry so.'

'As soon as she's over this,' John told Winnie privately, 'and the weather cheers up, I think we must get those tonsils out. She seems to get a severe bout of throat trouble every winter, and septic tonsils can lead to a number of complications.'

'Good heavens, John! What do you mean?'

'Oh, trouble with the retina at the back of the eye. Nodes on ligaments here and there. Sometimes infection spreads to the respiratory system. Best to have 'em out.'

'Of course, if that's the case. But surely it's rather a horrid affair, isn't it? Having one's tonsils out at Jenny's age?'

'Oh, she'll be all right,' John assured her. 'Not half as much blood these days. I'll get Pedder-Bennett to do it. He's getting a bit senile, but still manages a very neat little tonsilectomy.'

Winnie, despite having married a doctor, could not help feeling that the profession as a whole seemed remarkably off-hand about their patients' fears.

'Well, I shall say nothing of this to Jenny obviously,' she said. 'It's entirely your business. But I don't want her to have anything done until she is really fit. And if you think that there is anyone better – younger, I mean – perhaps more skilful—' she faltered to a halt.

'Than old PB? Oh, he'll be quite competent. As long as he remembers his spectacles, of course.'

It was that evening, when he had returned from surgery, that John read in the local paper about the court case.

It involved the two older men who had pleaded guilty to stealing cars and selling them. All three had appeared again before the Lulling magistrates who, in view of the number of charges and the large amount of money involved, had sent them to the Crown Court for sentence.

'I see they have given these chaps bail,' commented John to Ruth. 'I'd have put 'em inside.'

'Well, they might be there for months,' said his wife. 'Legal processes seem to take their time, and the gaols are full up, so one reads.'

'That's true. Evidently they've had to surrender their passports, so they can't nip over to their overseas customers, and their sureties will have to find a thousand apiece if they decamp. I wonder when the case will come up?'

'Will you have to appear?'

'I'm not sure. I can't be of any help with these two fellows. I shouldn't know them from Adam, and I've no idea what the cars were that they had in the barn. I could look up my records to establish the two dates when I called, but that's about all.'

'Well, that's one thing you need not bother about,' said Ruth comfortably.

John hoped that she was right. His earlier appearance at court had been an ordeal. No matter how often he had to attend in a professional capacity, it always made him nervous.

During this snowy period, Nelly Piggott was one of the unfortunate people who had to slither down hill to Lulling and struggle up again at the end of the day. It was true that the council men had salted the paths, but nevertheless Nelly wished that there were still a stout handrail at the edge of the pavement, as old photographs of the steep hill showed in times gone by.

On this particular morning, she was setting off early. Mrs Peters had telephoned the day before to say that she was smitten with the prevailing influenza, and was obliged to keep to her bed. Nelly was off to take charge.

'Don't you fret now,' she had said to her partner. 'Business is slack in this weather, and we can cope easily.'

'Fortunately there are no outside commitments this week,' said Mrs Peters, 'and with any luck I should be back by the weekend.'

Nelly's confidence had grown amazingly since starting work at The Fuchsia Bush, and the necessity of having to make decisions in her friend's absence daunted her not at all.

During the morning the snow took on a new intensity. There was a bitter east wind blowing, and the trunks of the trees lining the High Street were soon plastered with snow on the windward side. The few people who had braved the weather hurried by, bent against the onslaught. Windscreen wipers worked madly to try to cope with the flurries, and the window ledges of The Fuchsia Bush soon bore two or three inches of snow.

Just after twelve, Nelly hurried through from the kitchen. Only two tables were being used, she noticed, as she set a tray of freshly-filled rolls on the counter for the office workers and shop assistants who might be expected very soon.

The windows were steamy, but she noticed a figure studying the name above the shop. Soon the door bell gave its familiar tinkle, and a snow-plastered man appeared. An icy blast accompanied him. He took off his snowy cap and shook it energetically.

'You get some cruel weather up here, Nelly,' he said.

To that lady's horror, she saw that it was her old paramour Charlie, once visiting oil man at Thrush Green, who had turned her away from his bed and board when he had discovered a more attractive partner.

'And what,' said Nelly, in a tone as frigid as the world outside, 'do you think you're doing here?'

'You don't sound very welcoming,' replied Charlie, looking hurt.

'I don't feel it after the way you treated me,' responded Nelly. She became conscious of the interest of the two customers, and lowered her voice. A quick glance had shown her that this was not the spruce, confident Charlie that she remembered. Snow apart, there was a seedy look about his clothes, his shoes were cracked, he had no gloves, and the canvas hold-all was soaked. Despite herself, Nelly's heart was touched.

'Well, we can't talk here. Come through to the kitchen, and I'll put your things to dry.'

What a blessing, she thought agitatedly, that Mrs Peters was away! How to have explained this unwanted visitor would have been a real headache.

Charlie stood about looking awkward while Nelly hung up his outdoor clothes near the massive stoves. Gloria, Rosa and the two kitchen maids gazed at him open-mouthed.

'Just carry on,' said Nelly. 'I'll be with you in two shakes. Come through to the store room, Charlie.'

Here there was silence. Nelly pushed a pair of steps forward for Charlie's use, and sat herself in the only available chair.

'Well, Charlie, let's hear all about it. Where's Gladys?'

Gladys was her erstwhile friend who had usurped her place in Charlie's fickle attentions. It was Gladys who had caused Nelly's return to Albert a year or two ago. As can be imagined, there was not much love lost between the two ladies.

'She upped and left me. Went back to Norman, same as you went back to Albert. And how's that old misery?'

'You can keep a civil tongue in your head about my husband.

He's no Romeo, but he's treated me right since I got back, and we've settled down pretty solidly. Don't think you've any chance of getting me back, Charlie, because I'm not coming. Times have changed, and I'm doing very well for myself here.'

'So I heard. That's partly why I came. Thought you might have a job for me.'

'A job?'

'The fact is things went from bad to worse for me. Gladys was always at me for more money. In the end I sold the business.'

'But what are you living on?'

'Social security mainly. I flogged the furniture, so that brought in a bit. Now I'm looking for a job.'

Nelly took another glance at the cracked shoes and the wet ends of his trouser legs. For a moment she weakened, for she was a kind-hearted woman. But reason held sway, and she spoke firmly.

'Look here, Charlie. There's nothing here for you in the way of work. Lulling's as badly hit as all the other towns, and no one's going to employ a chap your age with no real qualifications.'

Charlie looked down at his hands, twisting them this way and that in his embarrassment. 'Well, if that's the case, I'd better be off. I thought I'd make my way to Birmingham, to see old Nobby.'

'Nobby?'

'Don't you remember Nobby Clark? Mary was his missus. They kept the ironmonger's on the corner. Nice pair.'

'Is he offering you a job?'

'Yes, in a way. When his dad died in Birmingham, he left Nobby his shop. A sweetshop, it is, with newspapers and postcards, and all that lark. He said he could do with some help if I needed work.'

'Sounds the best thing you could do,' said Nelly decidedly. 'Does he know you're coming?'

'No. I thought I'd see you first.'

And worm your way into my affections again as well as finding a job, thought Nelly.

'Before you set off,' said Nelly, 'you're going to have a good hot meal, and you can ring Nobby from here to say you are on your way. Where are you staying?'

'With them, I take it.'

'In that case, she'll need a bit of notice to make up a bed. You can use the phone in the office, and then go straight through to the restaurant. I've got to be getting back to my work. We're short-handed with the boss away ill.'

Charlie nodded his agreement, and Nelly ushered him into the office while she bustled back to the kitchen.

'That's an old acquaintance of mine,' she said to the girls. 'Down on his luck, and off to Birmingham this afternoon. Don't charge him, mind. Give the bill to me.'

Within the hour, just as The Fuchsia Bush's regular customers were beginning to struggle in, shivering with cold, Charlie had finished his meal.

He went through to the kitchen to fetch his clothes and to say goodbye to Nelly. He was looking all the better for his meal, she noted approvingly. There was a hint of the old chirpy Charlie who had first stolen her heart, but she had no intention of succumbing to his charms again.

She was alone in the kitchen, and she took advantage of their privacy to enquire about the state of his immediate finances.

He held open his wallet. It contained two five pound notes. 'I've got a bit of loose change,' he said, rattling a trouser pocket.

'That won't get you far,' said Nelly, opening her handbag. 'Here, take these two fivers. It'll go towards the fare. The bus to Oxford goes in ten minutes, and you'll have to get a train or bus on to Birmingham from there.'

He put them with the other two notes in his wallet, and muttered his thanks, so brokenly, that Nelly looked at him in surprise. To her amazement she saw tears in his eyes for the first time.

Much embarrassed, she hastened across the kitchen to the dresser where the remaining ham and tongue rolls lay in the wooden tray.

She thrust two into a paper bag and held out the package.

'Put those in your pocket, Charlie. It'll save you buying, and you can eat them on the journey.'

'You're one in a thousand, Nelly. I won't forget all you've done today.'

'That's all right. I'm glad to help, but take note, Charlie! It's the last time. Don't come trying your luck again. I hope you get on all right with the Clarks. Don't write, nor telephone. It's the end between us now, Charlie, and best that way.'

He bent suddenly and kissed her cheek.

'That's my old love,' he said warmly. 'Don't worry. I won't embarrass you.'

'If you want to get that bus,' replied Nelly, more shaken than she cared to admit, 'you'd best get outside to the bus stop. Thank the Lord the snow's stopped.'

She watched him cross the restaurant, humping his hold-all, and saw the door close. Much as she would have liked to see him board the bus, and perhaps give him a final wave, she was too upset to leave the haven of the kitchen.

Gloria came in balancing a tray on one hip.

'Your friend nearly missed the bus,' she said brightly. 'Got out there just in time.'

'Good,' replied Nelly huskily. She blew her nose energetically.

'Don't you go getting the flu now,' said Gloria, 'or we'll have to shut up shop.'

She spoke with unaccustomed gentleness, but forbore to make any more enquiries.

Later, she said to Rosa: 'The poor old duck was crying when

that chap went away. I bet she was sweet on him once, though what anyone could see in an old fellow like that, beats me.'

'One foot in the grave,' agreed Rosa. 'Must be nearer fifty than forty, poor old thing, *and* going bald.'

'He ate pretty hearty though,' replied Gloria. 'Steak and kidney pie, mashed spud, broad beans, and then the Bakewell tart.'

'Well, she said he was down on his luck,' Rosa reminded her. 'Maybe he didn't have no breakfast. Look out, she's coming back.'

The two girls began to stack plates busily by the sink as Nelly, now in command of herself, bustled into the room.

'Now, Rosa, you can cut the iced slab into squares ready for the tea tables, and there's some fresh shortbread to put out, Gloria. Look lively now, there's plenty to do.'

The two girls exchanged glances. It was quite clear that things were back to normal.

It was bitterly cold after dark. The wind had dropped, and the snow had not returned, but it was obvious that there would be a hard frost as the skies were clear.

At Thrush Green, Nelly was content to sit alone by the fire and ruminate. She felt completely exhausted by this encounter, and still worried by the pathetic shabbiness of the once dapper Charlie.

A pile of mending waited on the side table and the washing up remained on the draining board, but for the moment these jobs must wait, thought Nelly. Her head ached with thinking, her legs were heavy with standing all day, and her eyes were still sore from secret weeping.

To her surprise, Albert came in at nine o'clock, well before closing time.

'Perishing cold next door,' he told her. 'Got the fire smoking something awful. You're better off in here.' He bent towards the fire, rubbing his hands.

Nelly stirred herself.

'I'll just get the dishes washed, Albert, and make us a cup of tea.'

'Good idea,' said Albert. 'Did I tell you Miss Harmer give me a pot of jam for you? It's in the cupboard.'

'Thank her, won't you?' Not that we shall ever eat it, she thought privately, remembering 'Dotty's Collywobbles', a common Thrush Green complaint.

'She's not a bad old trout,' went on Albert, now seating himself by the blaze while Nelly tackled the dishes. 'She's promised me a sitting of duck eggs this spring. She's got two broody hens already.'

'But we've nowhere to keep ducks, Albert!'

'I can keep 'em down her place, she says. I'll enjoy that. And I'm to take both the goats to be mated when the time comes. Remind me to get some bran sometime this week. We're getting short down there.'

Nelly thought how much easier it was to live with Albert when he had animals to look after. It seemed to sweeten him somehow.

She put the last plate on the rack and filled the kettle.

'I'll take mine up to bed,' she said.

'Why? You ain't getting flu, are you?'

'No, just bone tired. There's a lot to do with Mrs Peters away.'

'Ah! There must be. Here, you go on up, and I'll bring you a cup in bed. How's that?'

Nelly could hardly believe her ears. She could not remember such a gesture from Albert in all their time together. In her present emotional state, it was too much, and the tears began to flow.

'Here, 'ere, 'ere!' said Albert, much alarmed. 'You've got something coming, my girl. Get you up to bed and wrap up warm.'

Weeping noisily, Nelly obeyed.

She woke some hours later. The bedroom clock said half past three, and the room was bright with moonlight. She got out of bed and went to the window. Her back room looked across the fields towards Lulling Woods. The larger room, where Albert now snored rhythmically, looked towards Thrush Green.

The whole world was white. The moonlight, reflected from the snowy fields, was intensified. In the garden of The Two Pheasants next door, the small cherry tree cast a circular tracery of shadows on the white lawn.

It was a tree which gave Nelly joy all through the year, from its first tiny leaves, its dangling white flowers, its scarlet fruit so quickly ravished by the birds, and then its final blaze of gold in autumn which it dropped, like a bright skirt, to the ground in November.

But tonight this rare beauty was a bonus. She gazed entranced at the tree's shadow. It looked like fine black lace cast around the foot of the trunk. Snow streaked the fragile branches, and lay like cake icing along the garden hedge. It was a magical night, calm and still, and Nelly, after her stormy day, drew strength from its tranquillity.

She shivered and padded back to bed, content to lie and watch the moonbeams moving across the ceiling.

She hoped that Charlie was somewhere safely asleep, and that he would settle with the Clarks and find a useful job. Poor old Charlie! It would have been so easy to give way and to say: 'Come back if things don't work out for you.' But it would never have done, she told herself.

The time with Charlie was firmly in the past, and she did not want to see him again. She was now a settled woman, with a good responsible job and money in the bank.

She thought of Albert, and his unexpected kindness that evening. If only he could always be as thoughtful! Perhaps, it occurred to her, he would be nicer if he had more interests, more animals, a better home. A lot of his moodiness came from too much drinking, she knew. Perhaps, one day, they could afford to move to a more cheerful house, well away from the pub, where Albert could keep ducks and hens, and a dog maybe, and be a happy man.

Who knows? He might even make a habit of bringing his wife a cup of tea in bed!

But at this flight of fancy Nelly's imagination baulked. With a sigh, she closed her eyes against the moonshine, and fell asleep again.

18. A HINT OF SPRING

At Lulling Vicarage, Charles and Dimity were congratulating themselves on the gradual improvement in their chilblains.

'I'm quite sure it's the calcium tablets,' said Dimity, beating eggs energetically. 'I don't care what people say. We started to get better as soon as we began to take them.'

'Egg custard for lunch?' asked Charles, watching his wife's efforts.

'Yes, dear, and bottled plums.'

Their little cat Tabitha appeared from nowhere, and gazed up expectantly at Dimity.

'Isn't she clever?' cried her mistress. 'As soon as she hears me whisking up something she comes for her egg and milk.'

She poured a little of the mixture into a saucer and put it on the floor. The cat licked delicately at this bounty.

'Dear thing,' said Dimity indulgently. 'So good for her, all those lovely vitamins.'

The telephone rang in Charles's study, and he hastened away to answer it.

By the time he returned, the egg custard was in a slow oven, and the cat's saucer was immaculately clean.

'Trouble?' asked Dimity, looking at his perplexed expression.

'No, not really, although I can see I shall have to make a hospital visit very soon. That was Mrs Thurgood. You know she's president of the Lulling Operatic Society. Well, the wardrobe mistress, whose name I didn't catch unfortunately, has some lung trouble and will have to have an operation which will put her out of action. Mrs Thurgood wanted to know if I knew of anyone who could help.'

'When is the performance?'

'Don't they take the Corn Exchange for a week? Sometime in March or April, I think she said.'

Charles appeared somewhat distracted.

Dimity spoke reassuringly. 'Oh, we'll think of someone, I'm sure. Can't her daughter Janet help?'

'Not with a young child.'

'We'll ask all our friends,' said Dimity, 'and something will turn up, you'll see. The only thing is, that our friends, like us, don't have much to do with the theatrical world. But don't worry, Charles, dear. Let's have our coffee early before you go down to the greenhouse.'

The time for Kit and Connie's return had almost arrived, and Vi found herself feeling quite sad about leaving her new friend.

Dotty, too, had found Vi's stay very stimulating. She had been able to indulge her love of television much more readily, for Vi was as much an addict, particularly of American serials, as Dotty was herself.

Kit and Connie were somewhat scornful of most of the television programmes, so that Dotty did not always see as many programmes as she would have liked.

She said as much to Vi, as they sat amicably gazing at the screen.

'Why don't you have a little set of your own in your bedroom?' suggested Vi. 'You're up there quite a bit, and there are often very good programmes late at night, when you know you are often wakeful.'

'I'll think about it,' said Dotty, watching a close embrace in vivid Technicolor. 'I really don't care for this modern way of kissing, do you, Vi? I mean, it goes on so long, and must be very unhygienic. When I was a girl, one was kissed on the cheek or forehead by relatives and close friends. I can't recall being kissed on the mouth, and certainly not *being eaten* like that!'

Dotty surveyed the couple with some distaste.

'Modern custom, I suppose,' said Vi, busily counting stitches on her knitting needle.

'Something to do with the Common Market, perhaps,' mused Dotty. ' "Common" being the operative word. You know, even quite nice men, like dear Kit, have taken to this continental way of kissing on both cheeks! I find it excessive. One tends to bump noses too. I really prefer to be kissed in the English manner.'

'Well, I'm sure Miss Bembridge will give you one of those when she comes,' said Vi. 'You remember she's coming to have tea with you while I call to see Jane and Bill?'

'Yes, yes, of course. Have you put out my sloe jelly?'

'I thought she might prefer the heather honey,' said Vi diplomatically. 'If you recall, you gave her a pot of the sloe jelly last time she came.'

'Quite right. Yes, I'm sure the honey will be better. After all, she's probably been tucking into my sloe jelly all the week.'

Vi forbore to comment on this hopeful remark, but directed Dotty's attention to the screen.

'Oh look! The Indians are massing on the horizon!'

'Good,' replied Dotty. 'Now we should get some good clean fun. Their horses always look in splendid condition, don't they?'

Jane and Bill Cartwright were sorry to be saying goodbye to Vi Ellis. Kit and Connie were due home at the weekend, and Vi was being fetched on the Sunday afternoon.

Naturally enough, the conversation turned to the vagaries of old people.

'I must say I've found Miss Harmer much easier than I first thought,' confessed Vi. 'She's so absolutely honest – embarrassingly so at times, but at least you know where you are with her.'

'Takes after her old dad in that,' Jane told her. 'Matron at the hospital had some hair-raising tales about him. He was always very punctilious about visiting any of his boys in hospital, but evidently the patients were in a fine state of nerves when the visit was over.'

'We had a headmaster like that when I was a boy in Yorkshire,' observed Bill. 'I believe he enjoyed caning us. Youngsters are lucky these days.'

'Now tell me about this job,' said Vi. 'Would it be the sort of thing that Ted and I might take on later?'

Jane looked thoughtful. 'You've got to have an enormous amount of tact – and sympathy. I must say that at times I've wondered if we're doing the right thing. They can be very awkward indeed, and over such trifles.'

She went on to describe the umbrage taken over Monty's deplorable sanitary habits, the petty upsets over neighbours' noises, and Carlotta Jermyn's irritating visits at the wrong times.

'It all sounds so trivial, I know,' she went on, 'but that's life here, and we have to remind ourselves how different it all is from the life they've had before. Gradually, *very* gradually, I think they are coming to terms with things here at Thrush Green, and becoming *integrated*, I think is the word.'

'It's a worthwhile job,' Vi said comfortingly. 'This fortnight with dear old Dotty has been quite hard work, but I've thoroughly enjoyed it, and I really would like to try my hand at something like this one day.'

'Well, if ever you do think seriously about it,' said Bill, 'come and stay for a few days, both of you, and see what it involves. Which reminds me, I must be off to sand the paths before they freeze.'

When Vi had made her farewells, Bill turned to his wife. 'I wonder if she means it?'

'Vi always meant what she said. I think they'd make a good pair of wardens, and heaven alone knows a great many are needed with so many in their seventies and eighties these days.'

The telephone rang and she walked quite briskly, and without her stick, to answer it.

Almost her old self, thought Bill with relief, setting about his sanding.

The bitter spell of weather abated slightly. The icicles fringing the Cotswold roof tiles and thatch grew shorter. In the middle of the day the puddles, once iron-hard, melted a little, allowing the ice to float above muddy water.

The winter days were beginning to lengthen. Now afternoon tea was enjoyed before the curtains were drawn at dusk, Betty Bell arrived in the light to sweep the school when the children had gone home, and Nelly Piggott found herself mounting the hill, on a good day, whilst the wintry sunset still glowed in the west.

The bulbs had pushed stubby noses through the soil, and the forsythia was in bud. Brave snowdrops were beginning to flower under sheltered hedges, and the signs of spring to come heartened everybody.

The invalids began to emerge, pale but hopeful. Tom Hardy, swathed in a woolly scarf over his overcoat, accompanied Polly and Johnny Enderby on a short stroll across the green. Young George Curdle, and other chickenpox victims, were allowed out for half an hour in the middle of the day to have a breath of fresh air, and very heady stuff they found it after being cooped up.

Even Edward Young, still suffering with shingles, felt more hopeful of recovery as he pottered about the garden, noting the first small leaves of the honeysuckle, and the buds on the lilac bushes getting plumper.

He was now much relieved to have made up the silly quarrel with John. Secretly, he knew that it was one cause of the tension which had helped to produce this most maddening and tormenting complaint of his. The Cirencester worry, annoying though it was, was all part and parcel of his professional life, and he had coped with far worse problems with officialdom in his time. He could overcome this one, he felt sure. But the rare upset with a relative, and one whom he respected as much as

John, was something different. He did not mind admitting that it had shaken him.

Another reason for its particular annoyance was the fact that he had a strong feeling that John was right about the steps. Something extra in the way of safety must be done. He had been turning this over in his mind ever since Jane's unfortunate accident, and much as he disliked altering the look of the shallow flight of steps which led the eye gently upward to the line of the building as a whole, he was forced to admit to himself that a central handrail would be an added precaution.

He felt pretty sure that this extra expense would be met willingly by the trustees, all of whom had been severely shocked by the fact that the youngest and most agile of the inhabitants had been the first to succumb to this unnoticed hazard. Not a word of complaint, with the exception of John's caustic comment, had been levelled at Edward's design by the trustees, which made him all the more determined to put the matter right as quickly as he could. Since making this decision he had felt a lot better.

The occasional card-playing evenings had been resumed, and it was during one of these sessions that Edward made his suggestion.

'A client of mine has a house on the Pembrokeshire coast and has offered it to me if I'd like to have it for a fortnight's holiday in the summer. He's going abroad evidently.'

'Lovely!' cried Ruth. 'And will you go?'

'I think so. Joan and I like the idea, and there's a wonderful beach nearby. We wondered if you would like to join us when the children break up. Perhaps the last week in July and the first in August. What d'you think?'

'Will the owner be agreeable?'

'I'm sure he will. He said: "Bring any friends", and as the house has six bedrooms it seems a great pity to have the place half empty.'

Ruth looked at John. Here, if anything further were needed, was another gesture of Edward's goodwill. The two men's estrangement had worried Ruth far more than it had her more self-reliant sister, and she was anxious to restore the harmony which had always existed until this little rift between the two husbands.

'Well?' asked John of his wife.

'I'd love to go. We haven't been that way for years, and it all sounds perfect. If you really want us,' she added diffidently.

'Then that's settled,' said Edward, rubbing his hands together briskly, and then giving a yelp of pain.

John gave him a quick anxious glance. 'Where did that hurt?'

'One of those damn scabs caught on my shirt.'

'That all? You'll live!' said his brother-in-law callously. 'Right then, Edward. Pembrokeshire it is, and very many thanks for asking us.'

The telephone call that Jane Cartwright answered was from Charles Henstock who explained that he had had a call from Mrs Thurgood.

Before he could proceed further Jane had said agitatedly: 'Oh, heavens! Mrs Thurgood! What's wrong?'

Of all the people who had interviewed them, the redoubtable Mrs Thurgood had seemed to Jane, and to her husband too, the most formidable. Luckily, she had not visited the old people's homes very often, but Jane had felt remarkably apprehensive when she had, expecting some trenchant criticism.

Charles laughed. 'She is rather awe-inspiring, I admit, but this is about a quite different job from your own.'

He explained about the operatic society's problem, and the discussion he and Dimity had had about a temporary replacement for the stricken wardrobe mistress.

'And we came to the conclusion that the only person we knew who had any connection with theatre work was Carlotta Jermyn. Do you think you could sound her out?'

'I will, of course. Shall I tell her to get in touch with you?'

'I think it would be best if she telephoned Mrs Thurgood if she wants to know more.'

'Much the best idea,' said Jane, sounding so relieved that Charles laughed again.

'Well, Jane, I think the two ladies can face each other quite successfully, and we can fade into the background.'

'It certainly suits me to be there,' replied Jane. 'I'll call on her this evening, or at any rate tomorrow. Frankly, I'd like to see her happily occupied. She's the one who is taking longer to settle in than all the others.'

'If she can't settle down with you and Bill as guardian angels, then it's a pity,' said Charles firmly. 'We could do with more couples like you. The Trust is always on the look-out, you know.'

Jane had half a mind to mention Vi Ellis's hopes, but decided that it was too early to confide even in such a discreet person as Charles Henstock.

'I'll do what I can,' she promised, and put down the receiver.

Kit and Connie had come back from Venice looking years younger and full of stories of that lovely city.

They had brought Dotty some lace mats from Burano and a pretty pale pink glass cream jug from Murano for Vi.

'I really think I must visit Venice again before I get too old,' said Dotty. 'I rather like the sound of that train that goes from Victoria. It looks very well equipped, and I always enjoyed train travel when I went abroad with Father. We always talked of going on the Trans-Siberian railway, but the trip would have taken up rather a lot of time in the summer holidays, and in any case we were obliged to visit my great-aunts in Broadstairs during August, which made things more awkward.'

'Well, we must think about a holiday for you,' said Connie diplomatically. 'Meanwhile, tell us how the workmen have been getting on.'

'Splendidly, splendidly!' cried Dotty. 'All should be finished by next month.'

'They've been saying that since before Christmas,' observed Kit, 'but let's go and have a look round.'

They left the room, and Dotty looked across at Vi.

'You know, they won't want me to go on that train – the Orient Express, isn't it? I can see that they think it will be too much for me. Perhaps you would think of accompanying me, Vi? I know they would be quite happy about me if you were going to be there. We have got on so well, haven't we?'

'We have indeed,' said Vi warmly. 'I've enjoyed every minute of my stay here.'

She did not respond to Dotty's tentative invitation, much as she appreciated her trust. A fortnight in Dotty's own home, with a certain amount of support from Betty Bell, Albert Piggott and innumerable kind friends, was one thing. A trip on the Orient Express, and the hazards of the waterways of Venice was another, and resourceful though she was, even Vi's stout heart quailed at the thought.

Much later, when she was safely back in her own home, Vi often thought of Dotty and her proposed holiday. Somehow, she could not imagine Dotty setting off for foreign parts even if

Connie and Kit accompanied her, but it was very comforting to think that she had been invited to share the adventures of that indomitable old lady, even if they had come to naught.

As well as the snowdrops, budding shrubs, and melting puddles, there were other signs of spring at Lulling and Thrush Green.

The most superior clothes shop in the High Street had removed the thermal underwear, woolly hats, scarves and padded jackets from the window, and had a tasteful display of frilly blouses, lightweight suits and pale handbags. A large placard adorned with daffodils exhorted the passerby to GREET THE SPRING, which though perhaps a trifle premature, was certainly hopeful.

At The Two Pheasants at Thrush Green, Mr Jones was cosseting his geranium cuttings and planting trays of lobelia and dwarf marigolds ready for bedding out.

He enthused about his seedlings to Albert, who seemed to have sunk back into his morose ways now that there was less to do at Dotty Harmer's.

'Seen old Perce?' Albeit enquired. 'Hasn't been bad, has 'e? Seems a long time since I bumped into him.'

'I think he's courting again,' said the landlord, twirling a snowy cloth inside a glass.

'More fool him,' grunted Albert. 'Who's he after this time?'

'One of the Cooke girls, I heard.'

'He must be off his onion,' said Albert flatly. 'Them Cooke girls is no better than they ought to be, and their old mum puts 'em up to all manner of mischief.'

'Well, Percy's not a bad catch. Got a farm and a house, and a bit put by I've no doubt.'

'That's as maybe, but them Cookes are proper bad lots. In any case, old Perce is still married.'

'And when did that stop a man running after others?' said Mr Jones, with unwonted cynicism.

'That's true,' agreed Albert gloomily.

He finished his glass and pushed it across the counter.

'Well, I suppose it's the spring,' he said. 'But I should have thought old Perce would have had enough of women by now.'

'Some,' replied the landlord, 'never learn!'

19. VARIOUS SURPRISES

With the end of February in sight, the countryside around Lulling grew greener. A mild westerly wind held sway, aconites and snowdrops adorned the cottage gardens, the chickenpox epidemic abated, and the village school had its usual quota of pupils.

The three teachers rejoiced as this gentle weather allowed the children to play outside, where they ran off their high spirits and returned to the classrooms slightly more ready for work than in the bleak weeks before, which had kept them confined indoors.

Little Miss Fogerty had discarded the silk scarf which had protected her neck throughout the winter, although she prudently retained her thermal underwear and some fine woollen stockings which Isobel had given her for Christmas. Dorothy, despite her more amply padded figure, felt the cold, and was still ringing the changes with her tweed suits, twin sets and hand-knitted jumpers.

She was engaged in darning the sleeve of one of the latter garments when the telephone rang one evening.

'Drat the thing,' she exclaimed, heaving herself from the armchair, and sticking the needle in the jumper sleeve. 'Now who can that be?'

Dorothy always said this when either the telephone or the front door bell rang, and secretly Agnes found it slightly irritating. After all, no one could know until the bell was answered, could they? However, she had never voiced her annoyance. It might upset Dorothy, and she herself, no doubt, had equally irritating little ways.

She held herself in readiness to go to the telephone if the call should be for her, but she heard Dorothy saying: 'But how kind, Ray! When did you say?'

Agnes relaxed, and studied the crossword. It seemed harder than ever today, and obviously was compiled by someone who knew far more about Charles Dickens' characters than Miss Fogerty did. She wondered about Ray. Very rarely did Dorothy's tone sound so affectionate towards her brother, although Agnes knew that there was a strong bond between the two, but made somewhat tenuous when Kathleen was involved. Perhaps Dorothy was subconsciously jealous? No doubt Freud would have made something of it, but whether his conclusions would be correct little Miss Fogerty had her doubts. Such over-emphasis on *sex*!

Dorothy returned looking pleased.

'That was Ray. They are going to spend a weekend with their Dorset friends, and want us to lunch with them at The Fleece on the Saturday on their way down.'

'How very kind!'

'He said they had decided to break their journey there as Harrison can be put up in the stables, and have a peaceful lunch and a rest. Really, one sometimes wonders if they are talking about a young child!'

'He is one to them,' replied Agnes percipiently.

'In that case, he and John Todd would have a lot in common,' retorted Dorothy, resuming her darning.

At the old people's homes, Jane Cartwright had cause to be hopeful about the outcome of her visit to Carlotta Jermyn.

It had not been an easy encounter, for Carlotta had become rather haughty at the outset, pointing out that an actress was in quite a different class from a wardrobe mistress, and that the exceptional qualities needed to create a character were definitely more rarified than such practical matters as theatrical costume, which were the concern of lesser minds.

'I think really,' said Jane, 'that they need someone more in the way of a *consultant*. Someone who would know the best costumiers and wig-makers to approach, or perhaps someone who could simply give a hand in adapting costumes.'

Carlotta considered this.

'Well, of course, I have had some experience in these matters when I gave some advice to amateur companies now and again. But I really don't know what to say. I know that the Lulling Operatic people have quite a good name for their little efforts,' she added graciously, 'and I believe they give quite a useful sum to local charities.'

'They do indeed,' Jane assured her.

'And of course I should not want a fee,' went on Carlotta. 'And if they employed a professional it might cost them a tidy sum.'

Jane thought that Carlotta was beginning to weaken, and made a swift move.

'Why don't you ring Mrs Thurgood and see what is involved? You need not commit yourself today. But I know she would appreciate any ideas you have. You might think of someone else that they could approach.'

At this Carlotta's face took on a somewhat obstinate expression.

'I shall ring her as soon as I've had my gin and tonic,' she told Jane firmly. 'This is a Worthy Cause!'

Jane would have loved dearly to hear the conversation between the two autocratic ladies later that morning. No doubt each was a model of frigid politeness. Carlotta would make it quite clear that such an undertaking would not do justice to her true worth, but that if she could assist lesser mortals in the theatrical sphere then she felt it her duty to do so.

Mrs Thurgood would be equally high-handed, gracious in her appreciation of Carlotta's feelings, but not in any way servile in her attitude.

But the outcome was a happy one. Carlotta agreed to give the Lulling Operatic Society the benefit of her expertise and also consented to help with such lowly but practical matters as altering costumes, should the need arise.

'One must do what one can in this world,' she told Jane. ' "We pass this way but once," as someone said.'

On repeating this to Bill his comment was typical.

' "Pass" is about right! Since she's got interested in this lark she's too busy to bob into our other old dears and annoy them.'

'That's true. Let's hope the Lulling Operatic Society makes her a permanent member.'

It was about this time that Jenny was admitted to Lulling Cottage Hospital for her tonsils operation.

The great man, Mr Pedder-Bennett, came down from the

county town once a week to perform straightforward opera-
tions at the local hospital.

Tuesday was his day, and the staff of the hospital was extra
alert. Castors on the beds were all turned to the exact angle,
throughout the wards. Sheets were tucked in so securely that
patients were unable to bend their toes. Hair was brushed,
dentures put in, noses wiped, pyjamas buttoned and night-
gowns adjusted for modesty.

Jenny was obliged to go in on the Monday evening, so that
she could be prepared for Mr Pedder-Bennett's ministrations
the next morning. It was one of the longest evenings of her life.
She had never before been into a hospital. Her foster parents
had slipped away some time earlier in the tender care of the old
people's home where they had lived their final years.

She was fascinated by the variety of women about her, and
full of admiration for the bustling nurses. The speed with which
they raced from bed to bed, yanking patients upright, pummel-
ling pillows, whisking vases, glasses, pens, spectacles, fruit,
talcum powder and scent from bedside tables and putting them
briskly below into cupboards which half the patients were
unable to reach, fairly took Jenny's breath away.

What energy these girls had! And how tired the patients
looked amidst all this activity!

She was allowed a light supper consisting of a bowl of some
milky white substance which might have been anything from
hot blancmange to thin porridge. It reminded Jenny of her
orphanage breakfasts, and like them could have done with a
spoonful of sugar. This repast was served at six-thirty which
Jenny found surprising as it was called supper.

'Last meal for you, love,' the nurse said cheerfully. 'No
breakfast before ops.'

Jenny cleared her bowl obediently, and lay back on the
pillows. It was still only seven o'clock, and she wondered how
Mrs Bailey was managing.

A few minutes later, the nurse came to collect her tray.

'Mrs Bailey's just rung up. Sent her love, and says she'll be thinking of you. Probably pop in and see you tomorrow evening if you feel all right.'

'Oh, I shall!' Jenny assured her.

'Well, we'll have to see, won't we?' said the nurse cryptically. 'Shall we have a bit of shut-eye now?'

Jenny slid down the bed, and closed her eyes, although sleep, she felt sure, would be impossible. Dear Mrs Bailey, she thought gratefully! How she longed to be back with her at Thrush Green!

The pillow was warm against her cheek, the porridge warm in her stomach.

Jenny was asleep in five minutes.

It was while Mr Pedder-Bennett was at his delicate work the next morning that Jane Cartwright went the rounds of the old people's homes and found all was well.

Polly and Tom were sitting in their porch enjoying the sunshine. Johnny Enderby was digging in Ella's garden across the road. Mrs Bates was making herself an apple dumpling. Miss Fuller was preparing to walk across to the school for coffee in the staffroom, and then an hour's reading practice with the slow readers. The Crosses were changing their bed linen with the radio on full blast. Jack and Sybil Angell were away for a few days with friends. Carlotta was at a sewing session with the other ladies connected with the Operatic Society, and her husband Eric was reading the newspaper, as best he could, with Monty on his lap impeding his view.

After a few words with each, Jane stood at the end of the building and looked across Thrush Green. The sky was of that soft tender blue which only early spring can bring. A hazel bush nearby shook its yellow catkins, the golden dust powdering some young dandelion leaves below.

Somewhere a lark was singing, and a blackbird winged by, its orange bill carrying a whiskery bundle of dried grass for its nest building. A beautiful brown and grey snail climbed slowly up the dry stone wall, leaving a glistening trail, and in the shelter of one sunny crevice Jane could see half a dozen ladybirds emerging from hibernation to enjoy this early sunshine.

Nathaniel Patten's benign countenance caught the sun's rays, and pink tipped daisies were already clustered about the plinth.

Jane breathed a sigh of delight. How good it was to be here, to see their charges beginning to enjoy their new surroundings, and, best of all, to be able to move again, perhaps not quite so nimbly as she had when she first arrived, but certainly with more confidence and with less pain as the weeks went by.

A figure loomed up beside her. It was Percy Hodge.

'Oh, hello, uncle,' said Jane. 'And how are things with you?'

'Could be worse,' said Percy cautiously.

'I was going to make a cup of coffee,' said Jane. 'Will you join me?'

'Just off over the road,' responded Percy, nodding towards The Two Pheasants. 'Got to have a word with Albert.'

'Then I won't hold you up,' said his niece, watching him set off, and went back through the dewy morning to her elevenses.

But through the kitchen window she noticed the young Cooke girl pedalling down the road from Nidden. She got off at The Two Pheasants, propped her bicycle against the wall, and vanished inside.

It certainly looked, thought Jane, stirring her cup, as if Uncle Percy was in the throes of love, yet again.

At Lulling Cottage Hospital, Jenny's recovery was steady, and she was promised a return home within a few days.

'Old P-B', as John Lovell called him, had done his usual neat surgery and, apart from an irritating little lump which Jenny imagined was a husk from the morning porridge, all was well. Mr Pedder-Bennett, on examining his handiwork, was quite hurt to discover that the irritation was caused by a minute knot in his exquisite needlework, and assured his patient that it was only a matter of hours and then all would be in perfect condition. And so, to give 'old P-B' his due, it certainly was.

When Winnie returned from a visit to Jenny that evening, she was slightly alarmed to see a light on in her sitting-room. Could she have forgotten to switch it off? Should she go into the Hursts and ask Frank to accompany her into the house, in case burglars had broken in? As long as they were free from stocking masks over their faces – which Winnie found unendurable – she felt that she could probably cope alone.

But while she stood at the gate, with all these thoughts whirling in her head, the front door opened, and there was her nephew, Richard.

'Oh, what a relief!' cried Winnie. 'I thought you were a burglar!'

'Not quite. I did try to ring you this afternoon,' he said, helping his aunt to take off her coat.

'I must have been in the greenhouse.'

'I had the key you gave me years ago. So here I am.'

'And very nice too,' said Winnie. 'Get yourself a drink, and me too, dear boy, and tell me what brings you here.'

There was silence for a time as Richard filled two glasses and carried them carefully across the room. It gave Winnie time to wonder if the spare bed had been made up should he want to stay. It usually stood in readiness for just such an emergency, and she was sure that Jenny would have left everything in apple pie order. Or was he the forerunner of the rest of the family? More than one person she simply could not accommodate.

She need not have worried.

'I'm afraid I'm homeless, Aunt Win.'

'Homeless?'

'Ever since I came back from China.'

'What happened?'

'When I arrived back I found that Roger had left his wife and moved in with Fenella.'

'What do you mean? Are they living together as man and wife? I thought you said they were cousins, or somehow related.'

'So they are. But very distant cousins.' Richard sounded

amused at Winnie's reaction, which made her cross, as well as shocked.

'But what's to be done, Richard? After all, you and Fenella are properly married—'

'So's Roger. The biggest snag of all is that the flat is Fenella's, and she can have who she likes there. At the moment she likes to have Roger, and not me.'

'But what about your baby?'

'That will have to be decided when we get a divorce.'

It all sounded drearily wretched to Winnie, and she turned to more practical things.

'So where have you been staying all this time?'

'With an old school friend. He has a service flat near Marble Arch, but it's much too small for the two of us. I moved into some digs in Notting Hill Gate last week, but there's such a racket going on from a pub next door, I felt I couldn't stand it any longer, and fled down here.'

'But what are your plans, Richard? For the immediate future, I mean? Of course, I can put you up for a day or two, and should be pleased to have you here, but things are a trifle worrying for me too at the moment.'

She explained about Jenny. To her surprise, Richard looked genuinely concerned.

'Poor old Jenny! So she can't make those delicious cheese scones at the moment.'

What a pity, thought Winnie, that he had not told Jenny how delicious they were at the time. But, in any case, she would repeat this belated compliment to the invalid.

'The thing is,' he went on, 'I'm having to get my notes together for another tour next month, and I simply can't work in those digs.'

'Well, I suggest that you settle in here for a few days, and we'll look around for quiet lodgings nearby until you set off on your travels again. That is, if you want to be in Thrush Green.'

'There's nothing I'd like more. I can work here, I know.'

Winnie roused herself. 'Well, that's settled. I'm just going to fill a hot water bottle for the spare bed, Richard, and you can take it up and unpack.'

Richard crossed the room and gave her a kiss. 'You are an angel. I can't thank you enough.'

'I'll be glad of your company,' she told him, much touched by this rare display of feeling. 'And while you're upstairs, I will get us some supper.'

'Lovely! I must admit I'm famished.'

'It won't be up to Jenny's standards,' she warned him. 'Scrambled eggs or sardines on toast, and some rather ancient cheese.'

'Delicious!' said Richard, making for the stairs. 'I'll come down for the bottle in two ticks. And, by the way, I brought a pork pie with me, in case I had to pitch camp under a hedge, so we'll add that to the supper table.'

Waiting for the kettle to boil, Winnie pondered on Richard's melancholy news. What a muddle some people seemed to make of their lives! And what would the future hold for this particular four?

More to the point, what would happen to that poor young baby and the unseen, but exuberant, Timothy? Would these marital troubles sort themselves out eventually? At times Richard, despite his brilliant brain, seemed absolutely helpless.

Nevertheless, thought Winnie, he had brought a pork pie with him. One must be thankful for small mercies.

20. RICHARD'S AFFAIRS

A week or two later, on a March day of wind and sunshine, Dotty Harmer, Connie and Kit celebrated the departure of the workmen with a particularly festive lunch.

They broached a bottle of claret from Kit's store, although Dotty had invited them to take their pick of her own home-brewed variety.

'I really can recommend the parsnip,' she assured them, 'and the wheat and raisin is quite heady stuff.'

'I think Kit particularly wants to try his claret,' said Connie. 'So let's keep yours for another time.'

'We ought to pour a libation to the household gods,' Kit said. 'Just to make sure they look after us after all we've been through.'

'Don't you have to do something dreadful to a chicken or pigeon, dear, if you make libations?' said Dotty becoming agitated. 'We really can't have anything like that here!'

'You're thinking of foretelling things, Dotty,' said Kit. 'The Greeks used to study the entrails of their sacrifice, if I remember aright.'

'It all sounds most unpleasant and messy,' replied Dotty, 'and I hope you won't speak of such things when the hens are present. They understand far more than you give them credit for, you know.'

Kit held up his glass. 'I promise you that, Dotty. And now, here's to the workmen!'

'And may they never return!' added Connie.

Dotty raised her glass carefully.

'To all of us in this house,' said Dotty.

'I'm not quite sure,' said Connie, 'what we are toasting.'

'Just drink, my dear,' replied her husband, 'and be thankful.'

The news of Richard's arrival had soon reached everyone in Thrush Green. The reasons for his visit were extraordinarily varied.

The old people at the homes were as intrigued as the other residents. Mrs Bates thought he might have been ill, and advised by his doctor to have country air. Miss Fuller had heard that he was studying for an examination. The Jermyns were nearer the mark with the correct guess that Richard's marriage was in jeopardy.

Nelly Piggott told Albert that the rumour going round The Fuchsia Bush was that Richard had lost his job and was now penniless. Winnie Bailey was supporting him until he found work.

Albert, who had spent the day at Dotty's refurbishing the coops ready for broody hens and was in a more mellow frame of mind than usual, contented himself with the rejoinder: 'More fool Mrs Bailey!'

Conjecture was rife in Lulling too. Charles Henstock, who had called at the Lovelocks' house to deliver a parcel from Dimity, was closely questioned, and had to reply, quite truthfully, that he really knew nothing about the matter.

'I fear it may be true that he has left his wife,' said Ada. 'He was never a very reliable character.'

'Do you remember when dear Donald Bailey called here one day when Richard was about six?' said Bertha.

'I shall never forget it,' trumpeted Ada, with a shudder.

'The child fingered *absolutely everything*,' Violet told Charles. 'And when he asked if he could play in the garden, of course we agreed.'

'But on his way through the kitchen he switched on every one of the burners on the stove,' said Bertha.

'And in the garden he found the hose, turned on the tap to its maximum, and swamped the flower beds,' added Ada.

'And, worse still,' continued Violet, 'he turned it on poor Mrs Jefferson who was pegging out The Fuchsia Bush tea towels next door, and drenched her to the skin!'

'And all in the space of five minutes!' Bertha said.

To Charles it really only sounded a childish prank, but obviously it had been a major disaster remembered, for many years, by the three sisters.

'What a lovely room this is!' he said, trying to change the subject. 'You get all the morning sun.'

'Yes, it is pleasant,' agreed Ada, 'but the whole house is getting too much for us. Far too big, you know. We have been thinking of applying for one of the new homes at Thrush Green.'

Charles was taken aback. No one could say that the Love-locks were in any need of such accommodation. They had this splendid house already, and a certain amount of domestic help, The Fuchsia Bush next door, and all the shops in Lulling High Street hard by and, above all, far more money than they could ever need.

'I doubt if you would qualify for a place,' said Charles. 'And in any case, the largest of the homes is only for two people.'

'Oh, we really thought of the *single* apartments. One each was our idea.'

'That, I'm sure, would be quite impossible,' said Charles firmly. 'You would be taking up three-quarters of the single people's accommodation at one blow.' He stood up ready to depart. 'If I were you,' he ventured, 'I should think of closing one or two of your rooms to save work – and heating, of course.'

'We don't have the heating on much at all,' said Bertha. 'We just put on thicker vests or our winter spencers.'

They waved goodbye to their visitor, and then Ada, who was the most senior of the sisters, turned to Bertha with a reproachful expression.

'There was no need to speak of our *underwear*, Bertha! In very bad taste! Even if he is of the cloth, you must remember that Charles is a MAN!'

At Winnie Bailey's house, upon which so much attention was being focused at this time, affairs were settling down. Richard was on his best behaviour, helped with the washing up, straightened his bed, and did his best to be unobtrusive.

He worked quietly upstairs for most of the morning, and took a walk in the afternoon. In fact, he was so little bother, Winnie found, after a few days, that she decided that he might just as well stay under her roof rather than go to the bother of finding lodgings for the fortnight or so which remained before he set off on his lecture tour.

The evening before Jenny was due back from hospital, she broached the subject. Naturally, Richard was delighted and grateful.

'But I must stress one thing, Richard. I'm not letting Jenny do any heavy work for a few weeks. I know she'll protest, but I'm going to be adamant. So that means you must pull your weight while you're here. Could you take on the boiler and this fire, for instance? Keep us stoked up, and cleaned out and so on?'

Richard brightened. 'I'd love to. You know I love dirty jobs.'

'You certainly swept the kitchen flue marvellously, I remember, and Phil Hurst still talks of the time you cleaned out her drains.'

'Dear girl!' said Richard affectionately. 'She's wasted on old Frank. I would have liked her for myself.'

'Maybe, Richard, but that time has gone,' said Winnie, with some asperity. 'Well, if you'll take on those jobs, it will help enormously.'

'I'm a dab hand at vacuum cleaning too,' said Richard, 'though I draw the line at dusting.'

'I can cope with that, and the cooking and shopping,' said Winnie. 'I'm glad you're going to stay, dear boy. We shall manage very well, I'm sure. But what about your family affairs? Do you want to try and meet Fenella before you go?'

Richard looked pensive. He took up the poker, and turned over a beech log on the back of the fire.

'I don't think so. I rang her last night and she was as off-hand as ever. She knows where I shall be for the next month or two, if she wants to get in touch. I think I shall leave it to her for the time being, and try my luck again when I've done this tour.'

'So you think there might be some hope?'

'If Roger takes it into his head to move out, then I think there might be. But not as things are at the moment.'

'Well, you are all four grown up, and presumably sensible people. It's the children, I'm thinking about.'

'So am I, Aunt Win. Now, that's enough of my worries. To-morrow I start my fire-tending duties, and fetch Jenny from the hospital. Right?'

'From the look of that coal scuttle,' observed Winnie, 'your fire-tending starts immediately.'

Richard obediently collected the scuttle and set off for the coal cellar, followed by his aunt's amused gaze.

The bright March weather continued. The birds were resplendent in their mating finery, nests were being built, and the hedgehogs and squirrels were beginning to stir from their months of hibernation.

Yellow coltsfoot and early primroses starred the banks, and George Curdle found a little bunch of fragrant white violets to present to his adored Miss Fogerty. The trees, so stark throughout the winter, were beginning to grow hazy with swelling buds, and rosettes of young leaves were bursting on the honeysuckle's twining stems.

'It all seems so *hopeful*,' commented Dorothy to Agnes, as

they descended the hill to Lulling to keep their luncheon engagement with Ray and Kathleen. 'Somehow I feel we are in for a splendidly hot summer.'

Ray and Kathleen were at The Fleece to greet them, and Harrison was mercifully absent, presumably having his own repast and rest as arranged.

Affectionate greetings were exchanged and the menu studied whilst the four sipped their sherry.

'I wonder what "Sole Veronique" is?' wondered Agnes aloud.

'Grapes on it,' replied Dorothy succinctly. 'I don't think you'd like it, dear. What about these scallops of veal?'

'I can't eat veal now,' said Kathleen, 'after seeing how the poor darling calves are treated on television,'

'I do so agree,' said Agnes. 'That's why I'm having sole, if I may.'

'So shall I,' said Kathleen, 'but I do so hope they can supply plain boiled potatoes. My migraine is so easily brought on.'

'Well, I'll settle for the veal,' said Dorothy sturdily.

'And I shall have a rare fillet steak,' announced Ray, which Agnes thought suitably manly.

The Fleece dealt competently with their order, and Agnes thought how pleasant it was to be sitting with old friends, with good food before them, and the tranquil view of St John's across the green.

At a table in the window, she now noticed young Mr Venables and his wife. She waved to them, and Justin half-rose, gave a courtly little bow, and resumed his seat again. Agnes was touched to see that he was engaged in cutting up his wife's meat, so that she could eat it with her fork, held in her cruelly twisted arthritic hand. Poor Mrs Venables, thought Agnes, almost moved to tears, and she used to do such beautiful crochet-work!

Coffee was brought to them in the hotel sitting-room. It was warm and sunny, and for two pins Agnes could have dropped off into a refreshing snooze, but common courtesy compelled her to make an occasional comment on Kathleen's non-stop description of her ailments. At least it gave Dorothy and Ray a chance to have a heart-to-heart talk on a neighbouring settee, she noted with some gratification.

'And my new doctor,' went on Kathleen, 'is taking so much more interest in my case. There were times when I believe my old medical man simply *didn't listen*. I couldn't understand it.'

Agnes knew exactly how he must have felt, but naturally did not say so.

At last, Ray stood up, studying his wrist watch. 'About time we were off, Kath. I'll go and get Harrison.'

The ladies donned their coats and went out of the front door. The air was cool and invigorating.

A frenzied barking announced the arrival of Ray and his black labrador. The latter leapt upon Kathleen with such impetus that it would have felled any unsuspecting person, but his mistress stood up to his attentions with great indulgence.

'There, there!' she cried. 'Say "hello" to your two aunties.'

The ladies put out their hands civilly and patted the dog's smooth head.

'Now, into the car,' ordered Kathleen opening the back door, and the animal leapt upon a rug there spread out, while farewells and thanks were given.

The two ladies waved goodbye, and then set off for home.

' "Aunties" indeed!' snorted Dorothy. 'Really, Kathleen takes the biscuit!'

'But what a pleasant party,' said Agnes. 'I enjoyed it so much. And I really think that Harrison's behaviour has improved, don't you?'

'Fat chance of it doing anything else,' said Dorothy, 'when you recall our last meeting with that creature.'

*

Charles and Dimity Henstock were eagerly awaiting a visit from Anthony Bull. Charles's predecessor had telephoned to say that he was on his way to Gloucester.

Charles hurried to the front door as soon as the bell rang.

'Come in, my dear fellow. What a pleasure this is! Are you alone?'

'Yes, on my way to a conference at Gloucester, and I thought as I was so close, I must call and see you both.'

Dimity now appeared in the hall, and was soon enveloped in a loving bear hug and the delicious scent of Anthony's after-shave lotion. Really, thought Dimity, emerging from the embrace, Anthony smells as gorgeous as he looks, and that's saying something.

'Coffee? A drink?'

'Nothing, thank you. Just a sight of you both, and the dear old church and vicarage. How's it going?'

They spent some time exchanging news, and the two men

went out into the spring sunshine to look round the garden. Charles told him about the new homes at Thrush Green, and the alterations to the church almshouses hard by.

'And where is my friend Mrs Bates then?'

Charles explained that she had been the first to be housed afresh.

'She was the best silver cleaner I ever met,' said Anthony.

'She still is,' Charles told him.

They began to stroll back again towards the vicarage. The church clock gave three sonorous chimes, and Anthony, pulling an elegant gold half-hunter from his waistcoat pocket, compared times.

'I don't need to be in Gloucester until six,' he said, 'and I would dearly love to see these new homes and my old friends again.'

'Let me take you up there,' said Charles. 'I know they would all love to see you.'

'Come in my car,' said Anthony, 'and I'll run you back.'

'There's no need for that,' replied Charles. 'I shall visit one or two people there, and enjoy a walk back.'

'In that case,' said Anthony, 'I must make my farewells to Dimity. It has been so good to see you both again.'

Ten minutes later the two men approached Thrush Green. As they came within sight of the new homes, Anthony stopped the car, and looked across to the spot where Charles's rectory had once stood.

'I miss the old house still,' said Charles.

He sounded wistful, and Anthony shot a glance at his sad countenance.

'It was a dreadful shock,' he said. 'But now these new homes have arisen, you see, like a phoenix from the ashes.'

Charles smiled slowly. 'I like that idea.'

Silence fell as the two men gazed at Thrush Green, golden and tranquil in the afternoon sunlight. Both were engrossed with their memories.

'Well,' said Anthony at last, 'it's no good harking back, Charles. We have to go forward, you know. And with hope.'

They got out of the car, and stood a moment, enjoying the fresh breeze.

'Come on, Charles,' cried Anthony, stepping out. 'Let's go and see our old friends.'

EARLY DAYS
A Childhood Memoir
* * *
Miss Read

From the author of the bestselling
FAIRACRE and THRUSH GREEN series

'The larks were in joyous frenzy above. The sky was blue, the now distant wood misty with early buds, and the air was heady to a London child. A great surge of happiness engulfed me. This is where I was going to live. I should learn all about birds and trees and flowers. This is where I belonged . . . This was the country, and I was at home there.'

Early Days is alive with vibrant childhood memories of an extended family of grandmas, uncles, aunts and cousins, and their houses – full of mystery and adventure – where Miss Read lived in the shadow of the First World War.

At the age of seven, Miss Read moved to a small village in Kent, into a magical new world where her love of the English countryside grew – a passion that would be found in her much-loved novels. Her evocative descriptions of the village school, the joys of exploring the woods and lanes, toffee-making and riding on the corn-chandler's cart, vividly convey this time as one of the happiest of her life.

Full of unforgettable characters, tender memories and the colourful intrigues of everyday life, *Early Days* is a charming and affectionate insight into the childhood of a bestselling author, and a bygone era.